Titles by Ana Seymour

MASTER OF CASTLE GLEN
MAID OF KILLARNEY
IRISH GYPSY
THE BLACK SWAN
ROSE IN THE MIST

Master of
Castle Glen

Ana Seymour

JOVE BOOKS, NEW YORK

This is a work of fiction. Names, characters, places, and incidents either
are the product of the author's imagination or are used fictitiously,
and any resemblance to actual persons, living or dead, business
establishments, events, or locales is entirely coincidental.

MASTER OF CASTLE GLEN

A Jove Book / published by arrangement with
the author

PRINTING HISTORY
Jove edition / March 2003

Copyright © 2003 by Mary Bracho
Cover art by Marc Cohen
Cover illustration by Bruce Emmett

Visit our website at
www.penguinputnam.com

ISBN: 0-515-13490-2

A JOVE BOOK®
Jove Books are published by The Berkley Publishing Group,
a division of Penguin Putnam Inc.,
375 Hudson Street, New York, New York 10014.
JOVE and the "J" design
are trademarks belonging to Penguin Putnam Inc.

PRINTED IN THE UNITED STATES OF AMERICA

10 9 8 7 6 5 4 3 2 1

chapter 1

Land of brown heath and shaggy wood,
Land of the mountain and the flood,
Land of my sires! What mortal hand
Can e'er untie the filial band
That knits me to thy rugged strand!
—SIR WALTER SCOTT

Glencolly, Scotland, 1885

L ook, here it comes!" Robby MacLennan raced along the
wooden platform toward the approaching steam engine. "Isn't it magnificent, Fee?" He turned briefly back
to look at his stepmother.

Fiona MacLennan twitched her nose at the sudden
acrid smell, but couldn't resist craning her neck to catch
the first sight of the giant machine. It was like nothing
that had ever been seen in Glencolly, and she had to
admit it was impressive. Robby had reached the far end
of the platform and was now running back in her direction. Like any fourteen-year-old boy, he always seemed
happier when engaged in some physical activity. His
cheeks were ruddy with the exertion. She gave a wistful
smile as she noted how much he looked like his late fa-

ther. Alasdair had always flushed when he had become excited about something around the estate. Which was often.

Skidding to a halt in front of her, Robby tugged at her hand. "Come down to the end of the platform to see it, Fee. Why has it stopped, do you reckon? It's just sitting there puffing. Do you think something's wrong? Isn't it supposed to pull into the station? Is the usurper on board, do you think? Shall we smile at him when he gets off or turn up our noses?"

Fiona could hardly follow the boy's dizzying onslaught of questions. She was busy concentrating on not letting her curiosity over the railway show. If Alasdair were still alive, he would have forbidden them to come to see the arrival of this contraption he had so dreaded.

Only one of the boy's words had caught her attention. "Don't call him the usurper, Robby. We're beholding to Mr. Campbell for letting us stay on at Glencolly Castle."

"But you called him that."

"Aye, when I was fashed, but we must stop doing it."

"Aren't you angry anymore?" Robby asked.

Fiona sighed. Was she angry with the greedy American who was coming to rob her stepson of the estate that should rightly be his? No, she decided. The anger had turned into determination. Somehow she would see this injustice rectified. She owed it to Alasdair.

"It's moving!" Robby shouted, letting go her hand and running once again toward the end of the platform as the engine shuddered to life and started slowly forward. The reminder of their purpose for meeting the train had managed to kill any pleasure she might have in seeing this miracle of the modern age. She turned her back on the gleaming black cars and walked into the shadowy station.

•   •   •

Duncan Campbell had not been able to take his eyes from the windows of the train. So this was Scotland, he thought with an odd twinge. This was the lush green land he'd wondered about since he'd been old enough to recognize the yearning in his father's voice. Robert Campbell had been forced to flee his homeland after a youthful brawl led to an opponent's death. He had never reconciled himself with his exile. Now, ironically, the son he had rejected would be the one to make the journey to the land he had so loved.

Duncan pulled a gold watch out of his pocket to check the hour. The train was a full ninety minutes behind schedule. Tapping the timepiece with a hint of impatience, he turned his attention back to the window. Glencolly could not be far, and according to his solicitor's letter, the widow of the former owner would be meeting him, along with her son. The boy had been expected to inherit Castle Glen until Alasdair MacLennan's will had revealed the old papers turning the estate over to a Campbell descendant.

It would no doubt be a bit of a sticky mess to get rid of them, Duncan thought with a sigh. He had the law on his side, of course, but he supposed there might be some degree of local sentiment in favor of the boy and the old widow.

"Glencolly's just ahead, sir." The eager young porter had been most solicitous the entire trip after Duncan had given the lad a lavish tip for helping with his cases.

Duncan leaned toward the window as a newly built platform and station came into view. The train lurched and stopped. "Why are we stopping?" he asked the porter.

The boy hunched his shoulders. "Sheep on the line, maybe. I warrant the critters have yet to learn about such things as railcars."

Duncan had a sudden urge to throw open the car window and look down the tracks toward the little village that was about to become his home, but he tamped down his curiosity and remained seated. "Have you been to Glencolly, lad?" he asked.

The boy nodded. "I've kinfolk there. My cousin Rufus is the blacksmith. He goes up to the castle regular-like for the shoeing." He leaned over Duncan's seat to peer out the window. "That's it yonder—Castle Glen. 'Tis a splendid place, my cousin do say."

Duncan followed the direction of the boy's pointing finger. In the distance he could see a series of hills. Atop the highest one was the outline of an imposing stone castle. A high, round turret dominated the north end of the structure. Another, smaller tower was at the opposite end.

"There's been a MacLennan at Castle Glen for well nigh two hundred years—since afore the days of the Bonnie Prince," the porter added, straightening up.

Duncan's notions of Scottish history were vague, but even he had heard the tales of the ill-fated young Stuart heir who had tried to wrest the Scottish crown back from the English. However, Duncan was more concerned with the current climate of the town than old wars.

"I heard that Alasdair MacLennan died recently," Duncan said. "Has your cousin mentioned anything about the new owner?"

"I reckon the old MacLennan's son is laird now," the lad answered with a shrug. "I reckon 'twill be hard for a young lad like that to fill his father's shoes. Cousin Rufus says that Lord MacLennan was the most respected man in all Glencolly. But I reckon one day they'll come to respect the son, too. He's laird of the castle, after all."

Duncan did not bother to correct him. The villagers would know about the new heir to Glencolly Castle soon enough. The train jerked and began to move again.

"Is someone meeting you, sir?" the porter asked.

"Yes." He deliberately avoided looking out the window as the train pulled alongside the platform. If the widow and boy were here, he did not want their first sight of him to be craning his neck out the window like an eager schoolchild. That was one lesson he'd learned early in the cutthroat atmosphere of New York business. When you weren't sure of an adversary, you never wanted to look too eager.

Duncan closed his eyes and sat back against the seat. It smelled pleasantly of new leather.

Fiona *twisted the cords of the silk reticule fastened to her* belt. It had probably been only a couple of minutes since the train had steamed to a halt, though it seemed longer. Through the small window of the station, she could see Robby running alongside the cars, stopping at each one to examine the windows for any sign of the new arrival, but the reflection of the sun on the glass made it difficult to see inside.

Of course, they had no idea what Mr. Duncan Campbell looked like. The only thing they really knew about him was that he was an American. She gave a little shudder. No doubt he would have slicked-down hair and brash, cheap clothing. Or perhaps he would resemble the mountain men in the adventure magazines Robby sometimes managed to find when his father had taken him into Edinburgh. The one thing he would *not* be was a gentleman. Gentlemen did not rob young boys of their birthright. In any event, she doubted there *was* such a thing as a gentleman in America.

Robby turned toward the window and shrugged his shoulders as if to ask why they had yet to see anyone come off the train. She motioned him to be patient, though she was as anxious as he. Their midday meal had been seriously delayed, but the unsettled feeling in her stomach was due to more than hunger.

Suddenly Robby turned and ran down the platform. Discreetly Fiona stepped closer to the window in order to see to the end of the train. A young lad in a blue railway uniform had stepped down from the last car and was piling suitcases and boxes on the platform. The bundles were being handed down to him by a man standing at the door of the car. She squinted. In a rare moment of vanity she'd left her spectacles at home. Now she was paying the price by missing out on her first look at the visitor.

She watched as Robby stopped a few feet back from the bundles and said something to the man at the top of the train steps. The man straightened up and looked at the boy. She couldn't see his expression, but the unloading of the bundles stopped as he and Robby had some kind of brief exchange.

Fiona willed her feet to stay planted firmly in place. Mr. Campbell could come to her, she told herself firmly. She wasn't going to go out to him as if she were some kind of supplicant looking for his favors, even if, she supposed, that was exactly what she was.

Once again she felt the familiar catch in her throat. Castle Glen had been her home for ten years—ever since Alasdair had taken her as a wife when she was only fourteen. She'd come to love the drafty old place. It had been Robby's home his entire life. It simply wasn't fair that they may now be forced to leave it.

She stiffened as she saw that Robby was pointing toward the station, evidently in response to a question by the new arrival. The man turned to give some money to the porter, then started walking toward her. Fiona watched him approach as though he were the hangman come to pull the gallows lever.

She tried to summon her late husband's voice. *What*

ails ye, Fee? 'Tis not like you to be fretful. He's just a man. He may have some paper that says the castle is his, but this is MacLennan land, and a Campbell will never be a true laird here.

She took a deep breath and drew herself up to her full height, which unfortunately was not to say much. From her glimpse out the window, Duncan Campbell looked to be tall.

From the way he filled the frame of the station door, he looked towering.

"Lady MacLennan," he said with a bow of his head that could have passed nicely in Queen Victoria's drawing room. "I'm pleased to make your acquaintance."

Her jaw went slack for a moment. She had not expected that he would be impeccably dressed, nor that he would greet her in a deep, calm voice using just the right tone of disinterested politeness that she had sometimes heard among the very rich. Most of all, she had not expected that he would be, well, *young*. For some reason, she'd expected a man of Alasdair's age. Duncan Campbell looked to be not much more than thirty.

Suddenly realizing that she was staring at the man, she stumbled over her words. "Ah—likewise, I'm sure."

Robby poked his head around the doorway. "Mr. Campbell says I may climb up to see the inside of the train car, Fee." He gave her an uncertain glance, as if wondering if accepting the invitation might be considered disloyal.

"What if the train begins to move again?" she asked.

"No need to worry," Duncan Campbell replied. "There's plenty of time. The train will be here for twelve minutes." He pulled a watch out of his pocket and looked at it, as if to emphasize his words.

"Go on ahead, then," she said to her stepson. "But don't tarry. I'd not like to be sending Malcolm to fetch you all the way to Carter's Brae."

Robby grinned at her, then whirled around and sped out of the station. She turned her attention back to the American and forced a smile. "You've had a long journey," she said.

"Yes." He glanced again at the watch in his hand. "Though not as bad as I had feared. If the train hadn't broken down just outside of Glasgow, we would have been nearly on schedule. Admirable for a new run." He looked around the station house, which was furnished with roughly hewn benches that still smelled of cut pine. "I'd expected worse," he ended with a shrug.

Fiona felt a tug of irritation. He'd expected worse? Then why hadn't he stayed in his own country where he belonged and left them in peace?

"How far is it to the castle?" he asked.

"We brought the wagon," she told him. "That makes it half an hour. 'Tis less on horseback, but we expected you would have luggage."

He nodded without offering thanks. He appeared to be studying her. "You are much younger than I had expected."

Fiona flushed. Though she'd had the same thought about him, the observation seemed far too personal from a man who was still a stranger, no matter what his status. It was just the kind of impertinence she would expect from an American. And she wouldn't give him the satisfaction of showing that it had unnerved her. "I was younger than my husband," she confirmed calmly.

"I should say so. According to the estate papers, Alasdair MacLennan was nearly seventy. You could be his granddaughter."

Fiona struggled to keep her voice even. "I was, nevertheless, his *wife*."

"So the boy informed me. It's a surprise, that's all. I'd

expected a shriveled old widow instead of a beautiful young woman."

Fiona's cheeks grew hotter, but she gave the newcomer a wary glance, trying to see if his offhanded flattery was meant to ingratiate himself with her. However, his expression held not the least hint of flirtation.

"I'd been warned that I'd find some odd customs here in the Highlands," he continued. "Such things happen in New York, but more and more seldom these days. No matter how good the fortune, women no longer stand for being sold off in marriage to lecherous old codgers."

For the second time Fiona's jaw dropped. Of all the insulting, infuriating . . .

Duncan Campbell turned as Robby bounded back into the station, his face aglow. "You should see inside the cars, Fee!" he cried. "There are beds that come right out from the wall, and tables, even a little water closet. I wish we could take a ride somewhere." His voice trailed off as he saw his stepmother's stormy face. "I don't suppose Father would approve," he ended, with a more subdued tone.

Duncan smiled at the boy and clapped a hand on his bony shoulder. "Your father's generation has passed, lad, and now, sadly, so has he. The world is changing. You will surely have your train ride. I'll take you with me when I go down to Glasgow to meet with my solicitors."

Fiona was only now recovering her voice. "Mr. Campbell, you may be the new owner of Glencolly Castle, but I'll thank you to remember that Robby is *my* responsibility. Now that my husband is no longer with us, I am the one entrusted to see that his son grows into the kind of person his father would have wanted him to be."

Duncan Campbell tilted his head, regarding her. One black eyebrow lifted as he said, "From what I have heard of Alasdair MacLennan, he would want his son to be a man who is ready to face the challenges of the future, whatever it may bring."

Fiona's temper snapped. "You know nothing of what Alasdair would have wanted, Mr. Campbell. But I can tell you this, the last thing he would have wanted was to have some upstart American come into his town and his home and take over the position that should rightfully be his son's."

Robby gave a little gasp. "Fee," he said in an anguished half whisper. "I thought you said that you were over being fashed."

She looked at him. "I'm sorry, Robby. I just want to make it clear from the beginning that this man is not your father. He has no authority over you, and he's not to be telling you what you can and can't do."

Outside the station windows the train hissed and clanked as it slowly pulled away from the station. Fiona took the opportunity to take in a deep breath. The meeting with the new owner of Castle Glen had begun even more dreadfully than she could have imagined. She'd intended to be dignified and distant, but pleasant enough so that Duncan Campbell would have no reason not to allow them to stay at the castle until she had time to sort out the coil of the old Campbell clan rights. Instead, she'd lost control.

Alasdair had cautioned her about her quick temper.

She turned to face Duncan Campbell. "Forgive my comment about the upstart American," she apologized. "As you can imagine, we've been through a difficult time with my husband's death, and it was not easy to learn that the castle was not to be passed to his heir. Frankly, I have no idea whether you're an upstart or not. I don't know anything about you."

For the first time she thought she saw a glimmer of amusement in Duncan Campbell's dark eyes, but his voice was serious as he answered, "No, you don't. But since we are about to share living quarters, I suspect that situation will change."

She stopped twisting her reticule strings. At least it did not appear that he intended to run them off the place. "I suspect it will," she agreed. She made no further apology for her words. After all, *he* had insulted her first, bringing up rude questions and assumptions about her marriage. He knew nothing about her marriage or about her husband, who had most certainly *not* been a lecherous old codger.

Tears stung her eyes. Alasdair MacLennan had been the most decent, noble gentleman Fiona had ever known. He'd waited nearly two years after bringing his young bride home before he'd taken her to his bed, and even then it had been more at Fiona's insistence than his.

"If we are to live together, perhaps we should agree to make an effort to get along," he said, taking a step toward her and extending his hand.

She moved closer to put her hand in his. Instead of shaking it, he lifted it to his lips in a gesture so smooth that it appeared he had just arrived from the Continent.

"I believe we have established a guarded truce, Lady MacLennan," he said, releasing her hand and stepping back.

She looked into his face, searching for the slightest bit of warmth, but his dark eyes were impassive.

chapter 2

D uncan *looked around the castle dining room with ap-*
proval. Some of his business colleagues back in
New York had questioned his decision to leave his lux-
ury Park Avenue mansion for a crumbling old castle in
the wild Highlands of Scotland, and Duncan had to
admit that he himself had wondered if he wasn't com-
mitting the height of folly. But except for the frigid temperature throughout the place, Glencolly Castle had been
a pleasant surprise. The seemingly endless rooms were
richly furnished, the walls covered with quite extraordi-
nary tapestries. Of course, some of the trappings appeared to be as old as the castle itself and were showing
their wear. But age had not altered the carved oak beams
that stretched across the ceiling of the dining hall. Nor
had the years damaged the magnificent dining table,
whose rich wood had only been enhanced through generations of polishings.

The large table looked a bit absurd for the size of the
dinner party. Lady MacLennan sat at the opposite end, far

enough away to make conversation difficult at normal levels of speaking. The boy, Robby, sat halfway between them.

"Do you eat here every night?" Duncan asked loudly, breaking a long stretch of silence. "I mean, do you eat at this big table, just the two of you?"

Robby looked at his stepmother, then turned to Duncan and replied, "Most nights everyone eats here."

"Everyone?" He looked down the table at Lady MacLennan. She remained silent. Duncan's eyes narrowed. He hadn't quite made up his mind about the attractive widow. After her outburst at the railroad station, which he supposed he had partly deserved, she had turned into the perfect hostess, cool and dignified, yet saying all the correct things to welcome him to her home. He'd felt like a guest visiting for tea rather than the new owner of the estate.

She had changed clothes for the evening meal, but her dress was still a conservative dove gray, high-necked and stiff, appropriate for a mourning widow.

He turned back to the boy. "Who is everyone?" he asked.

"Why, *everyone*—Malcolm and Lizzie and the Bandy twins and—" He paused. "We sit at table together at Castle Glen. 'Tis the way my father wanted it."

Now Duncan was thoroughly confused. According to his papers, the boy was the only direct descendant MacLennan left in Glencolly. "Who are these people?" he asked her directly.

Even from a distance he could see her tight expression soften into a smile. "Robby is talking about all the people who work here at the castle. Most of them are kin in some loose-handed way. My husband always considered us to be a family, and, as such, all were free to dine at our table whenever their duties permitted."

Duncan blinked in surprise. Servants eating at the master's table? He wondered if he'd understood correctly. "Forgive me, but—are you referring to maids and, er, the elderly gentleman who brought us from the station and—"

"Aye," she agreed. "We call Malcolm the butler, but he really manages the place. He usually joins us for dinner, as does Lizzie, the upstairs maid, and May, the buttermaid, and our gardeners, and Baird and Blair Bandy, who run the stables. My husband enjoyed having a full table."

Duncan took a moment to digest the odd revelation. "Where are they all tonight?" he asked.

"I believe it was a unanimous decision to wait and see how the new owner cared to run the household."

Duncan pushed away his half-eaten plate of mutton. He'd had little appetite since arriving in London a week ago, and the English fare had not particularly helped in boosting it. Servants at the dinner table? That was one decision he hadn't expected to be making. "It would seem an unusual practice," he said slowly.

Fiona MacLennan's expression had frozen up again. "Perhaps, but it's always been the way here. As I say, these people are kinfolk in some way or another. We don't think of servants and masters. We're just . . . family."

Back in Manhattan, Duncan would have jumped naked into the Hudson sooner than he would have sat down at a table with his butler. "I suppose we should follow your regular custom, at least until I have a chance to learn the operation here," he said finally.

Robby's face brightened. "Shall I go fetch people, Fee?" he asked.

Fiona shook her head. "Not tonight, Robby. But you may tell Malcolm that they are free to join us tomorrow." She looked at Duncan and said, "Thank you. I know it will reassure people to learn that things are not to change."

Duncan traced a design on the embroidered tablecloth with his fingertips. He had noticed that the fine stitching was frayed and the rich linen was stained. The lovely widow's assumption was not entirely correct. He was quite sure that a number of things would change around Castle Glen. Servants dining at the table may or may not be one of those things. But he saw no need to make waves on his first night. Tomorrow would be soon enough to begin the process of bringing some order and efficiency to his new home.

"So what do you say, Mr. Campbell?" the boy was asking.

Duncan had not been listening. "I beg your pardon?"

"Shall I take you around the estate tomorrow morning? I reckon you could pick any horse in the stable since they belong to you now." The boy's statement appeared to be utterly without resentment. He looked to Fiona for confirmation. "Don't they, Fee?"

Fiona nodded stiffly. She appeared to be much more aware than her stepson of exactly what he had lost.

"I would be pleased to have you show me, Robby," Duncan answered smoothly, "though I'll warn you that I'm not much of a rider. Perhaps Lady MacLennan would care to join us?" he added.

She shook her head, her expression stern. Duncan was beginning to believe that he had dreamed that brief smile. "I will let Robby do the honors," she said.

Fine, he thought. Let her be as haughty as she liked. He'd come to take over Glencolly Castle and get it running with the efficiency he'd used with his businesses in New York. If Fiona MacLennan got in his way, he was under no obligation to continue to offer her shelter under his roof.

He gave a brisk nod, then pulled out his watch and looked at it. "The boy and I shall leave at ten o'clock and return by noon. Lady MacLennan, would you please arrange for me to meet with the estate warden at that hour?"

He thought he could see her flinch. "My husband ran the estate himself," she said.

"Oh—er, I had understood that he was ill and—" He paused. "Who has been handling things since his death?"

Her pointed chin rose. "I have."

Another surprise. He supposed he would have to get used to them. "Very good. Then I should like to see *you* at noon tomorrow."

"You may see me whenever you choose, Mr. Campbell," she said softly. "I live here."

He began to make a quick retort, then stopped as he heard a faint, distant sound, oddly like a wail. "What's that?" he asked, slipping his watch back into its pocket. "Is someone in distress?"

The sound grew slightly louder, then seemed to dip and swell in a curious way. Robby clapped his hands together and shouted, "It's Jaime! He's playing the Stuart pipes again. We haven't heard him for ages!"

"Jaime?" Duncan asked. "Is he another servant?"

"Nay, Jaime's not a servant, he's a true MacLennan laird." Robby was squirming in his chair. "May I go, Fee?" he asked. She nodded, and in an instant Robby had shot out of the room.

Duncan waited for an explanation from the opposite end of the table, but when Fiona remained silent, he said, "I don't remember reading anything about a Jaime MacLennan."

She gave a dab to her mouth with her napkin, then stood, shaking out her full skirt. "I'm not surprised, unless you read history books. Jaime MacLennan died at the Battle of Culloden in 1747."

Duncan frowned. "I'm not sure I understand—"

"You should be pleased, Mr. Campbell," she answered. "It's your first night here, and you've already been honored with an appearance by the ghost of Castle Glen. If you'll excuse me, Malcolm will see you to your room."

Then she turned around with a swish of taffeta and walked out of the dining hall.

Fiona sat at Alasdair's old desk in the castle library. Even with the cushions she'd added to raise the seat, she was dwarfed by his massive carved chair. She'd been managing the estate for nearly a year, ever since Alasdair's cough had weakened him so that it was difficult for him to go up and down the steep stairs. But every time she considered bringing in a chair that would be more suitable to her size, she would feel a pang of guilt. This was Alasdair's office, and to her, it always would be. It was here that the two of them had shared their love of books and learning. Here that he had spent hours comforting her after her mother's death.

Her father had died in a riding accident when Fiona was five, leaving his wife and daughter with only a modest estate just north of Glencolly. Alasdair had helped out through the years, but by the time her mother died nine years later, the family debts were greater than the value of the small estate.

Alasdair had brought her to live at Castle Glen and eventually had gently offered her marriage as a solution to her need for a home and money to pay off the debts her parents had left.

She looked around the cluttered room with its book-lined walls. Duncan Campbell did not appear to be a man who would enjoy this kind of cozy chaos. Soon he'd be sitting in Alasdair's chair. At least it would fit him, she thought with a sigh, plumping up one of the pillows beneath her.

She supposed it had been ungracious of her not to go on the estate tour this morning, though she had no doubt that Robby would do perfectly well as a guide around the vast MacLennan lands. He'd begun making the rounds of the estate riding on the front of his father's saddle before he'd learned to walk. In fact, Robby was no doubt a better choice for the task of showing the estate off to its new owner. It appeared easy for the sunny-natured boy to forget the injustice involved. Whereas she, as had been amply demonstrated the previous day, seemed to have trouble keeping a civil tongue.

Alasdair had warned her about her temper a time or two, but his words had had little effect since she'd always known that secretly he had admired her spirit. She smiled at the memory.

It was nearly noon—the appointed time for the meeting with Mr. Campbell. She had a feeling that the meticulous American might not think much of her management. As usual, her papers were strewn across the desk. She'd never seen much point in trying to put things in some kind of artificial order when she always knew where everything was when she needed it.

Now, for example, she knew exactly which papers she needed to extract from the piles and put away before Mr. Campbell's arrival. She'd found the documents in the window seat a fortnight ago. By then, of course, the courts had already awarded the title of the Castle Glen estate to Duncan Campbell and the new owner was already en route to take possession. But if these new documents proved to be authentic, they would provide the means to overturn the court's decision.

She'd written immediately to her lawyer, Hampton Sinclair, and asked him to investigate, but so far she'd had no reply.

She gathered up the newly discovered papers and stuffed them into a brown folder. Then she crossed the room to the seat underneath the big office window. Though it wasn't apparent from looking at it, when the cushions were removed, the top of the seat could be pried open to reveal a compartment underneath. Duncan Campbell would never think to look there.

Quickly she crossed the room, pushed aside the cushions, opened the seat, and put the brown folder inside.

She had barely had time to replace the pillows when the door opened behind her and Duncan Campbell entered the room. Turning around, she spoke quickly, her voice slightly higher than normal. "Ah, Mr. Campbell, you're here. I trust your morning tour was satisfactory?"

"Quite," he replied. He glanced around the room for a moment, then, without asking, walked over to Alasdair's desk and began to take a seat behind it. The cushions Fiona had piled in the chair to make up for her small stature raised the height of the seat, causing him to teeter. He put his hands flat on the desk for balance and looked down in confusion. "What the devil?" he muttered.

Fiona stifled a laugh. "I'm sorry. I'm afraid the chair is full of pillows. I need them to reach the desk."

Though her explanation made it obvious that *she* had been the one using the chair, he didn't offer to let her resume her seat there. Instead, he stood up, threw the offending pillows to one side, then sat down again. The big chair fit him perfectly, she noticed with some annoyance.

Her heart gave one of the twinges she'd become accustomed to since her husband's death. With an inner sigh she took a seat in the smaller chair in front of the desk, just as she had so often when Alasdair had been alive. "Did you and Robby manage to see most of the place?" she asked, trying to get her mind off the past.

He shifted in his seat with a quick flush of embarrassment that didn't seem to fit on his strong features. "We, er . . . the horse and I had a disagreement a bit into the ride. Robby said we saw about a third of the place."

"That's odd. Glencolly horses are known for their training."

Duncan apparently did not want to pursue the topic. He cleared his throat and observed, "Robby seems to know everyone on the estate."

"Aye," she agreed. "He's a sharp lad."

"Though he apparently believes in *ghosts*," he added with a sardonic raise of his eyebrows. "But I suppose no one is perfect."

"He told you about Jaime, then?"

Duncan nodded. "How many other people here believe in that piece of foolishness?"

Fiona shrugged. "It's not a matter of believing or not. It's simply a fact of life here. Jaime makes himself known now and then. He's no bother."

"I'd heard that the Highlands were still rampant with legends and superstitions, but I hadn't expected an example so close to home. A castle ghost. It seems appropriate somehow." He grinned at her. The change in expression startled her. Duncan Campbell was an attractive man, she decided. She was glad that her mission to defeat him put her out of danger of being charmed by him. "Now tell me the truth, Lady MacLennan," he continued, still smiling. "You don't truly believe in ghosts, do you?"

She clasped her hands tightly in her lap. It wouldn't do

to lose her concentration simply because for perhaps the first time in her life she was engaged in a private conversation with a handsome young man. "I thought we were here to discuss the business of the estate," she said.

His smile faded. "Yes, we are. I'll admit that I was surprised to hear that your late husband had not appointed someone to manage things."

"But he did," Fiona corrected. "He appointed me."

"Yes, but I mean—"

"You mean a man?"

"Frankly, that would have been my expectation."

"Over the years my husband taught me many things, Mr. Campbell, including the management of Glencolly Castle. By the time of his death I had already been running his affairs for quite some time. I think you'll find that things are in order."

Duncan looked down at the stacks of paper with a doubtful expression. "Yes, well—"

"In fact," Fiona continued, her voice rising, "Alasdair had every expectation that I would *continue* to manage Glencolly Castle until such time as his son was ready to take over the task. It was that expectation that allowed him to go to his Maker in peace."

She bit her lip as more hot words threatened to tumble out. She simply could not continue to lose her temper around Duncan Campbell, no matter how infuriating the situation nor how exasperating he decided to be.

Duncan appeared to be studying her. After a long moment he leaned toward her over the desk. His tone was warm and cajoling. "Lady MacLennan, I realize that this must be difficult for you, but I'm hoping that together we can make this transition as easy as possible for everyone concerned. I'd like you to consider me a friend."

He appeared to be sincere, and she had to admit that sitting across from him, watching the sunlight from the bay window flicker in his dark eyes, she found her anger softening.

"Perhaps you could start by calling me Duncan," he said, his smile returning.

"Very well," she agreed, though such familiarity was a little more than she would have wanted.

"Good." He leaned back in the chair and waited.

After a moment she asked, "What exactly do you want to discuss?"

He looked down at the papers again, and she expected a question about estate finances, but when he lifted his gaze to her again, he said merely, "Let's start with you."

She frowned. "I beg your pardon."

"Tell me about yourself. You bristled in the station yesterday when I made the comments about your husband's age, and I suppose you had a right to think me impertinent. So I'll try a more decorous approach. How long were you married to Alasdair MacLennan?"

It was not the topic she had expected, and she shifted in her chair in confusion. She'd never before had to answer questions about her marriage. Everyone in Glencolly knew the circumstances.

"We were married for ten years," she said finally.

His eyes widened. "Ten years. You must have been a mere child, since you could not be much more than a score of years now."

The confusion was turning to irritation. "Mr. Campbell—"

"Duncan," he corrected.

"Very well, Duncan. I realize that you have certain rights to my husband's estate, but I don't believe those rights give you any kind of authority over me. Nor do I see that the circumstances of my marriage are any of your business. But I was fourteen, of legal age to marry, when I wed Alasdair."

"Which would now make you four and twenty."

"I'm happy to see that you learned sums in America," she retorted.

He smiled. "Was your family content to see you marry a man so much your senior?"

"I had no family, Mr. Campbell, and if Alasdair had not been kind enough to take a penniless orphan into his home, I have no idea what would have become of me."

"Ah," he said, leaning back in his chair.

She bit her lip. She hadn't intended to tell him that.

"At the risk of seeing the hair stand up again on that lovely neck of yours, I'll make the observation that it was probably not much of a hardship for MacLennan to find himself with such a beautiful young woman under his roof."

Fiona sighed. She was having difficulty dealing with Duncan Campbell's odd mixture of insults and compliments. "Could we change the topic to something of a less personal nature?" she asked.

He hesitated a long moment, studying her with those intense dark eyes. Finally he said, "Very well. Tell me about this ghost of yours. Robby said the tale has been around for generations, yet no one now living has ever seen the thing."

She had little desire to discuss the ghost, either, but at least it was less uncomfortable than answering questions about her marriage. "There are some in the village who claim to have seen Jaime MacLennan walking in the Stuart Tower and playing his pipes, but it has been many years since he's been sighted."

"The Stuart Tower? That's the one at the north end of the castle?"

"Yes. The story is that Charles Stuart himself once stayed there."

"Bonnie Prince Charlie? That Charles Stuart?"

"Yes. That's how the tower got its name."

"And Jaime MacLennan?"

"Was a supporter of the Bonnie Prince," Fiona supplied. "He was killed fighting for him at Culloden." She'd heard Alasdair tell the sad story many times. "He was a young man and had just taken a new bride not a month before the battle."

Duncan cocked his head. "So now the ill-fated Jaime walks this Stuart Tower and plays the pipes in mourning for his lost love." His expression was serious, but his tone was mocking.

Fiona had had some doubts herself about the validity of the ghost story, but now she found herself wanting to defend the MacLennan legend. "You yourself heard it last night."

"Yes, and Robby told me that he went racing up to the tower, but unfortunately, old Jaime had packed it in for the night by the time he arrived."

Let him mock, she told herself. If Mr. Sinclair could authenticate the new papers she'd found, Mr. Duncan Campbell would soon be on his way back to New York, where he could laugh with his American friends about the quaint Scottish Highlanders who believed in ghosts.

"I thought you wanted to talk about the estate," she snapped.

"I want to know everything about it," he agreed. "I'm merely starting with some of the more curious aspects."

"Meaning the ghost."

"The ghost, yes, and the mistress of the castle."

"Well, if we've dispensed with those *curious* subjects, then perhaps we could move on." She picked up the pile of papers nearest her.

"I've not dispensed with them yet," he said.

She looked up, ready to fend off another impertinent question.

Duncan was standing up. "I believe I'd like to see this Stuart Tower."

Puzzled, she told him, "Jaime never makes an appearance during the day."

He grinned at her. "Good. Then he won't mind if we take a tour of his quarters."

chapter 3

Duncan took long strides to follow his hostess as she hurried across the great hall that led out of the castle entryway. Oil paintings lined the sides of the large room.

"Ancestors?" he asked.

Fiona slowed her pace. "Aye. We call this the Portrait Room." She pointed to a large painting in the middle of the left-hand wall. A glowering Highlander in furs and fierce battle attire glared out at the room. "That's Black Guin, the first MacLennan laird. Next to him is his son, Geordie the Meek." She smiled briefly. "I suspect there was not the best of understanding between father and son."

She continued along the line, giving him the name and ranking of each one of the portraits. Though she'd come into the family by marriage, she appeared to know a great deal about the MacLennan family history.

"The MacLennan ancestors apparently were warriors," he said, pointing to the far wall that held an impressive display of axes, crossbows, pikes, and swords.

"Men like to fight," she commented.

His eyebrow rose. "Nowadays I believe we use more civilized means to settle our differences."

"Such as courts and judges?"

There was a tinge of bitterness to the words, so he decided it would be best to change the subject. "Are you MacLennan kin as well?" he asked as they reached the far door of the long room.

"Kin? Of course not. I married Alasdair MacLennan."

"I was just curious. You say most of the servants are kin. I wondered if there was anyone in Glencolly who was not related to the MacLennans."

Without reply, she turned away from him and continued leading the way toward the tower.

Duncan gave a last glance back at the wall full of formidable Scottish faces, then followed her. From the stiffness in her shoulders, it appeared that he had managed to irritate her again. He knew that he had stepped over the line of propriety more than once in his questioning of Fiona MacLennan, but something about the woman piqued his curiosity and brought out a roguish side that would probably surprise his friends back in America.

Though he'd never been one to mince words in his various businesses, he knew how to behave in proper society. The doyennes of the New York social scene would no doubt be appalled by his lack of manners toward a gently born widow.

They would definitely be gossiping behind those ridiculous Japanese fans that were suddenly the rage this season if they could see how his gaze lingered on Lady MacLennan's delectable backside as she led the way up the winding stone stairs to the Stuart Tower. In New York a society lady would give away half her trousseau rather than let a man follow directly behind her while she mounted a steep stairway, her hips swaying enticingly in

front of his face. Lady MacLennan's hips were diminutive, but nicely rounded, just like the rest of her. A com-
pact package that promised delights and surprises if the
wrappings were carefully opened by the right man. He
frowned. It was difficult to believe that Alasdair MacLennan, at over three score years, had been that man.

"Have a care with this section," Fiona turned to say
over her shoulder. "Some of the stones are loose."

Duncan quickly shifted his gaze from her hips to her
eyes. "What is this part of the castle used for?" he asked
her.

"It's not used at all. Robby comes up here to play
sometimes, but most of us avoid it."

"Because of Jaime the Ghost?" he asked with a sardonic grin.

The eyes flared blue fire. "Aye."

She was offended again. Why did he keep doing that?
"I only meant to say is there not some good use it could
be put to?"

She continued on up the stairs, holding the oil lamp in
front of her instead of to one side, apparently no longer
concerned whether the beam reached behind her to light
Duncan's way. "The disposal of the rooms is the province
of the master of the castle, of course," she said coldly. "If
you'd prefer sleeping here, I'll have them bring you up
some bedding."

He was unaware of the sarcasm of her reply until they
reached the end of the long stairway and entered a single
round room that occupied the entire top of the tower. The
chamber was anything but a comfortable sleeping quarters. It had narrow slits to the outside every three or four
feet, as if the room had once served as a battlement. The
sun slanted through the narrow openings all along the
west side, making an odd crisscross pattern of shadows on
the gray stone floor. A settee covered in tattered purple

velvet was pushed awkwardly against part of the round wall. The only other furniture was a heavy table in the exact middle of the room. It was draped with what looked like a flag.

"The Stuart banner?" he asked, pointing to it.

"Nay," she answered without offering further explanation. She walked across the circle to the far side of the room and peered out one of the window slits, squinting. "From here you can see the village of Glencolly."

He followed her over and looked out the opening, bracing himself on the icy stone wall that surrounded it. From a distance the little village of Glencolly looked like a picture from a traveler's stereopticon collection—a quaint jumble of gray tiled roofs nestled into gentle green hills and split crosswise by the river in one direction and the railroad tracks, gleaming new, in the other.

"It's quite a view." He stepped back and studied the opening. It was a diagonal cut that narrowed from about fifteen inches on the inside to no more than five at the outside of the thick wall. "It's a shame these windows aren't larger," he said. "This room would be spectacular with a wider vista."

To his side he heard that annoyed click of her tongue. He'd only been making an observation, he thought, irritated. There was no need for her to bristle at his every word. Particularly when this was *his* castle. Ignoring her dark expression, he walked around the room slowly, stooping to see the view from each of the slits.

"What's that over there?" he asked when he reached the east wall. The river gave a sharp turn north alongside a large estate with a spectacular house that was obviously of much more recent origins than Castle Glen.

She walked over beside him. Surreptitiously, she slipped her hand into a pocket and pulled out a pair of silver-rimmed spectacles. Putting them on, she looked out the window. "That's Maitland Manor," she said. "Our nearest neighbors."

He looked at her in surprise. The spectacles did nothing to alter the loveliness of her even features. In fact, they seemed to enhance the blue of her bright eyes.

She seemed unaware of his scrutiny. "Logan Maitland received a knighthood from the queen for service in India," she continued, "and returned here about twenty years ago to build that house."

Finally he took his gaze away from her face and followed the direction of her pointing hand. Even from here he could see that the Maitland house had windows that gave proper display to the beauty of Glencolly Valley. Back home the wealthy owners of the manors one of his companies had built along the Hudson would kill for views like this. And they wouldn't have been happy looking out at them through five-inch openings. Of course, none of them had ever entertained Bonnie Prince Charlie.

"Not too many places here for a ghost to hide," he observed with a smile, turning back to the circular chamber.

She shrugged. "I reckon ghosts can hide wherever they like. Part of the bargain in being a ghost."

He resisted the urge to make another flippant comment. He'd no doubt offended her enough for one day. It would be wise to remember that her cooperation was important to him until he learned everything he needed to know about Castle Glen. It had always been his way with every new venture. Learn. Listen. Play dumb, if necessary. Then, when you have mastered the subject, the mentor becomes disposable. He had a feeling that he'd be wise to make the prickly Lady MacLennan disposable as soon as possible. But at the moment he needed her.

He walked over and put his hand on the banner draping the table. Surprisingly, the cloth was quite cold to the touch, even colder than the stone wall. "If this isn't a Stuart flag, is it a MacLennan banner?" he asked.

She hesitated. Finally she walked over to the table, briskly pulled the cloth out from under his hand, and held it up for display.

It was a royal blue color with two insignias. In the upper left was a golden lion wrestling with a bear. In the center was a circle of stars surrounding a crown and what appeared to be a goblet. "It's a special ensign," she said stiffly. "The Campbell design is in the center, and in the corner is the old MacLennan coat of arms. We believe the flag dates from the time of Culloden, when the MacLennans were forced to swear fealty to the Campbells."

Beginning the process that made him legal heir to Castle Glen rather than her stepson, he finished silently. No wonder she'd been reluctant to show it to him.

He took the cloth from her. His fingers brushed against her hands, which were also cold. Was there nothing warm in this country? He spread the flag back on the table, then pointed at the MacLennan insignia. "Why a bear and lion fighting?" he asked.

She gave a fleeting smile that gave the icy room a sudden warmth. "I reckon 'tis a family trait."

"Was your Alasdair a fighter?"

"When he believed something was worth fighting for."

"I detect no undue belligerence in his son."

"Robby's mother was a Mungo. They're reasoning people. In Robby, the MacLennan stubbornness was sweetened by the Mungo strain."

It was another thing he'd have to get used to in this place, Duncan realized. In New York a man could make his own mark. Here your reputation was predestined by the deeds of ancestors going back for centuries. "He's a good boy, whatever made him that way."

"Aye," she said. She leaned over to make a barely noticeable adjustment to the way he'd replaced the flag on the table.

"Perhaps we should hang it somewhere now that the Campbells and MacLennans are united, so to speak," he offered.

"To be truthful, I've always felt it an ugly banner. The two insignias are a poor match. Have you seen enough?"

"Unless you think ol' Jaime will make an appearance."

She ignored his comment and turned to lead him back down the winding stairs.

*B*y the time Fiona had gone through the estate papers to the new owner's satisfaction, she was feeling more weary than she had since the days of nursing Alasdair before his death. It would not do, she told herself briskly. If she was to do something about the situation facing her and Robby, she had to have energy, and she had to keep her wits about her.

Duncan Campbell was not the brash American she had thought him. He was thorough and obviously clever. He'd quickly grasped that Castle Glen was no longer sustaining itself. In recent years Alasdair had begun selling off little sections of MacLennan land to raise the funds to maintain the place. She suspected that he'd also borrowed money, though he'd never mentioned this, and she'd found no record with his papers.

She had a theory that the necessity to sell his family land had hastened Alasdair's death. Each sale had been like another stone on his grave. Now the grave in the far corner of the MacLennan cemetery behind the castle was fully covered with stones, in the ancient way. Alasdair was gone, but the problem of keeping the castle was no closer to being solved.

To his credit, Duncan had not appeared discouraged by

the figures she'd given him. He'd pursed those strong lips of his a time or two and once gave a low whistle at the cost of salaries paid to estate retainers who were too old to do any more work. But he'd not become excited or angry.

"The problem is that the days of feudal tributes are long past," he'd observed. "A laird no longer has minions to pay him annual funds in return for his overlord protection."

Alasdair had explained the situation to Fiona in much the same terms. Her throat closed as she remembered her husband's apology as he lay dying. For the first time ever she'd seen tears gather in his dear eyes. "I've left ye a muddle, Fee," he'd told her. "Ye'll need to hope the woolen market picks up. Then ye could expand the sheep business . . ." His crackly voice had trailed off in despair. Life was ebbing too fast for him to be of any further help to her.

She'd been so lost in her thoughts she practically ran straight into Malcolm, who had been standing silently, waiting for her at the end of the hallway.

"Are you quite sure the new master wants us at the table for supper?" he asked when she'd looked up at him with a tired smile.

"So he said. I get the feeling he's trying his best not to cause too much disruption." She'd give him credit for that much.

Malcolm nodded approval, then observed, "He's not as dreadful as we had thought. In fact, some of the lads are calling him a rather decent chap."

"I know." Did that make her task easier or more difficult? she wondered. "Do they need help in the kitchen?"

"No, milady. You look as if you could use a rest before supper. You and the new master have been at those numbers all afternoon."

"I'll find Robby and see how his ride went this morning."

"He's in the schoolroom, still at his lessons."

Fiona felt a surge of pride. He could have used her absence as an excuse to ignore his studies that day, but he was a diligent student.

"Learning is important," he'd told her many times. "I'm to be laird, and need to know more than anyone."

The memory brought another pang. Would Robby ever be able to assume his rightful place as laird? Duncan Campbell appeared to be winning approval from some of the people on the estate. Even Malcolm seemed to be softening toward him. But that didn't mean he deserved to be here.

She reached the second floor and continued up the winding stairs of the Scholar's Tower. The tower was on the far end of the castle from the Stuart's Tower. Looking at the castle from the outside, the two towers gave the structure a certain symmetry, though the Scholar's Tower was much smaller than the Stuart Tower and lacked the battlement-like openings. The daylight in the Scholar's Tower came from two louvered openings, one on each side of the circular room.

Fiona had never liked the room and had suggested that she and Robby move their lessons down to a more comfortable parlor on the lower floor of the castle, but Robby had insisted on keeping the tradition. The Scholar's Tower had served as the schoolroom for generations of MacLennan lairds.

He was sitting at his schoolroom desk squinting at a book of maps. The late afternoon sun lent little light to the room.

"You should have lit the lamps, Robby," she chided.

He looked up. "I was nearly finished."

"That's not your lesson."

He turned the book around so that the page was facing her. "There's New York, Fee," he said, pointing. "Duncan says it's on an island, just like England and Scotland, only much smaller."

"I know."

"And Duncan says that there's more business done on that one little island than all of Scotland. Can you believe it?"

"Well, that I'm not sure of. It hardly seems likely. People are usually overly proud of their own towns."

"I'm proud of Glencolly," Robby agreed. "But it's *nothing* like New York City. Duncan says people are back and forth in the streets all day and all night. It never stops. Duncan says that one day it's going to become the most important city in the world and that he would take me to see it some day."

Fiona had heard entirely too many *Duncan says*.

"You should be calling him Mr. Campbell, Robby. Duncan is disrespectful."

"Duncan says I should call him Duncan."

She sighed.

"When do they sleep if people go around all day and all night, Fee?"

"I don't know. I imagine New Yorkers need to sleep just like everyone else."

"Duncan says—"

"It's time for you to put the books away and come downstairs," Fiona interrupted with a touch of irritation. She'd sought Robby out to ask what he'd thought of his morning ride with Duncan Campbell, but the boy's eager recital of the newcomer's every utterance told the story more plainly than words. "We should check with Malcolm and Emmaline to see if they need any help with the supper, since it's the first night we'll have everyone at the table with the new master."

Robby seemed to belatedly sense his stepmother's annoyance. "I'll go straight down to the kitchens," he said. Then he got that adult look in his eyes that she had not quite become accustomed to. "You look tired, Fee. Why don't you lie down for a spell?"

Fiona gave herself a shake of irritation as she made her way down to her bedchamber. Malcolm and Robby had become her two protectors since Alasdair's death. It was comforting at times, but today she found it annoying. She looked tired, they'd both said. What was that supposed to mean? She smoothed her hands over the gray linen gown she'd been wearing all day long. Alasdair had hated her in black, so she'd taken to wearing gray since his death. She hadn't yet had the heart to resume donning the bright MacLennan plaid he'd loved to see her wear.

But she knew the gray was not flattering. It dulled the sparkle of her blue eyes and made them look shadowed against her pale skin. She closed the door to her bedroom with a hard push.

Tired, indeed. She'd show them that Alasdair MacLennan's widow was not too tired to serve as hostess in her own castle. With sudden determination she walked across the room to her wardrobe cupboard. Opening it, she pulled out a dress that Alasdair had had made for her shortly before he'd taken ill. It was a yellow taffeta, designed to be the perfect showcase for the bright reds and blues of a length of MacLennan plaid that was stitched across one shoulder and around the waist. She'd hardly worn the dress. The truth was she'd been embarrassed by the rather shocking décolletage which left the entire top of her breasts covered by the barest strip of tulle. Tonight she didn't care. Let Duncan Campbell be shocked, she thought. It was time that he saw what the widow of Alasdair MacLennan was made of.

• • •

D uncan *was surprised when he glanced at the window of* the comfortable office to see that the sun was setting. After Fiona MacLennan had left him, he'd become engrossed in the castle accounts and had not noticed the passage of time. The situation was much more bleak than the attorney in Glasgow had painted. The income from Glencolly Castle had dwindled to practically nothing. Tenant rents had steadily fallen as Alasdair MacLennan had sold off the best portions of the estate lands.

Decreased profits from the Glencolly woolen mill, which was owned by the estate, were apparently a major source of the problem. The mill still processed all the MacLennan wool and wool from the entire Glencolly Valley, but the cost of running the mill appeared to be overrunning the income earned from the end product in Glasgow. It was one area that his business sense told him needed immediate attention.

Of course, Duncan himself had sizable reserves. He'd built Campbell Enterprises into a conglomerate of a number of companies, all of which produced substantial income. He could well afford to subsidize the castle operations for a number of years. But he hadn't become one of the shrewdest businessmen in New York by investing in losing ventures.

He closed the big account book with a sigh of exasperation. The oversize ledger appeared to be decades, if not centuries, old, just like everything else in Alasdair's office. Just like everything else in this entire moldering place. What the hell was he doing here?

He'd as good as usurped the place of the lad everyone had expected to be MacLennan's heir. The man's widow was frostily polite when she wasn't letting her obvious hostility show through. He knew nothing about this country or its people. They weren't his family, no matter what some ancient land feud had dictated.

There was a timid knock on the door. At his response it opened to admit a mousy serving girl.

"The mistress says be ye coomin' to supper, sir?"

"Yes, I'll be there directly."

The girl bobbed and disappeared.

The truth was that Duncan knew very well why he was here. No matter how high Duncan had risen in New York, his father, Robert, had never been impressed. To Robert, everything about the New World had been cheap and second-rate. The fact that Duncan had embraced that world had simply widened the gulf between father and son. Eventually the arguments, which had started when Duncan was just a boy, hurting from the loss of his mother, had turned into an estrangement. Duncan had wanted to patch things up with his father, but the demands of his businesses always seemed to keep him too busy to deal with the situation. When Robert died, Duncan had not spoken to him for five years.

He gave a humorless laugh. "Can you see me from beyond the grave, Father?" he asked aloud. "Can you finally accept that the son you refused to acknowledge has made something of himself? I've come back to the homeland. I've a castle and a moldering, bankrupt estate to run. Is that enough for you?"

His father made no answer. His words for his only son were no more generous from beyond the grave than they had been in life. Perhaps he would ask Jaime the castle ghost to relay a message if he made another appearance tonight, Duncan thought with a sad smile.

He pushed his chair out from behind the desk and stood. As he started to leave, he stepped on a pillow, which reminded him that Fiona MacLennan had been occupying the chair before his arrival. The seat didn't fit her, he thought, in more ways than one. She might not see things that way, but it was lucky for her that he *had* arrived. Whether she knew it or not, Castle Glen was on a sure path to ruin. He wasn't yet sure exactly how he would do it, but he knew it was time for a dramatic change of course.

chapter 4

They had evidently been waiting for him, Duncan realized as he entered the castle dining hall. Unlike the previous evening, the huge table was nearly full. He'd met some of the people on his tour with Robby, but many of the faces were unfamiliar.

Everyone was still standing, apparently waiting for the new master to take his seat at the end of the table. But Duncan delayed sitting as his gaze went to the far end of the table where Fiona stepped from behind the back of the ornate carved chair. It had nearly hidden her, but now he could see that she had abandoned the dull gray she'd swathed herself in since his arrival. In its place was the most outlandish set of colors he'd ever seen. Her dress and the tartan wrapped around it stood out like a sudden bright sunbeam in the midst of the dark old wood of the dining hall. She'd be a laughingstock in New York, but here somehow the outfit suited her.

Even from the far end of the table, he could see the light dancing in her eyes as she smiled at Robby on her right. She looked young, and the specter of the tired, sad widow was suddenly banished.

She shifted her gaze to meet his and flushed as she saw that he had been studying her.

"I'd like to introduce you to the household, Mr. Campbell," she said. Even her voice sounded younger.

She gestured along the table, pronouncing the names far too quickly for him to remember.

"The Bandy brothers, Baird and Blair, run the stables, with several of the village lads. Then there's Lizzie, you've met, and Jane, upstairs maids, and Elspeth and May, downstairs, and May's new husband, Gavin, who's to start in the garden, with Hamish, the gardener . . ."

Duncan waved her to a stop. "Why don't we all sit down and each of you can introduce yourself while we're eating?" he suggested.

The previous day, when Fiona had talked about eating with the servants, he'd wondered if he hadn't quite understood the situation, but to all appearances, these people were humble folks who served the castle by day and dined with the master and mistress by night. Remarkable.

Even more remarkable was the fact that by halfway through the dinner, he was enjoying their company immensely. They were a bright and happy group who seemed not the least awed by the newcomer who had come to take over their home.

Hamish, the gardener, had the most to say. An older man with a rusty mane that was beginning to streak gray, he asked well-directed questions about both gardening and education in New York State. Apparently he'd had a letter from New York University when the University of Glasgow had referred his query regarding a new blight that was threatening the Highland meadows.

The four housemaids said little, but had not taken their eyes off Duncan the entire meal. Lizzie, the one who had come to his office to fetch him earlier, stared at him sideways through a big lock of brown hair that had come loose from her coiled braid and hung at the side of her face. She regularly opened and closed her mouth, as if she were going to speak, but no words came out.

He recognized one of the other maids, the one called May, from the tour with Robby. She'd introduced herself as the buttermaid, and Duncan had reflected that the job seemed to suit the pleasingly plump girl. During the meal, she spent most of her time smiling and casting adoring looks at the dour-looking young man by her side—Gavin MacTavish, her new husband. Gavin himself did not utter a word during the entire meal, but every time he glanced at his round little wife, a blush rolled up his face.

Gardener Hamish had been a widower for a number of years, Duncan gathered from the conversation, though often the man referred to his late wife in the present tense.

"Rufus here won the shoeing competition over to Glenmoor last spring," Hamish was saying.

Duncan eyed the muscular man who sat across from Robby at the far end of the table. He remembered the name from the boy who had helped him with his luggage.

"I met a cousin of yours on the train," he told the man. "He seemed a bright young lad."

Rufus gave a kind of grunt. "H'ain't nae business workin' fer sich a comp'ny. His ma tried to steer 'im to 'n honest trade like smithin', but he'd have nae part o' it. Lads today have nae sense."

"I'd love to work for the railroad," Robby piped in, ignoring the blacksmith's deepening frown.

"Nothing wrong with a lad being a mite forward-looking," Duncan agreed. "Railroads are the future, no doubt about it."

Rufus turned back to his plate of stew without comment. He was by far the least agreeable person at the table, Duncan decided. At least he didn't live at the castle. Fiona had explained that Rufus was up from the village for the day. He came twice a week to shoe horses and tend to any other of the castle's needs at the small forge behind the stables.

Duncan supposed that there had been a time when Castle Glen was self-sufficient, not needing the outside world for anything. But those days were over. Everyone needed the outside world these days.

"My husband was none too fond of the idea of the railroad coming through, either," Fiona said. "He was afraid it would ruin the land and bring undesirable elements to disrupt the peace of the Glencolly Valley."

Duncan wondered if the comment was directed toward him. But if the widow of the former master was calling the new master an undesirable element, no one around the table seemed to react to it. Perhaps he was being too sensitive, he decided.

"Progress always brings changes," he said briskly. "But generally it means a better life for everyone concerned."

"My seed sent up from Glasgow arrived in two days," Hamish agreed. "The contraption's something of a miracle, I should say."

"It puffs and huffs like a big ol' bull lookin' fer a ripe cow," May added with a giggle, and the flush started traveling up new husband Gavin's face.

Duncan expected chiding from her mistress at the randy remark at the dinner table, but Fiona was laughing along with the rest of the table. In New York such a comment would never have passed in polite society. Of course, a maid wouldn't be seated at the table in the first place. In New York . . . hell, he wasn't in New York anymore. Suddenly Duncan felt a wave of loneliness.

"I'd like a look at the stable tomorrow," he told the stable men, who sat halfway down the table to his left. He had yet to be able to tell the two apart or even to get their names straight. Bandy? Was that the surname? Baird Bandy? Or was it Bandy Baird? And the other was Blair? Jesus. There sure as hell was nothing about their appearance to distinguish them. They had on identical gray smocks and trousers. Handsome enough faces with happy dark eyes. Black hair of identical length.

"You'll be pleased, sir. The Castle Glen horses are a fine lot," one of the two said. Baird?

"I'm afraid my knowledge of the beasts is limited, but I understand that Lord MacLennan took quite an interest—"

He stopped as both the twins turned their heads toward the door, as if expecting a visitor. The doorway remained empty, but now Duncan could hear the distant sound of a faint wail.

"Two nights in a row, Fee!" Robby said, jumping up. "I do believe he's lonely. May I go?"

Fiona nodded and the boy took off, racing.

Duncan felt a surge of totally unanticipated excitement. He threw his napkin down on the table and stood without thinking. No one else at the table had moved. Perhaps it was not the most dignified way for the new master to act, he thought, looking around at their faces, but he couldn't help it.

"If you'll excuse me, ladies and gentle—er—*everyone*. I believe I'll join Robby in the Stuart Tower. Perhaps we can catch ourselves a ghost."

By the time Duncan exited the dining room, Robby had crossed the big castle entrance hall and was halfway down the long portrait gallery. Feeling a little foolish at his eagerness, Duncan broke into a run to catch up to him. He shook his head in bemusement. It was only his second night in Glencolly, and he was racing through his new property in search of a ghost that he knew did not exist. If he stayed in this place, he'd likely become as balmy as the rest of them, he thought with a grin.

He turned at the sound of light footsteps behind him. Fiona was following him, her bright skirts hiked up around her knees and her tartan flying behind her. She caught up to him easily.

"The ghost won't appear if you go storming up the tower like a warden after a fox," she told him.

"I don't expect he'll appear in any event," he said, but slowed his pace. "Didn't you tell me that no one living has ever seen the wily old spirit?"

Fiona let her skirts fall and smoothed them back into place. "You hear whispers, but there have been no confirmed sightings in recent years, no. Just the piping."

"Which could be any prankster sneaking up from the village to bedevil the castle residents for his own amusement."

"Think what you like, Mr. Campbell. But Glencolly folks do not take the legend of Jaime MacLennan lightly."

They had started up the winding stairs of the Stuart Tower. Robby was out of sight, but they could hear his steps above them. At least, he assumed they were Robby's steps, Duncan corrected himself with amusement. When ghosts walked, could you hear their footsteps?

"The wailing has stopped," Duncan noted.

"Aye. It always stops before anyone reaches the top of the stairs. I reckon Jaime plays for his bride, not for a bunch of curious descendants he doesn't even know."

She was ahead of him again on the stairs, holding a candle that flickered wildly in the drafty stairwell. Duncan glanced up at her face to see if her words were serious, then joined in her laugh when he saw the candlelight reflect a mischievous glint in her eyes. She was different tonight, he decided. It wasn't just the clothes. She'd been much less stiff at dinner, no doubt more comfortable sur-

rounded by the castle folk who obviously regarded her as
highly as they had their departed laird.

"Maybe we can change his mind," he answered with a
smile.

Robby came clattering down the stairs toward them,
holding another candle. "He's not there," he said. There
was little disappointment in his voice. Evidently the years
of looking had dimmed his expectations.

Fiona turned around to Duncan. "Do you want to go on
up?"

"As long as we're here, we might as well take a look.
Where do you think he goes?" he asked Robby.

The boy shrugged. "The piping always seems to fade
away just as I round the last turn to the Tower Room."
Then he moved past them down the steps.

Duncan had no idea why he wanted to complete the
climb when the boy had told them there was nothing to be
seen, but Fiona continued upward, and he followed her.

The Tower Room looked much different at night without the sun's rays from the slotted windows. The light of
Fiona's single candle did not reach across the big area,
which left the outer walls of the circle in shadow. In spite
of the warm summer evening, the room felt icy.

"It's frigid up here," Duncan observed. "It must be bru-
tal in the winter."

Fiona smiled. "Not always. The temperature seems to
depend on Jaime's mood. But the room appears empty to
me. Are you satisfied?"

He reached to take the candle from her and walked to
the other side of the circle. "I suppose you see nothing at
night from these windows."

"You may see some lights from the crofts over at Glencolly. It's too early for people to have retired for the
night."

She moved next to him to look out the slot that pointed

directly to the village. He moved the candle to his other hand to allow her to crowd close to him. A whiff of fragrance from her hair drifted up to compete with the smell of the burning wax. Duncan felt an odd and not entirely welcome stirring.

Lord Almighty, the last thing he wanted was to feel attracted to the quick-tempered widow. It was, however, difficult to avoid the fact that when he looked downward, his gaze had little other place to go than her breasts, gleaming white in the candlelight and pushed into tantalizing fullness by the tight bodice of her dress. He moved slightly to one side.

"Aye, there they are," she said, pointing and inching next to him to fill the space he'd vacated. She seemed unaware that he had deliberately moved. "Lights dancing in the darkness like faeries in a meadow. I've always loved to look at them from up here."

"You've come here before at night?"

She laughed. "I used to come running up with Robby every time Jaime played. We never caught him, of course. I tired of the game eventually, but Robby still comes to check, every time. He's sure that Jaime will show himself one of these days."

Duncan moved the candle farther away to keep the candlelight from flickering across her chest. The change of position didn't help.

He stepped back. "What about on the other side? Can you see the neighbors' estate that you showed me this morning?"

"The Maitlands? Aye, they're over here."

She led the way around the circle to the western windows and leaned out one. "Way off in the distance. Can you see it?" She took his arm and directed him toward the slot of the window. His face brushed against her hair as he leaned forward, but she didn't seem to notice. Her firm side pressed against his as she pointed in the distance to a faint spattering of lights in the darkness. If he turned even slightly, Duncan calculated, those full breasts he'd been admiring would be pressed against his chest.

From behind them came a sudden blast of cold air. Duncan turned around with a start. "What was that?"

Fiona did not appear startled. "These slanted windows create odd drafts at times. That's probably why it's so cold up here tonight."

Duncan stalked around the circle, but felt not the least breath of air entering from any of the slotted windows. "Odd" was all he said.

"Odd things happen in a castle, Mr. Campbell," she said, her voice suddenly tense. "Look." She pointed to the table in the center.

The flag was still draped over it, but the Campbell and MacLennan insignias were nowhere in sight. Duncan walked over to the table, set his candle on the floor, and picked up the cloth. As he suspected, the insignias were still in place on the other side. The flag had been laid on the table upside down. "One of the maids must have been up here dusting," he said.

"The servants don't come up here. I clean myself occasionally, but there's really no need."

"Perhaps Robby turned the flag around."

Fiona hesitated before answering. She had no intention of letting Duncan Campbell know that the upside-down flag had disturbed her. As far as she knew, no one else had ever even touched the banner in the ten years since she'd come to live at the castle. She herself had aired it out on several occasions, but she'd always put it carefully back in the place it had probably occupied for generations. Even though the two united emblems had always made her uneasy, just as she'd told Duncan earlier. When she'd turned and noticed that the cloth was turned over, she'd felt a strong chill along her spine, and it had nothing to do with any cross breeze from the slotted windows.

But Mr. Campbell had already made his skepticism about castle ghost tales clear. She wouldn't give him another reason to scoff.

"Aye, perhaps 'twas Robby," she said. She took the flag from him and spread it out with the insignias once again facing up. "Shall we go downstairs?"

"Will everyone still be at the table?"

"I reckon supper has finished by now."

He hesitated. "Then what? Do you invite these . . . er . . . people to spend the evening in the parlor with you?"

"These, er, *people* are hardworking folks, Mr. Campbell. They've toiled all day long, and I'd wager that most of them seek their beds rather directly after supper."

He looked relieved, and she had to shake off the feeling that he was *insulting* her family. He was a newcomer, she reminded herself. He couldn't be expected to understand Glencolly ways or to appreciate the generations of kinship and friendship that had forged the bonds of unity at the castle.

"Then perhaps I could persuade you to join me in the parlor for a glass of . . ." His brow furrowed. "I suppose you do have brandy here?"

The invitation was polite, but once again there was a hint of insult to his words that made her bristle. "I'm sure you'll find the castle wine cellar satisfactory, Mr. Campbell. My husband took great pride in it."

"Splendid. Then will you join me?"

For just an instant she thought she could detect a look of loneliness in his expression. She recognized it because she was feeling it, too. She'd always looked forward to her evenings with Alasdair. When most of the castle folk had gone to bed and the big old place had gone quiet, the two of them would retire to the library and read together by the cozy lamplight. Or they would sit on the floor in front of the fire discussing the day's events. Sometimes she would lie with her head on Alasdair's lap, and he would gently stroke her hair as they talked.

Eventually it had become difficult for him to lower himself to the hearthstone, and they had taken to sitting at his desk. At the end, of course, he'd been confined to his bedroom, and the comfortable library evenings had stopped altogether.

She hadn't yet grown accustomed to missing him. Since his death, she'd spent late nights by herself in the library, reading the books they had loved and letting the memories wash over her. She understood loneliness all too well. Her own was burden enough—she wanted nothing to do with Duncan Campbell's.

"I should see to Robby," she said, forcing a smile. "He sometimes has trouble settling down to sleep after Jaime's playing."

If Duncan was disappointed, he didn't show it. "Very well. I may just spend some more time with the books, then."

She nodded. Apparently her late nights in the library were at an end now that Duncan was taking possession. "I'm sure my husband would be impressed with such diligence," she said, not trying to soften the edge in her tone.

He looked at her a long moment. "Your husband is deceased, Lady MacLennan. Unless you intend to expand the gallery of Castle Glen ghosts, he's unlikely to be in a position to judge what a new owner of his property is doing. Whatever actions I take are directed toward the future of this place, not toward satisfying a man who lies in his grave."

If she'd felt even the slightest sympathy for that moment of vulnerability she'd glimpsed earlier, his words removed all traces.

"Have you never lost someone you loved, Mr. Campbell?" Her voice shook.

"I've lost *everyone* I loved, Lady MacLennan," he answered with a fleeting smile. "Permit me to give you some advice. Mourning is a useless exercise. So is living your life in order to make a dead person happy. They're dead. If you go to church, you may believe that they're in a better place. But they sure as hell are not going to be affected one way or another by what's happening to the folks they've left behind."

He leaned over to retrieve the candlestick and handed it to her as she stood there listening to him with her mouth open.

"Would you like to lead the way?" he asked, gesturing toward the stairs.

She looked from the candle flickering in her hand to his impassive face. For once, words failed her. With a swish of her skirts she turned and started toward the stairs.

chapter 5

"You do understand that Castle Glen is in trouble?" Duncan's tone was harsher than he had intended.

Fiona's expression didn't change. "My husband explained to me that the revenues have fallen. He suggested that we'd have to find some additional revenue, perhaps increase the sheep—"

"A few sheep are not going to solve the problem. Especially with the cost of processing the wool right here in Glencolly. The first thing we have to do is shut down that ancient woolen mill. I don't know how your husband kept it open this long. Once we begin shipping the wool to the city on the new railroad—"

She was shaking her head vehemently. "The Glencolly mill provides a living for many of the people of the village. If we shut it down, they won't be able to survive."

"And if you continue to insist on outdated systems, the castle itself won't survive."

They were glaring at each other across the big desk in the library. They'd been working at the books most of the morning, and the gloomy picture had not helped their humors. Every time Duncan had proposed a solution for improving the situation on the Glencolly estate, Fiona had thrust out that stubborn lower lip and given some kind of reason that the action was simply impossible. It would deprive the Glencolly townsfolk of their livelihood. It would violate the ancient pride of the MacLennan clan. It would go against some kind of oath sworn by her late husband. Duncan was growing weary of the litany.

She was dressed in her stern gray again, and the attraction he had felt in the moonlight of the tower the previous evening had been replaced by an urge to throttle her.

"Perhaps the Glencolly mill can be"—she hesitated, scrunching her forehead—"updated. Glencolly folks are hard workers. Surely there's nothing that can be done in a big city mill that we can't do here."

Duncan shook his head in exasperation. "It's not a matter of working hard. It's a matter of raw material economics and plant efficiency and product volume and . . ." He could see that she was hardly listening. Her eyes had taken on a sudden gleam.

"We can talk to the mill manager this afternoon. His name is Jock. Jock MacLennan—he's my late husband's double cousin by way of his uncle Herbert, who married a Spratton, who was a cousin of the sixth Lady MacLennan—"

Duncan waved her to a halt. "No more family genealogies," he said. "If the people of this valley are to join the modern world, they'll have to learn that things move based on economics, not on family ties. You'll have to learn it, too. It doesn't matter a whit who's cousin to whom if the castle and the estate and the entire bloody town are going bankrupt."

Fiona was silent for a long moment, but her expression

was no longer stubborn. She looked more . . . forlorn. And
it was suddenly possible for him to remember that she
was inexperienced and recently widowed. She'd had a
heavy burden placed on her young shoulders. His voice
softened. "I'm planning changes because they are necessary, not because I'm some kind of ogre."

Her pointed chin went up, and he could see that she
was making an effort to hold back tears. He stood up
abruptly. "Perhaps we've done enough for today." He'd
always considered himself a brave man, but he'd flee
faster than a sneak thief in the dark to avoid being sub-
jected to female tears.

She stood more slowly. "I want you to talk with Jock,"
she said, holding her voice steady. "Perhaps if we all put
our heads together, we can come up with a solution to
keep the mill running."

He tried not to let his doubt show. In the world of
business he'd sometimes had to make difficult decisions,
but at least he hadn't had to deal with female sentimentality and a town full of cousins in making them. "We'll
continue talking tomorrow," he told her. "Perhaps by
then—"

He stopped at the sound of a knock on the library door.
Before he could say anything, Fiona said quickly, "Enter."
It was as if she wanted to say, "I still am mistress here,"
and he couldn't decide if the notion annoyed him.

The knocker was Jane, the maid, who bobbed curtsies
to each of them, then raised her eyes to Fiona and said,
"You have a visitor, milady. Er"—she looked over at Duncan—"I reckon 'twould be a visitor for the master as
well."

"Who is it?" Fiona asked.

" 'Tis Master Maitland, ma'am. The young'un, not the
sir."

Duncan watched as Fiona's face brightened with a

smile for the first time all day. This time there was no doubt about his annoyance. "The neighbor?" he asked.

"Yes. I suspect he's come to pay his respects to the new master of Castle Glen. Or else he's curious to see what an American Campbell looks like."

Duncan ignored the mild sarcasm. He was interested in meeting the visitor. If he was to carry out his plans for the Glencolly Valley, it would be helpful to have the neighbors' support.

In New York he would have offered a lady an arm to escort her to another room, but such courtesies didn't seem natural when dealing with Fiona. They walked side by side in silence without touching, following the little maid to the front parlor.

The visitor had remained standing. He was a burly man, almost as tall as Duncan himself. His thick hair was dark blond with a glint of Highland red. He would have looked perfectly natural in a kilt and tartan, but he was wearing a business suit with a cut as fine as any to be found in London on Saville Row. He walked to the doorway to meet them and held out a thick hand.

"You'll be Duncan Campbell," he said, his voice booming. "Welcome to Glencolly."

His grip was strong enough to force Duncan to hide a wince. "Thank you. I understand you are my neighbor."

"Graham Maitland, at your service," he said, giving Duncan's hand a final shake before he turned to Fiona. "How are you farin', lass?" he asked.

Duncan was surprised at the informality and even more surprised when Graham Maitland took both Fiona's hands and leaned forward to kiss her on the mouth.

Fiona's only reaction to the gesture was a smile. "I'm well, Graham," she answered him. "It's good of you to come."

He grinned. "Ach, Fee, you well know I'd be camped

at the end of the castle drawbridge if I didn't think you'd have Malcolm run me off with a hayfork."

She gave a happy little giggle that Duncan had never heard from her before. "You're welcome here anytime, Graham. You know that."

Duncan felt excluded from the exchange. It appeared that the newcomer's visit was in fact intended for the former mistress of the castle rather than the new master.

"I hope you can stay for dinner, Master Maitland," he said, then realized that he'd spoken loudly, perhaps trying to match his visitor in volume.

"Thank you, but my call must be brief today. I just wanted to be sure"—Graham glanced from Duncan to Fiona—"to be sure that you were settling in well."

Duncan suspected that the visit was directed more toward discovering if his arrival had caused any hardship to Fiona. This was something he hadn't expected. It appeared that the mistress of the castle had a champion.

After a few minutes of polite conversation, it was obvious that Graham Maitland wanted to speak with Fiona alone. Duncan stood and excused himself. There would be time to talk to his neighbor later, he decided on his way back to the library, after the man had heard from Fiona's own lips that the new master of Castle Glen was not a monster.

Fiona knew that the meeting with Graham had made Duncan Campbell uncomfortable, and she found that the idea gave her a little twinge of satisfaction. If she wanted to be honest, she had greeted Graham more warmly than she was accustomed, and the reason had been that Duncan had been watching her. However, after Duncan had excused himself and left her alone with her burly neighbor, she was the one who began to feel uneasy. She had sus-

pected for some time that Graham's attentions were somewhat more than neighborly. He'd always been completely
circumspect when Alasdair had been alive, but now that
her husband was gone, he'd been less reluctant to make
his feelings known.

"You've not had trouble with the man, have you, Fee?"
he asked. "I've heard that Americans can be a rude bunch,
and if he doesn't treat you with the utmost respect, he'll
have to answer to me."

"Mr. Campbell has been nothing but courteous, Graham," she assured him. "I must admit that I was pleasantly surprised by his manners."

Her companion looked less than pleased with her answer. "Perhaps he's trying to impress you."

"He doesn't have to impress me. The castle is already
his. It doesn't matter whether or not I approve."

Graham's eyebrows were as thick as the rest of his
bright hair. When he scowled, they nearly touched,
forming a bridge of hair all the way across his brow. "He
may have other reasons for trying to dazzle you, Fee."
He leaned closer and said in a low voice, "I know
you've not had too much experience with the ways of
the world. Alasdair did a good job of protecting you
from all that. But 'tis wise to be a bit suspicious of a
man's motives when he pays too much attention to a
woman."

Fiona shifted slightly away on the sofa they shared.
"This is your third visit to Castle Glen in less than a fortnight, Graham. Shall I be suspicious of your motives as
well?"

Graham leaned back and cleared his throat. He looked
embarrassed and a little hurt. "I suppose I let myself in for
that, Fee, but you must know 'tis unjust. If I've not spoken of it before, it's only been out of respect for Alasdair.
It has seemed too soon to speak of a future for us. But,

God forgive me, I've thought of little else since the good man's passing."

Fiona wished that she had made her own excuses when Duncan had left. Now, short of feigning a sudden swoon, she had little choice but to listen to Graham's declaration.

"You're too young and full of life to be a widow, Fee," he continued. "And my greatest hope is that when a decent period of mourning has passed, you'll begin to think about loving again. This time with a younger man who can show you—"

She sat up straight and reached out to put her hand over Graham's mouth. Playing the courteous hostess had its limits. She was not ready to hear Graham Maitland or anyone else belittle the love she and Alasdair had shared.

"As you say, Graham, it's far too soon to speak of such things. I loved Alasdair deeply, and I'm not even thinking about looking for someone to replace him in my heart."

"Oh, I know," he hastened to assure her. "I'd not intended to say a word about it yet. It's just that when I think of you here alone with that—that American . . ."

She laughed. "I'm hardly alone, Graham. I've a castle full of people to defend me, if the need should arise."

He hesitated a moment, then reached to take her hand. "I know. Everyone at Castle Glen loves you, Fee. But I want you to know that you an count on me, too. If you should need anything, you must send word."

His hand was sweaty and she had an impulse to pull hers away, but she forced herself to let him continue to hold it for a moment before saying, "I appreciate that, Graham. You and your father have always been wonderful neighbors. I know that Alasdair held you both in great esteem."

Slowly she pulled her hand out of his moist grip and

stood. "Now I should go see to the dinner preparations. You're welcome to stay, of course."

Reluctantly he stood, shaking his head. "No, I'll be leaving now that I've seen for myself that you're well. But you will remember my offer, won't you, lass?"

"Aye, Graham, I'll remember. Thank you."

She sighed with relief as she closed the big front door behind him. What was wrong with her? she wondered. Graham Maitland was a good friend and neighbor. He was from a respected family with respectable means. She should be welcoming his attentions. His father was a knight. The Maitlands were in a position to be of help to her in her efforts to return Castle Glen to Robby. But when his big hand had closed around hers, she'd gotten a bitter taste at the back of her throat.

When Alasdair had touched her, it hadn't been so terrible. In fact she'd felt warm and comfortable when he had held her in his arms. The rest of it—the bed part—she'd gone along with in order to please him. He'd always been grateful—and quick. But she'd loved Alasdair. That's what had made his touches bearable. She had no desire for Graham Maitland to touch her.

A sudden vision of Duncan Campbell's lean, strong hands flickered across her mind. She gave herself a shake. She had no desire for *any* man to touch her, she told herself firmly. The only touch she wanted to feel was the one she would never feel again. Her Alasdair. Dear, kind, gentle Alasdair.

W*hat's wrong with her?" Duncan asked the old butler.* Malcolm had just informed him that his mistress would not be joining the staff for dinner. "She was all right a few minutes ago in the parlor."

But he'd left her with Graham Maitland. "Is she sick or

did she go off riding somewhere?" he asked with sudden suspicion.

The old butler hesitated. "I couldn't say, sir."

Couldn't—or wouldn't? Duncan thought. Why in blazes should he care if the troublesome woman had run off for a romp with the neighbor? he asked himself. It would keep her out of his hair.

He sat down at his place and looked around the table at the others who were watching him guardedly. "Well, what are you waiting for? Sit down," he said.

Benches scraped as one by one the odd assortment of dining guests took their seats. Fiona's place at the opposite end of the table remained empty, as did Robby's. Surely the wench hadn't taken her stepson along on her liaison.

"Where's Robby?" he asked Malcolm.

As if in answer to the question, the boy came sailing into the dining room, out of breath. "Sorry," he mumbled, and took his chair. After a moment he looked up and asked, "Where's Fee?"

Malcolm answered him. "She said she wasn't feeling well and wouldn't be coming into dinner."

"Not feeling well? Fee is never sick." Robby frowned. "Perhaps I'd better go up to her."

Surprising himself, Duncan put down his fork and said, "I'll go." He looked around the table of doubtful faces. "I was with her most of the morning. I'll just go up and ask what is wrong. Please"—he gestured along the row of plates"–continue with your meal. I'll be back shortly."

He could see that Robby had been close to insisting on accompanying him. In fact, he didn't understand why he hadn't let the boy go himself. If Fiona had gone off riding with the neighbor without telling anyone, it wasn't Duncan's business to protect her reputation with her stepson.

By the time he reached her bedchamber, the scenario was so fixed in his mind, that he could practically see the diminutive Scotswoman and the burly Scot galloping across the moors to some secluded spot out of sight of the castle.

And so what? He smiled at his own absurdity. He was acting like the old biddies who served as chaperones at the New York debutante parties—occasions he had done his best to avoid. If Fiona MacLennan wanted to ride off with Graham Maitland, it was none of his business. She was a woman grown. She'd been married for ten years . . .

An odd relief swept over him when her voice sounded from the other side of the door in response to his knock.

"May I come in?" he asked.

There was a long moment of silence, then she answered, "I'm not feeling well. I asked Malcolm to relay the message."

"He did, but Robby was worried about you. He said it's unusual for you to be ill."

After another silence she said, " 'Tis nothing serious, actually. Tell Robby I'll join him in the schoolroom this afternoon."

But this time there was a distinctive gulp in the middle of her words. She was crying. Had Graham Maitland done something to disturb her? Before he stopped to think further, he opened the door. Fiona was sitting on the edge of her bed. Her upturned nose was red and the thick lashes around her eyes were wet. Damnation. It appeared he wouldn't be escaping the tears after all. He took a step into the room.

"You're not sick, you're upset. What's the matter?" he asked.

Her gaze slid away from him. "I'm perfectly fine."

Walking closer to the bed, he observed, "Yes, I can see

that. Most perfectly fine people shut themselves away in their bedrooms in the middle of the day and cry their eyes out."

She looked at him again, her eyes angry and sparkling from the recent bathing. "I fail to see why it's any of your business what I choose to do."

It was the same point he'd been making to himself, but he continued, "As you yourself have been trying to convince me, when I received this inheritance, the welfare of everyone at Castle Glen became my business. That includes you, as long as you continue to live here."

She lifted an utterly soggy handkerchief and wiped her eyes, then stood and faced him calmly. "Very well, Mr. Campbell. I'll grant you a certain right of authority. But I'm telling you again, there's nothing wrong with me."

"Did Maitland say something out of place? Did he insult you? I'll not have—"

He stopped when she gave an icy smile. "Graham Maitland would cut off his arm before he would insult me. He's been in love with me for years."

Even though Duncan had suspected that something like this might exist between the two neighbors, the words hit with a thump in the middle of his chest.

"In love with you?"

"Yes. Graham has apparently been attracted to me since he came here to live with his father. He was always quite circumspect while Alasdair was still alive, but since my husband's death, his attentions have become more marked." Her smiled turned mischievous. "Are you finding that so hard to believe? Now who is being insulting, Mr. Campbell?"

"No, of course, not, I mean—" Duncan stopped and took in a breath. Never in his life had he stumbled over words in the way he seemed to at every other encounter with Fiona MacLennan. "It would not surprise me to discover that any number of men are in love with you, Lady MacLennan. But that still doesn't explain why this admiration sent you up to cry in your room."

All traces of her smile faded and there was a telltale tremble to her lip. "Have you ever been in love, Mr. Campbell?"

"No," he answered without hesitation.

She nodded her head as if his answer had confirmed something she already knew about him. "If you ever do love a woman and then lose her, you'll be able to understand. Until then, I'll ask you to leave me to my grief."

Apparently, she'd been crying about her dead husband, he realized finally. She was right—it was a hard notion for him to understand. Especially when he considered that Alasdair MacLennan had been an old man. But all at once he felt embarrassed that his suspicions about the neighbor had made him intrude on her private mourning.

Duncan's experience with women was not extensive. He couldn't remember his mother. He'd had no sisters. Growing up, they'd rarely even had a woman visitor in his home. His stern father had always disdained female "megrims," as he'd called them. Duncan's relations with women had been confined to the artificial interactions of the obligatory New York social scene and the occasional romps with obliging young women of the working class. The latter had usually been happy to exchange their laughter and their bodies for a night out on the town, followed by a long, pleasurable session in his bed.

None of it gave him the least clue about how to deal with a grieving widow.

"Would you like me to send you up some food?" he asked finally.

"No, thank you. In fact," she added with sudden resolve in her voice, "I should really go down to the dining hall.

It's not fair for me to hide away when everyone is still getting to know you."

"I'm sure everyone would be relieved to have you there," he agreed. He would, too, he realized. "Though I believe most of them are beginning to realize that I'm not quite the monster they had feared."

She gave a little laugh. "Nay, you are not, Mr. Campbell," she agreed. After a moment she added, "Thank you for coming up to get me."

The words gave him an odd warmth.

chapter 6

Fiona lifted the last of the big textbooks to the shelf and dusted off her hands. Robby had already left, clattering down the stairs to seek some fresh air outside after an afternoon of study. He'd left pencils and papers scattered across the desk, she noted with a rueful smile. Evidently the pupil had developed some of the teacher's propensity for clutter. She straightened the desk, then turned to walk down the stairs.

Her sadness from earlier in the day had dissipated. She hadn't allowed herself to give into grief often since Alasdair's death, but something about Graham's visit and his obvious intention of making an offer to take her former husband's place had made it all seem overwhelmingly sad. She couldn't imagine feeling about another man as she had about Alasdair.

Even as the thought entered her head, she had a sudden image of Duncan Campbell at her bedroom door. Why had he sought her out? she wondered. And had she really seen a disturbing flicker in his eyes as she had told him of Graham's love for her?

She ran her fingers along the cold stone walls as she slowly descended the curving stairs from the tower. For the past few months her life had seemed like a spiral as well. There had been Alasdair's illness, then his inexorable march toward death, then the shocking news from her lawyer of the old Campbell inheritance documents that had been included with Alasdair's will. It seemed as if she'd been whirled along the twists and turns without any control.

Her foot jarred on the flagstone as she reached the bottom of the stairs. Well, it was time she began to regain some control, she told herself. Alasdair would have expected it of her. It was time she stopped letting her mind be distracted by Graham's attempts at wooing and Duncan's disturbing mixture of authority and solicitude. It was time she got this mess straightened out—for Robby and for Castle Glen and for the people of Glencolly. Once the inheritance ruling in Duncan's favor was overturned and Castle Glen was safely back in Robby's hands, she could afford to think about how she was going to fill the rest of what at the moment appeared to be years and years of a lonely life stretching out before her.

"D*id we underestimate the man?" Logan Maitland took a* pull on his long pipe and regarded his son with an eagle-eyed gaze. "I'd expected a backwoods bumpkin, fresh from the New World."

Graham laughed. "New York is hardly new anymore, Father. And I'd wager that Duncan Campbell has had to be a shrewd operator to be successful there."

"Well, it wasn't shrewdness that got him Castle Glen. It

was sheer dumb luck and a ridiculous ancient grievance that should have been forgotten generations ago."

Graham nodded agreement. "Aye, the pearl fell into his lap without any effort on his part, though he'll see soon enough that the condition of the estate is precarious at best. If he was forced to abandon his holdings in New York to come here, he made a poor exchange. Perhaps he's not so shrewd after all."

They were sitting in Logan Maitland's comfortable dressing room at Maitland Manor, the sumptuous home Logan had built when he returned from the India wars. His military adventures had earned him a knighthood, but it had been his ability to deal behind the scenes that had earned him the fortune that had contributed to the richly appointed manor house.

"Did he mention the loans to you?" Logan asked his son.

"No. If he's aware of the amount of debt owed by the estate, I doubt he would bring it up on first meeting with a neighbor."

"Unless he had discovered that the neighbor was holding the largest portion of those debts."

Graham shook his head and reached for his glass of brandy. "The tracks are carefully covered through more than one bank. You know I wanted to keep Fiona from discovering that we hold the debt to her husband's home."

Logan shrugged. "A precious sentiment I never truly understood. If it were me, I'd just tell the chit that it would be in her best interests to throw her lot in with you, since you and your father already own the very chair she's sitting on."

Graham finished his brandy in one big gulp. "That's not the way I want her, Father. When Fiona agrees to become my wife, it will be because she's in love with me."

Logan Maitland had straight bushy eyebrows that

matched his son's. They did a little dance as he grinned and said, "She'll be ripe for the plucking, however you manage to convince her. Considering Alasdair's age and health, I'd wager there was never much juice in that marital bed."

Graham grimaced. "I can't bear to think of the old lecher's hands on her. If he hadn't managed to conveniently pop off when he did, I'd have been tempted to help the bugger along."

Logan took another long pull on his pipe and gave a sigh of satisfaction. "This tobacco was Alasdair's last gift to me. One thing I'll say for him, he did know something about life's delectable luxuries. He managed to snare the most tempting little virgin in the valley. I can't wait to get my hands on his wine cellar. I'll bet it's magnificent."

Graham held up his hand. "Don't count your castles before you've got them, Father. Castle Glen is now legally in the hands of a Campbell, and in spite of being an American, he just might prove to be a more formidable foe than the MacLennans."

"I doubt it. Castle Glen is so far in debt, it would take a financial wizard to save it now."

Graham looked thoughtful. "I hope you're right. 'Twould be a fitting setting for our wedding. I believe Fiona would like that."

Jock MacLennan had been the manager of the Glencolly woolen mill since before Fiona was born. He knew more about the process of creating cloth from fleece than anyone Fiona had ever known, and he certainly needed no advice from her to run the business. But Alasdair had paid regular monthly visits to the mill, so she had decided to continue the practice.

Of course, the mill was now officially Duncan's property, along with the rest of the estate. After his comments about closing it down, she'd suggested that the two make a visit together. Though she had yet to see a tenderhearted side to the American, she was convinced that even he couldn't fail to see the dedication of the workers, the pride they took in producing their product. At the very least he had to be impressed with Jock. There was not a more experienced wool man in all of Scotland.

The mill manager met them at the entrance to the little factory. "Welcome to Glencolly Wool, Mr. Campbell," he said, offering his hand. Much to Fiona's surprise, he appeared to be nervous.

Duncan gave the man a brisk handshake. He towered over the little manager, who was not much taller than Fiona, though Jock made up for his short stature with a considerable girth. "I'm looking forward to the tour," Duncan said.

"Have ye e'er seen wool weavin' afore?" Jock asked.

"The only think I know about wool is that it keeps me dry while I'm waiting for the hack on a rainy day."

Jock grinned. "Aye, that it would. A fine-wove tweed'll keep ye warm 'n' dry in any weather."

He ushered them in and led them into a long room, where a number of women were sitting at spinning jennies.

"You still spin by hand?" Duncan asked in surprise. "I'd expected a machine of some sort."

"A spinning machine? Aye, in the big city mills they have machines with many bobbins each. I reckon each machine spins twenty or thirty times what one of these ladies does. But the work is not as fine," he added, smiling at the women, who were studiously trying to continue working while being watched by their employer and the new master of the castle.

Fiona recognized the elderly woman sitting at the wheel closest to them. "Hello, Margaret," she said.

"How d'ye do, Lady MacLennan? How're me boys doin' up at that stable of yers?"

"It's Mr. Campbell's stable now." She gestured to Duncan, then said to him, "This is Margaret Bandy, mother of our stable men, Baird and Blair."

He gave a gracious nod. "I've met your sons. They're fine men, though I'd not be the one to call them boys," he added with a smile.

"They be brawny lads," Margaret agreed. "But they'll always be my boys." Then she started her peddle again to set the wheel into its monotonous motion.

From the spinning room they went to the weaving room, where the weavers were working their magic with the long coils of yarn. They watched the heddles move rhythmically up and down and the shuttles slide back and forth as the delicate patterns slowly emerged.

"It's quite remarkable," Duncan said.

Jock beamed with a proud smile. "Some o' these weavers hae been here for years," he said, "and their fathers and grandfathers afore them. They say there's art in the rhythm and the fingers."

"Just men work here?" Duncan asked.

Jock nodded. "Aye, women do the spinnin', men do the weavin'. 'Tis the way it's always been."

Duncan walked close to one of the looms, where a handsome young man was weaving a length of MacLennan plaid with such speed that you could hardly see his hands move. Fiona recognized him as their maid Elspeth's beau, Hugh, who came up to the castle to court her every Sunday.

"Why is this piece so flat?" Duncan asked the young man. "Some of the others are thick."

Hugh's eyes widened as he realized that he was being

addressed, but he answered promptly, " 'Tis the sheep it do come from and the spinnin' style that make the thickness o' the yarn, sir. This be Shetland wool."

They lingered a few more minutes, watching the fascinating process, then moved to Jock's office, where he invited them to sit and have some tea.

When they were seated, Duncan leaned toward the mill manager and said, "Mr. MacLennan, I've already spent a deal of time going over your books."

"The market's not been good the past couple of years," Jock responded quickly.

"By my reading of the figures, the mill's in serious trouble."

Jock's taut face showed his distress. "Glencolly hasn't been able to keep up with the big mills down to Glasgow. They've got spinnin' machines and power looms that can produce material many times faster than we can. It's hard to compete. Many o' the folk from the little villages around here are no longer bringin' us their fleece. They can fetch a better price sendin' it to the city."

Fiona listened to the manager's recital with surprise. Whenever she'd visited, Jock had always been enthusiastic about the mill's progress. "I've never heard you mention any of that, Jock," she commented.

The stout manager smiled sadly and gave a pull to his full gray beard. "I didna want to fill that pretty head of yers with·worries, lass. Yer late husband and I discussed the matter often eno', but we knew there was little to be done. There's simply no money left in Glencolly to outfit this factory the way it should be. E'en if there had been money, the new machines wouldna hae made it all the way here on the Highland roads. Of course, now that the railroad's coom, 'tis a different tale. But that doesna solve the problem o' the money."

Fiona felt the heat rising in her cheeks. She'd been indignant when Duncan had talked about the antiquated mill. She'd been coming here every month, seeing nothing but happy workers and hearing nothing but Jock's glowing reports. Alasdair had never mentioned conversations about new machines, about losing out to more efficient factories in the city. She thought she knew everything there was to know about the MacLennan estate. Now she wondered what else Alasdair had failed to share with her.

She could see each of the men looking at her as if she were too much of a *female* to be expected to understand business matters.

"You should have discussed it with me, Jock," she told him stiffly. "What kind of investment are we talking about? If we don't have the money available, surely we could find the credit. The MacLennan name alone—"

She stopped as Jock began to shake his head sadly. "That's just the thing Alasdair was wrestlin' with, lass. There's no one willin' to give credit anymore based on the MacLennan name alone. And without credit, you canna buy new equipment. Without the equipment, you canna expect to make enough money to keep up in today's market. I don't doubt that the whole situation was one of the things that hastened yer poor husband's death."

Fiona sat in stunned silence. She couldn't believe that Alasdair would have kept all this from her. They had been so close, and she'd always assumed that he shared everything with her—all his thoughts, all his worries.

Evidently Duncan had been right when he'd told her that the financial condition of the mill was dire. She'd jumped on him without justification. To his credit, he did not attempt to throw it in her face as they rode back to the castle in the little two-seater spider phaeton.

It had been Duncan's choice to take the carriage to town. Fiona used it seldom, preferring to ride horseback.

The flimsy vehicle was not a good choice for the rutted road from Glencolly to the castle. She bumped against his shoulder after a particularly violent jolt.

"It's more comfortable to come by horse," she said, straightening herself.

"I'll remember next time."

She turned to study him as he concentrated on the road ahead. "Most men prefer riding anyway, even on smooth roads."

"Highland men, perhaps, not New Yorkers."

"Didn't you ride in New York?" All the men she'd known in her life had been practically born in the saddle.

They both shifted to the right as he steered the horse around a huge hole in the road. "No. That is, not if I could avoid it. In New York it's easy to walk most places. Or nowadays we take the streetcar."

"The streetcar?"

"Yes, it runs on rails, like the train. Right down the center of the street. You can cross most of Manhattan in just a few minutes."

Fiona shook her head in wonder. She and Alasdair had spent most of the evenings reading, but the books he had chosen had always been classics. When she thought about it, she really knew very little about the modern world. Perhaps it was time she started learning.

"I didn't know about the equipment at the mill being outdated," she confessed. "Alasdair never told me."

"He probably thought there was little point in discussing it if the new machines couldn't be transported over the highways. He died before the railroad reached Glencolly."

She had a feeling that even if he were still alive, Alasdair would not have considered using trains to bring in improvements to the estate. "Alasdair didn't like the railroad. He called it a smelly, chugging abomination."

Duncan turned to her as the phaeton took another wild bounce. "This is kind of fun," he observed with one of his rare grins.

She smiled back. "I wasn't sure you knew the meaning of fun, Mr. Campbell."

He was apparently in a good enough humor not to be insulted by her remark. "I've been known to enjoy myself a time or two."

This intrigued her. "And just how did you enjoy yourself?"

He raised one eyebrow and cast her a sideways glance. She blushed as she realized the subtle implication.

"Why, Lady MacLennan," he said with mock reproof. "What are you thinking?"

Her blush grew hotter.

"Very well," he continued, "I'll admit that what you were thinking about *is* fun, but I'd not be so impolite as to bring it up. Even though you're a married woman."

She was at a loss how to respond to his wicked teasing. Obviously the *fun* he was referring to had to do with relations between a man and a woman. He was right—she was a married woman. She'd had experiences with sexual relations, but the last word she would have applied to the practice was *fun*. Nor would she ever have thought about discussing the matter freely and out in the open. Her sessions in bed with Alasdair had been carried out mostly in silence and had never been mentioned by either of them once they were finished.

"I'm afraid I'll have to ask you to change the topic, Mr. Campbell."

"Duncan."

"I beg your pardon?"

"I'll change the topic if you'll call me Duncan."

They had started up the hill that led to the castle, and the jouncing had become nearly intolerable, almost throwing her out of the carriage with every bounce. She gripped the seat underneath her as the motion rocked her back and forth.

"Perhaps we'd do better not to talk at all," she told him. "You need to keep your attention on your driving."

He pulled on the reins and the big carriage horse slowed to a stop. The phaeton came to rest at an angle, sliding her almost on top of her companion.

"Are you criticizing my driving?" he asked.

His tone was indignant, but once again she could tell he was teasing. Where had his sudden good humor come from? she wondered. It was as if the visit to the woolen mill had given him immense satisfaction, which she found exceedingly odd. Hadn't the news from Jock been entirely gloomy?

She pushed herself away from him and tried to slide back up the slanted seat. "I have no problem with your driving," she answered carefully.

"Hmm." He was studying her. "I could swear I heard you call your neighbor by his first name, so I think I'll press my case. Repeat after me, 'I have no problem with your driving, Duncan.' "

"I've known Graham for several years."

"Yes, but you've slept under the same roof with me. And a moment ago you practically threw yourself into my arms."

"That was the carriage—" she began with a huff, then stopped when she saw his grin. "What's put you in such a good mood?" she asked finally.

He sat back against the seat, pondering the question. "The gallant answer would be to tell you that riding with a beautiful woman always puts me in a good mood, but that wouldn't be the truth."

"So what is it?"

"You asked me earlier what I did for amusement."

"And then I asked you to change the topic."

He looked apologetic. "I shouldn't have teased you, but it's a question I always hated to answer."

"Why?"

He leaned toward her and she saw a different kind of light shining in his eyes. "My amusement is solving problems. Especially business problems."

It finally started making sense to her. "Like the woolen mill."

"Exactly, like the Glencolly mill. It's a business with serious problems, and I'd like to solve them."

Fiona shook her head. To her mind, it was an odd form of amusement. "How do you intend to do that?" she asked. "I thought Jock said the mill couldn't compete with new looms, and without them there's no way to make the money to get them. It seems insurmountable."

"That's what makes it a challenge," he said.

She wasn't used to this kind of thinking. Alasdair had never shirked his responsibility for taking charge when it was necessary, but problems had always made him unhappy. She'd never seen him with the same light she was now seeing in Duncan's eyes. Of course, by the time she'd met Alasdair, he was already old. It was not an admission she'd often made to herself.

"What do you plan to do?" she asked.

"First of all, I need to spend some time with Jock going over exactly what equipment he thinks is needed. Then I might have to make a trip to the city to search out the best possible buys."

"But if there's no money—"

"Then we find the money."

He flipped the reins to start the horse plodding up the hill again. For a few moments Fiona was silent as she contemplated this new side of Duncan Campbell. She had to admit that there was some comfort in the idea of having his help in solving the estate's difficulties. Especially when he seemed so confident that no problem was insurmountable.

"Thank you for coming with me today," she said impulsively.

He looked down at her with some surprise. "I was pleased that you asked me. In fact, I'm grateful for all your cooperation as I've been learning about the estate. It couldn't be that easy for you to see me taking the reins that had belonged to your late husband."

"And that should now belong to his son," she reminded him, but her tone was not as vehement as it had been in their earlier encounters.

It looked as if he was going to reply, but suddenly the carriage lurched violently to the side and the left front wheel slipped into a ditch at the edge of the road. Fiona was bounced all the way across Duncan's lap and, before he could get a hold on her, tumbled out the far side of the wagon into the dirt. She twisted in midair in an attempt to land upright and halfway succeeded, coming down hard on her right foot before falling to the ground.

Duncan was at her side instantly.

"Are you all right?" He put his hands on her back but didn't attempt to move her.

She closed her eyes and took a quick assessment. The upper half of her body seemed normal, but her hip was sore from the impact and an incredible pain radiated up from her ankle.

"What is it?" Duncan asked. She opened her eyes. His expression was full of concern.

She managed a smile. "I think I'll live, but I believe I've sprained an ankle."

"Can you sit up?"

Cautiously she let him help her to a sitting position. The suddenness of the impact had left her heart racing, but slowly she began to relax as she realized that except for her ankle, she appeared to have come through the tumble without serious harm.

"Perhaps you were right to doubt my driving," Duncan said ruefully. "I swear I've never been on such a road."

"You're in the Highlands now, Mr. Campbell, not New York City."

"Next time I'll let you choose the mode of transportation," he told her with a smile.

She could see that in spite of his lighthearted comment, he was worried about her and feeling guilty about the accident. She wasn't sure exactly why, but his concern pleased her. "Do you think we'll be able to get the carriage out of that ditch? I'm not sure I'd be able to walk up the hill at the moment."

"You'll not be walking anywhere. If the carriage is stuck, I'll carry you to the castle."

She laughed. "That would be a feat, Mr. Campbell. Duncan. You'd not get more than a few yards with such a burden."

In response he stood and lifted her easily, juggling her to a comfortable position as if she were no heavier than a rag doll. "Burden? Why, you may be a grand Highland lady, but you're no more than a tidbit in my arms."

He smiled down at her, and Fiona's heart gave a kick inside her chest. Alasdair had cradled her in his arms many times, but it had never felt like this. She'd never been so aware of the taut muscles as he held her, of the side of her breast pressing into a hard male chest, of the stubble of whiskers across a square chin, just inches from her mouth.

"You can't hold me," she protested, surprised that the words came out raspy.

Duncan's smile had faded, replaced by an expression she hadn't seen before. She could see a hard swallow travel the length of his strong neck. She had an absurd impulse to reach out her fingers and touch him there.

"Yes, Fiona MacLennan," he said softly. "I can."

Her gaze seemed locked to his dark eyes, and the breath stopped in her throat.

"Whoa there! What's happened?"

The shout came from the road above them up the hill. Fiona turned her head, startled. Graham Maitland was coming toward them, urging his horse to a precariously fast trot over the bumpy road.

Pressed against Duncan's chest, she could feel him draw in a long stream of air. She shifted in his arms, trying to put more distance between them. A twinge from her ankle surprised her. For a few moments she'd forgotten that she'd hurt it.

Graham pulled his horse to a halt in front of the lopsided carriage. "I never did understand why Alasdair bought this contraption," he said, dismounting. "It's no damn good up here, that's for sure."

Duncan continued to hold her as Graham walked around the carriage toward them. "Are you hurt, Fee?" he asked.

"Just my ankle."

"Lucky I found you," he said with a glance at Duncan that could be described as condescending. "I was up at the castle looking for you, and they told me you'd gone down to the mill."

Without asking, he reached to take her from Duncan's arms. She could feel the American's arms tightening around her. A slightly hysterical giggle escaped her as she pictured herself being the subject of a tug-of-war between the two men.

"Please, put me down," she murmured to Duncan.

With obvious reluctance he set her back on her feet, but

as soon as she felt weight on her ankle, she realized that there was no way she was going to be able to walk on it.

Graham looked irritated. "I'm taking you up the hill, Fee. Don't argue. One step over these ruts and you'll do further injury to yourself."

Fiona first looked at Duncan, whose face had returned to its usual cool expression, then at the listing carriage. It would not be easily righted, she decided. With a nod of apology, she said to Duncan, "I should probably ride up the hill with Graham and send down a couple of men to help you."

He gave a stiff nod.

Graham wasted no time. He scooped Fiona off the ground and walked with her to his horse. "I want you to promise me you'll not ride out in that thing again," Graham told her.

She wasn't sure she liked his possessive tone, but her ankle had begun to throb and she was in no mood for an argument. She allowed him to boost her up on his horse, then sat quietly while he swung himself up behind her.

"I'll have someone come immediately," she said to Duncan. Neither man said a word as Graham turned the horse around and headed up the hill. She looked back to offer Duncan an apologetic wave, but he was already kneeling by the carriage wheel, studying how to get himself out of his dilemma.

chapter 7

"W hat possessed you to travel out in that blasted carriage, Fee?" Graham asked as they made their way
up the hill toward the castle.

"It was Duncan's choice. Apparently he didn't have
much of a chance to ride in New York City."

"Duncan? It sounds as if you've become friends with
the man. I thought you resented his coming to take over
Robby's inheritance."

"I did. I do, but we're stuck with the situation for the
moment, so I see no reason to be hostile."

"What twisted Highland feud caused this reversal of
MacLennan fortune anyway?" Graham asked.

Fiona had read and reread the old papers. "The way I
understand it, when Bonnie Prince Charlie made his play
to gain the throne, King George formed the Highland
clans who were loyal to him into a special band called the
Black Watch."

"And the Campbells were Black Watch."

"Aye. While the MacLennans were Jacobites, trying to restore the Stuart monarchy through the Bonnie Prince."

"But what has all this to do with Glencolly Castle?"

"The castle was to be forfeited because Jaime MacLennan had fought for the Stuart at Culloden. But apparently the Black Watch captain, one Fergus Campbell, who had come to seize the place, fell in love with Jaime MacLennan's widow, Bethia. When she pleaded to save the inheritance of the baby she was carrying, the captain offered a concession. If she had a boy, the MacLennans would keep the estate for her son's lifetime, but would cede the castle to the Campbells within five generations."

"And Robby is the fifth generation," Graham added.

"Aye," Fiona said. "According to the old agreement, he loses his rights, and the castle is to be turned over to the oldest direct descendant of Fergus Campbell."

"The American who neither rides nor knows how to manage a carriage," Graham added dryly, steering his horse expertly around a fallen branch on the road.

"He's used to pavement, not Highland roads," Fiona said.

Graham's arms stiffened around her waist at her defense of the American. "But now you've found a codicil reversing the original agreement."

"Aye, apparently after Fergus Campbell married Bethia, he gave all rights back to the MacLennans in perpetuity."

"It's odd that the codicil wasn't included with Alasdair's papers."

"Apparently the codicil was never filed in Glasgow. That's why Hampton Sinclair is investigating to discover where it was registered."

"I don't like you having to live here with the American," Graham said with a scowl. "When do you expect to hear something from your attorney?"

"Mr. Sinclair sent a message that he hoped to have

news within a fortnight. If he has been able to find corroboration for the papers we found, we should be able to reverse the judgment that gave Castle Glen to Duncan."

"And send him back to New York City," Graham added with a note of satisfaction.

It was what Fiona had been hoping for ever since she'd found the old codicil in the window seat, but to her surprise, the thought was not as welcome as it once had been.

Her foot had begun to throb in earnest. She turned around in the saddle and said to him, "Forgive me, Graham, but could we discuss this at another time?"

He looked instantly contrite. "Of course. The important thing now is to get you to bed and wrap up that ankle. Though I wish you'd come to Maitland Manor with me. My father and I would be happy to have you with us until you're fit again."

"That's kind of you, but I feel my place is at the castle."

"Ah, Fee, I wish you would let me take care of you."

She knew he was sincere. She could hear the yearning behind his words, but she had no desire to be taken care of. Alasdair had taken care of her, but that had been different. She'd been little more than a chid when she'd married him. From now on, she intended to take care of herself.

They were nearing the castle. She could see Baird Bandy walking toward them from the stable yard, ready to take Graham's horse.

"I know your sense of duty is strong, Fee," Graham continued in a determined tone. "But if Hampton Sinclair doesn't get the information he needs soon, it might be time for your neighbors to step in and help you straighten this out. I'm ready to send your American packing. And in the meantime, I think you should move to Maitland Manor."

He gave a nod to the stable man and swung off his

horse. Then he held out his arms so that Fiona could slide into them.

"What happened, Miss Fee?" the strapping young man asked.

"A mishap on the road, Baird. I've hurt my foot."

Baird cast a suspicious glance at Graham, as if wondering if the neighbor had somehow been the cause of his mistress's misfortune. "The phaeton slipped off the path," she explained.

Baird gave a huff. "I told that Yankee that he didn't want to go to town in that thing."

She smiled. "I know, but what's done is done. I'll be fine. Would you and your brother go down to help him bring it up?"

The stable man agreed and went off at a trot, leading Graham's horse. Like everyone on the estate, he was fiercely loyal to her. She had a whole castle full of protectors, she realized. She didn't need another one in Graham Maitland.

"I appreciate your offer, Graham," she told him as he lifted her high in his arms and strode into the castle, "but I'm staying here."

Duncan's good humor had disappeared. He'd enjoyed the visit to the woolen mill, in spite of or, as he'd told Fiona, perhaps because of the old factory's problems. Business problems were something he knew, something he could fix. For the first time since he'd arrived in Scotland, he'd felt in his element. Then had come the disastrous carriage ride and Fiona's accident, for which he blamed himself. He'd been warned by one of the twins who managed the stables not to take the carriage, and he hadn't listened.

Then there had been that odd moment when he had

lifted her in his arms. He could have sworn that she'd looked at him with that special look that females only gave when they were reaching the moment of capitulation. It was hardly credible. She'd said nothing, done nothing to show that she regarded him as anything other than an adversary. If she was being pleasant, it was only because she had decided that a guarded truce was the best for all parties.

But for just a few moments as he held her, it had appeared that the battle had been called off completely.

It had him baffled.

"Ho, Mr. Duncan," came a voice from up the hill. The two stable twins were running down the road toward him. Either Baird or Blair had shouted.

He waited until they were closer, then took his chances by addressing the one on the right. "I should have listened to you, Baird. This carriage was not designed for a Highland hill."

The man nodded. "I be Blair, Mr. Duncan. But if I'd seen ye take off this morning, I woulda tole ye the same as me brother."

Duncan smiled and shook his head. "Forgive me, but how does anyone ever tell you two apart?"

"I be the handsome one," Baird replied at once.

"I be the smart one," Blair added quickly.

Their engaging grins told him that he was not the first to confuse them and that they were not the least offended by the mistake. He could see now that there was a slight difference. Baird, "the handsome one," was a hair taller, and Blair had a slight curvature to his nose, perhaps a legacy of a friendly fight.

He liked them both immensely and felt a certain camaraderie, which seemed odd. He'd had a stable man back in New York, but for the life of him, he couldn't even remember what the man looked like.

"I seem to have gotten myself into a muddle, gentlemen," he told them, nodding at the tilting phaeton.

"We'll have that out o' there in no time, Mr. Campbell," Baird said, walking to the front of the carriage. "The trick will be making it the rest o' the way up the hill wi'out tumblin' it again."

"We may have to cary the danged thing up on our backs," Blair agreed solemnly.

Duncan shook his head in apology. "Good lord, I'd not have you carry it—" Then he stopped as he saw that the two men were grinning at him again.

"The road smoothens out a bit nearin' the castle," Baird told him with a friendly cuff to Duncan's arm. "We'll hae her up in a trice. Then I suggest ye let us chop the bloody thing up fer firewood."

He was right. With three men working, the carriage was easily pulled from the ditch, and, with Baird at the reins and Blair walking alongside the horse, they had no further trouble climbing up to the castle.

Duncan thanked them both as they reached the wagon shed. "Next time ye take a fancy to go into town, ye'd best take a horse," Baird told him with another grin.

Duncan hesitated. "So I understand. The problem is that I'm not much better at riding than I am at steering a carriage up a hill."

Baird and Blair exchanged a glance as if they found this difficult to believe, but neither one spoke.

"Perhaps 'tis just a matter of practice," Duncan said, feeling a rare lack of self-confidence.

"Ye should ride out on Daisy, Mr. Campbell," Baird said after a moment. "She'll ride ye along so gentle-like, ye'll think ye're in a bloomin' boat."

"Daisy?" It was hardly a name for a man's mount.

"Yup," Blair confirmed with a nod. "If 'tis practice ye're wantin', Daisy's the gal."

Duncan wasn't sure that it was practice he *wanted*, but practice was definitely what he *needed*. "Very well," he said. "I'll come tomorrow morning and take a ride on . . . Daisy."

"We'll have 'er ready for ye, sir," Baird told him.

Duncan began to turn toward the castle, then hesitated. "Er, you don't have to mention to anyone that I'll be riding out on her."

"Mum's the word, sir," Baird told him. "A few rides out on Daisy and ye'll start to feel that ye were born in a saddle."

"That sounds like exactly what I need," Duncan agreed. He almost reached to shake the man's hand, then remembered that Baird was his stable man. "I'll see you in the morning, then."

The twins made identical salutes with their right hands as Duncan turned to leave.

T*he mood at the supper table was subdued. It appeared* that everyone was feeling the absence of the mistress of the household. With the usual chatter cut down, the meal finished quickly, and Duncan was not inclined to prolong it. He made his excuses and left the table before Emmaline had even brought in the trifle.

"Did you send some supper up to Lady MacLennan?" he asked the cook as she passed with the big dessert bowl.

"A course I did, sir. Poor little lamb. She was sittin' with her foot up on a pillow. All swolled up it was like a pig's bladder."

Duncan looked back at the row of somber faces still at the table. He wondered briefly how many of the assembly blamed him for Fiona's misfortune.

"Did she get trifle?" he asked.

"I beg yer pardon, sir?"

He nodded toward the big bowl she'd placed on the table. "Lady MacLennan. Did you send up some of the trifle with her dinner?"

Emmaline looked at him in wonder. "Why, no, sir. I surely did not. What a kind thing fer ye to think o' it." In a moment the plump little cook had scooped a portion of the sweet pudding into a dish and plopped it into Duncan's hands. "Tell her I expect her to finish every bite," she added with a dimpled smile.

Duncan looked at the dish. He hadn't intended on visiting Fiona in her bedroom, but it appeared that he had just been given duties as a serving maid. Emmaline had begun preparing dishes for the others at the table. One look at her authoritative, weathered face dissuaded him from attempting to decline the assignment.

The truth was, he admitted as he climbed the castle stairs and turned down the east wing toward Fiona's bedroom, he did want to see her. He told himself that it was only to assure himself that her injuries were not worse than they had feared.

When he'd returned that afternoon from bringing up the carriage with the Bandys, Malcolm had informed him that Fiona was doing well and that Graham Maitland himself had carried her up to her bedroom. This news had sent Duncan off to the library, where he'd spent the rest of the day looking through books of figures without the concentration necessary to make sense of them. The call to supper had been a relief.

Now he stood in front of Fiona's closed bedroom door, wondering if her attentive neighbor was still inside with her. There was no sound from within. Would he find them in a compromising position, in spite of her injury? he wondered. Would she be bold enough to act with such impropriety right in her own household?

This was his household, damn it, not hers. His knock was louder than he had intended.

She answered at once. His shoulders relaxed as his suspicions faded. He opened the door and went in. She looked up in surprise, and he was grateful for the excuse of the trifle. He held it out to her. "Your rather ferocious cook says you're to eat every bite."

She smiled. "I'm not hungry. Jane gave me a powder for the ache in my foot, and I believe it's working. I feel more sleepy than anything else."

Duncan frowned. "Jane gave you a powder? Isn't there a doctor in Glencolly?"

"Jane's something of a healer, as was her mother and grandmother before her. It's how things work here. The nearest doctor is two villages away."

"What if someone gets really sick?"

"Then we fetch the doctor. But, as you yourself saw, it can take some time to travel over the Highland roads."

He gave a rueful nod. "It's one of the things I'm learning about this place." Motioning to a chair that was already in place beside her bed, he asked, "May I sit down?"

She nodded agreement. She was sitting propped against several pillows, her billowy comforter pulled up around her. When she shifted position, Duncan realized that underneath the covers she was wearing no more than a night rail. It was made of some kind of silky material that allowed tantalizing glimpses of flesh up and down her slender arms and below her neck.

"What else have you learned?" she asked.

He blinked. "I beg your pardon?"

"You said the road travel is one thing you've learned here. What else have you learned?"

"Ah." He thought for a moment. "I've learned that including everyone at the dining hall is an interesting custom that works quite well, but only when the mistress of the castle is there to preside." At her confused look, he continued, "Supper was quite subdued tonight without your presence. I think people were afraid to talk much, and everyone seemed to be worried about you."

She sat up straighter and let the covers fall all the way down to her waist. Duncan sat up straighter as well.

"They're protective of me," she said. "I'm lucky to have such a family around me."

He had no idea what she'd said. He'd been busy trying to keep himself from staring at the pert dark circles underneath the fabric of her night rail. Clearing his throat, he held out the dish he still held. "You really should try the trifle or you'll disappoint Emmaline."

She leaned closer to take the dish from him. Her unbound breasts swayed gently with the motion. Duncan quickly put the dish in her hands and leaned back in his chair. There was no help for it, he realized with some irritation. He was fully aroused.

The state represented a dilemma. In the past, when he'd wanted a woman, the decision had always been easy. If she was an eligible debutante, he'd turn tail and get as far away as possible. If she was someone who would not be in a position to somehow coerce him into the fatal state of matrimony, he would arrange a discreet rendezvous and satisfy their mutual desires.

Fiona MacLennan was a different story.

He watched as she lifted a spoonful of creamy trifle to her lips.

She wasn't even the type of woman that usually attracted him. She had the sparkling blue eyes he liked, but her diminutive size was unlike the tall, elegant women he generally preferred. She had a smattering of freckles across her nose that gave her a little-girl look. When her brown hair was coiled up on her head, she sometimes had the aspect of a schoolmarm.

At the moment the hair fell loose around her shoulders in soft honeyed waves. He had a quick image of how it would look draped over her trim, naked breasts. The breasts he could practically *see* through that night thing she was wearing.

Damn it all, she was prickly and stubborn and he knew very well she wished he'd never left New York. She was a widow and a lady and had a son to raise. She was his responsibility as a member of this household. The choice between delight or flight had never been more clear in his head. Starting tomorrow, he would begin to stay clear of the former mistress of Castle Glen.

"Perhaps I should send for this doctor to look at your foot," he said briskly. All business. The master of the household tending to household needs.

She wiggled the limb under the covers. "That's not necessary. Jane's powder did wonders. I'll be up on it tomorrow."

"No," he said firmly. "You'll not. It needs rest, and I intend to inform everyone else in the castle that you are not to be allowed out of bed for three days."

"But I—"

He held up a hand. "No argument. You know very well that your family, as you call them, will support me in this. They can get along perfectly well without your help for that long."

After a moment she nodded. "Very well. I'll stay in bed tomorrow. Then we'll see how it's improving. Honestly, I don't think I'll need as long as that. I'm even getting my appetite back. This is delicious." She took another bite of trifle, licking the last bit off the spoon with enthusiasm. Her lips glistened.

Duncan watched, his erection growing tighter against his wool trousers.

"I should leave you to rest," he said, standing.

"It was kind of you to come." She looked up at him with genuine warmth in her smile. It reminded him of the glimmer he'd seen in her eyes when he had held her in his arms by the carriage. She felt it, too, he realized suddenly. This thing between them.

A slight bit of white cream remained at the corner of her mouth after her attack of the trifle spoon. He leaned over and wiped it away with his finger, then brought the finger to his own mouth. "You're right," he said. "It's delicious."

Her eyes opened wide in surprise. "Oh, dear," she said, bringing her hand up to wipe at her mouth. "Is there more?"

"Unfortunately, no," he answered. He'd steer clear of her, he'd told himself. *Starting tomorrow.* He bent over her again and, pulling her hand from her mouth, replaced it with his lips.

She gave a startled murmur, but he could feel her lips soften under his. He straightened and took in a ragged breath. She looked up at him, her long lashes moving furiously.

He watched her for another moment, then turned to leave. At the door he paused to look back at her once more. "Take care of that foot, Fiona MacLennan."

She was still sitting with a dumbfounded gaze, the bowl of trifle clasped tightly in her hand.

Duncan walked slowly down the long corridor to his own room, the taste of trifle still sweet on his lips.

chapter 8

Fiona sat without moving for several minutes. *She looked down* at the dish of trifle in her hand. Had he really wiped her mouth, then licked his finger? Had she dreamed that he had leaned over and kissed her?

Her lips still tingled. It had been no dream.

Her head buzzed. Perhaps it was from Jane's powder, but it may just as well be from Duncan's kiss. What had possessed him? What had possessed *her* to let him? The odd thing was, it hadn't been entirely a surprise. Ever since he'd lifted her in his arms on the road this afternoon, it was as if something had shifted between them. She'd had a churning in her stomach, and she had it again now. And it wasn't from her ankle pain or the powder or any of that. It was from being near him. From feeling him against her. Lordy.

She jumped and almost spilled the trifle as a knock sounded on the door. Had he come back?

"Are you awake, Fee?"

It was Robby. "Come in," she called.

"Are you better?" he asked when he had entered the room and jumped up on her bed, jarring her injured foot. At her nod he continued, "It was ever so dull at supper without you. I think Duncan missed you." He gave her a sly smile. "I do believe he likes you, Fee."

She didn't know what to answer. What would her stepson say if he knew that the American had *kissed* her, with Alasdair not four months cold in his grave. Of course, he'd taken her by surprise. She hadn't kissed back. Had she?

Robby frowned. "That's not a bad thing, Fee. He obviously wants us to stay here, and since Castle Glen belongs to him now, it's much better if we can all get along. Don't you like him?"

She hesitated. "I like him well enough, Robby, but—"

"I wouldn't be surprised if he's starting to fall in love with you, Fee. You're ever so pretty."

She didn't know whether to be touched by the boy's innocent compliment or horrified by the idea he was proposing.

"I hardly think Duncan Campbell is a man who is interested in love, Robby," she said finally. "He's mostly concerned with business matters."

Robby nodded. "I know. He's going to take me to Glasgow to purchase the new equipment for the mill."

This was news. Duncan had wasted little time in following up on his plan to update the mill. "When did he tell you that?"

"This afternoon before supper. We're going to go on the train, Fee. Isn't it exciting? I may go, mayn't I? Please do say aye."

"I don't see any reason why you shouldn't go."

Robby beamed. "Perhaps he'd take you, too."

Robby was too young to see the ramifications of her

traveling alone with a man who was not her husband. "No, Robby," she said gently. "That's not possible."

"Then I'll bring you back a present, Fee. What would you like?" In his excitement he gave a little bounce on the bed, bumping her foot. She grimaced, and he was immediately repentant. "Oh, Fee, I'm so sorry. Does it hurt very much?"

"No, just when I move it."

"The Bandy brothers were teasing Duncan a little at supper about the accident. I think they like him, too."

Everyone seemed to like him, Fiona thought with a frown. Except Graham, who had his own particular reasons. And she herself had to admit that she was becoming thoroughly confused on the subject. Duncan had come to strip Robby of his inheritance, and she was still committed to rectifying that. But she was intrigued by these odd feelings she was getting when she was near the man. Intrigued and more than a little frightened.

"So could I, Fee?"

"Could you what?"

"I asked you if I could sleep up in the Stuart Tower."

"Whatever for?"

"Weren't you *listening*?" he asked with some exasperation. "I said that since Jaime has come to play his pipes two nights in a row, I think it means he wants to make a connection with someone. If I'm up there all night, perhaps he'll show himself."

Between the medicine she'd taken and the buzz that Duncan's kiss had created in her head, she was having trouble thinking clearly. "It would hardly be comfortable, Robby."

"I don't care. I'll take some bedding. Are you going to eat that?" He pointed to the dish of trifle.

She handed it to him and watched with amusement as he downed the entire dish in seconds. Though he was still a slender lad, these days it seemed impossible to fill him up.

"Wouldn't you be afraid alone all night in the tower?" she asked when he'd finished.

"Why should I be afraid? I've waited ever since I can remember for Jaime to decide to make an appearance. You know, he wasn't all that much older than I when he went off to fight at Culloden. Just imagine."

The thought was sobering. "Aye, imagine. I'm glad there are no wars for you to fight, Robby," she added fervently.

He grinned. "I wouldn't mind a *little* war. It sounds kind of exciting."

"It didn't turn out to be exciting for Jaime MacLennan."

His smile died. "Nay. But may I stay up there, Fee? Jaime may have something to say to us, especially now that the MacLennans are no longer the owners of the castle. I think I need to be up there to listen to him."

Fiona had little faith in the boy's fancies, but she saw no harm in his adventure. She agreed to his plan to sleep up in the tower, and tried not to wince when once again he moved her foot as he jumped up from the bed.

"I'll see you in the morning, then," he told her, his voice high with youthful good spirits. Just as he was about to leave, he stopped, remembering her condition. "Take care of your ankle. I hope it feels all better tomorrow."

She watched him leave with a smile. He was a wonderful mixture of boy and man, and it was a joy to watch. As always, she felt the pang, wishing that Alasdair were here to see his son growing and changing.

She slid down the hill of cushions to arrange herself in a more comfortable position to sleep. Robby was her most important responsibility, she told herself firmly. All this stomach-churning nonsense with Duncan had to stop. To-morrow, bad foot or not, she intended to find a way to send a letter to Hampton Sinclair asking about the progress of his investigation. If he had not yet been able to find the documentation for overturning Duncan's inheritance of Castle Glen, perhaps it was time she looked for help elsewhere.

Y*ou do understand that these machines work with much less labor than the older ones,"* Duncan said soberly, leaning across the desk toward the mill manager. "We'll have to let people go. That's one of the major ways we'll be saving money."

Jock MacLennan winced. "We've never done things that way in Glencolly. When someone gets too old fer one job, we move 'em to an easier one. And when they get too old fer that, we just kinda help 'em along a little until they're called away to their blessed reward. We think of ourselves as family here, Mr. Campbell."

"So I've heard," Duncan said dryly. "But tell me, Mr. MacLennan. Would you rather have a profitable mill that can pay wages to half the town or no mill and no wages for anyone?"

Jock bent his head. "I feel as if I'm betraying the old laird. Glencolly Wool has never once dismissed an employee in all my time here."

Duncan gave a brisk nod of sympathy. "I know it's unpleasant, but it's what managers do."

"It's what they do in New York, I reckon," Jock muttered, but he was cordial enough as he showed Duncan out the door. As they stood on the front stoop, he pointed to Duncan's horse. "So ye decided to ride down today? I heard about yer mishap yesterday. How's Miss Fiona doing?"

Duncan hadn't seen her since he'd left her room the previous evening, but at breakfast Emmaline had told him that she had looked "a mite perkier" this morning. "I believe she'll be fine. Fortunately, it was no more than an ankle sprain."

"Give her my best, then," Jock said.

Duncan waited, hoping the man would go back in the building, but Jock made no move to leave, so finally Duncan went down the steps and over to Daisy, the horse Baird Bandy had saddled for him that morning. Drawing in a breath, he steeled himself and swung up into the saddle. To his relief, Daisy stood still as a statue. He gave a little smile. Perhaps he could master this after all. Though it somehow seemed uncivilized to him to get right up on the back of an animal. He lifted the reins and gave Jock what he hoped was a confident wave.

"Are ye forgettin' somethin', Mr. Campbell?" the mill manager drawled.

"Forgetting something?"

Jock ambled down the steps and walked over to the hitching post. "It's easier to ride 'em if they're not tied to a post," he said, his expression deadpan.

Duncan gave an embarrassed laugh. "Thank you, Mr. MacLennan," he said, taking the lead rope Jock had untied. "I'll try to remember that next time."

G raham Maitland *was always impeccably dressed, but* today his attire seemed to have been put together with extra care. He was wearing a fawn-colored tweed riding suit and a stylish bowler hat with a silk hatband. His brown boots were polished like a mirror.

"I can't tell you how pleased I was to get your note, Fee," he said. "Though I'm not happy to see you up on that foot. You should still be in bed."

He bowed over her hand as she welcomed him in the solar at the rear of the castle. Late afternoon sun shone in through the ceiling panels, warming up the chill that pervaded most of the castle rooms.

She'd had Malcolm assist her to hobble down the stairs. After twenty-four hours in her bed, she'd become restless, and when she'd made the decision to request Graham's help, she had also determined that she did not want to receive him in her bedchamber. Her only concession to her injury was that she sat on a sofa with her foot on a cushion.

"I'm fine, Graham. In fact, I can almost walk on it now. By tomorrow I'll be running you a race."

" 'Tis no joke, Fee. With the wrong care, you could end up lame."

She shook her head as he pulled a chair near her and sat down. "You worry too much, Graham."

"I worry about *you*," he corrected.

She smiled. "I know you do. You've been a good friend. In fact, that's why I sent for you. I'm going to presume upon that friendship and ask you to do me a favor."

"Anything you want, Fee. Just name it."

What irony, she thought. This was a perfectly nice man who would do anything for her, and when he'd taken her hand a moment ago, she'd wanted nothing more than to snatch it away. Yet Duncan Campbell, who was here to take Robby's inheritance, who had had the impudence to *kiss* her, and then to compound the impudence by not even showing his face to apologize or inquire after her health all day . . .

"Is something wrong, Fee?" Graham asked, concerned.

She took a deep breath. "Nay. That is, just the same thing that's been wrong since Alasdair's death."

"The inheritance?"

"Yes. I've heard nothing from my solicitor. I can't ride down to the city myself with this blasted foot, and I—"

Graham raised his hand. "Say no more. I've been hoping you would ask for my help. I wish you'd let me handle it from the very beginning. I'll take the train to Glasgow first thing in the morning."

Fiona had a slightly uneasy feeling. She didn't want Graham Maitland to "handle" her affairs. "I'm just asking you to talk with him, Graham. To see what progress he's made in verifying the old papers. If he's reaching dead ends, I want to begin inquiries somewhere else. We can't let this situation go on indefinitely."

"I'd as soon not see it go on another day," Graham replied forcefully. "I don't like to see that American settling in here as if he's truly the master of it all. And I certainly don't want to see him act as master over *you.*"

"Just bring me a report from Mr. Sinclair, Graham. I'd be grateful."

Her doubts remained as Graham made his farewells, still obviously buoyed by the task she had entrusted to him. It may have been a mistake to involve him, she decided, but it was too late now. At least she would now get prompt word from Mr. Sinclair. Then she would thank Graham for his help and proceed on her own from there.

Duncan was glad to round the last curve and see Castle Glen looming before him. He'd been in a saddle enough for one day, he decided. Who ever said that horseback riding was a comfortable way to travel?

Both Bandys were waiting for him at the stable. "Didn't I tell ye that Daisy would treat ye well, Mr. Duncan?" Baird called as Duncan pulled the horse to a stop with a sigh of relief.

"That ye did, Baird," Duncan answered, affecting a brogue that brought a smile to both the stable men.

"I bet she gave ye a real smooth ride up and down that hill," Baird continued, giving the animal a pat on its flank.

Duncan dismounted clumsily. His legs refused to move normally. "Smooth as silk," he said.

"Though ye did look a bit tense on that last patch up the road," Blair added, moving to join the two men next to the horse. "Ye need to relax more. Move with the animal. Otherwise ye'll be stiffer than a dead varmint."

In case the Bandys were still watching him, Duncan tried to walk with a normal gait as he went toward the castle. He might not be quite as stiff as a dead varmint, he thought ruefully, but he felt as if he smelled like one. The pungent scent of horse clung to his clothes.

He shook his head with a smile. It was just one more thing he had to learn in this country. He wasn't sure he'd ever become completely comfortable with riding, but it was better than that harrowing trip in the little carriage. Better than tumbling his passenger out on the ground.

He wondered how she was. Several times during the day he'd remembered the moment when their lips had touched the previous evening. Each time it had made his body swell. Each time he'd wondered what in hell he was going to do about it.

There was no help for it. He'd put off the encounter all day, but he had to go see her. It was only common courtesy to inquire about her injury, especially since he'd been the one to cause it. He wasn't sure what he was going to say about the kiss. Perhaps she would ignore the subject. But knowing the forthright Fiona, he doubted it.

"Is Lady MacLennan in her bedchamber?" he asked Malcolm after he had changed out of his riding clothes.

The old butler's tone of voice never seemed to change.

Duncan had yet to see him excited or angry or happy. "I believe she's in the solar, Mr. Campbell," he said.

"Downstairs?"

"Yes, sir."

"Her ankle is better, then?"

"You should ask Lady MacLennan herself, sir. But I don't think she put much weight on it when I helped her downstairs."

Duncan hesitated a moment. "Did she seem . . . is she in good spirits?" If he was in for a battle, he'd like to be forewarned.

"Lady MacLennan is always in good spirits," Malcolm answered. For just a moment his long face warmed with a smile.

"You care for her a lot, don't you?" Duncan asked.

"Everyone at Castle Glen loves Lady MacLennan." The old man looked to be struggling with a decision of whether to say more. Finally he added, "This place was very sad before she came here. Lord MacLennan had lost his wife and Master Robby had lost his mother. The new Lady MacLennan brought the light back to Castle Glen."

Duncan nodded. It was an apt description. Fiona was not stunningly beautiful or sophisticated like the women he had sought out in New York. But she brought a kind of light . . .

"I'll go see how she's faring," he told the butler.

"Very good, sir," Malcolm said with a stiff bow. Then he turned to walk down the hall, his back ramrod straight, even though his careful steps showed the weight of age.

Duncan knew where the solar was, but he'd never been inside the room. This place was entirely too big for one family, he thought again as he made his way through the maze of corridors. It was another idea he was pondering. Three-fourths of the castle sat empty day after day. There may be a way to use some of this space to good advantage.

Fiona glared at him as he entered the room. Not a promising start.

"How's your ankle today?" he asked in a neutral tone.

"Nice of you to ask, Mr. Campbell."

That seemed unfair. He *was* asking, wasn't he? "Malcolm told me that he helped you downstairs. He didn't seem to think you could put weight on it yet."

"It's fine." She was lying against some cushions on a comfortable-looking sofa, a book in her hands.

He walked closer. "Perhaps it was a good thing, in a way. You always seem so busy around the castle, doing more than you should. You manage the household and help Emmaline in the kitchen and do the estate books and go to the mill. It was time for you to have a bit of a rest."

"I enjoy being mistress of Castle Glen," she said, then corrected, "Or should I say, I *enjoyed* it when I was mistress."

"You still are in everything but name. And I'm grateful you're here. I'm not sure I've told you this, but I would have had a difficult time managing all this without your help."

He was trying his best to soften that hard shell she had once again wrapped around herself, but it was not working.

"In everything but name?" she repeated. "Ah, but name *is* everything, isn't it, Mr. Campbell?"

He sat down in the chair next to her, uninvited. If she wasn't going to respond to his roundabout attempts to please her, he'd have to face the subject directly. "Are you waiting for me to apologize for kissing you?"

She flushed. "I'm not waiting for anything."

"Well, would you *like* an apology? It might be the gentlemanly thing to do."

"Heaven forbid that you should try to act like a gentleman. I'd not want you to hurt yourself."

The insult was so quick and pointed that he couldn't help a short burst of laughter. She evidently had been surprised by it herself and, after a moment, gave a grudging smile.

"'Twas not a gentlemanly thing to do," she concluded a bit defensively.

"No, but I can't apologize for it."

"Why not?"

He grinned. "Because I'm not sorry."

This brought another reluctant smile. "You should be. But in the name of peace, I'm willing to forget it ever happened. We'd both had a hard day what with the accident and all—"

"What if I don't want to forget it?" he interrupted.

"Why, I . . . I . . . that—" She stumbled for an answer.

He leaned closer in his chair. "I may even want to do it again sometime."

"Please don't." All traces of her smile had disappeared. Duncan leaned back again and studied her, wondering what had put that frightened tone in her voice.

"Why not?" he asked softly.

She turned her gaze away from him. "I don't think . . . I can't . . . I don't much like kissing," she ended finally.

"You don't *like* kissing?" he repeated with a frown. "If that's the case, my dear Lady MacLennan, you haven't been doing it right."

chapter 9

*S*omehow *she'd known from the moment he walked into* the room that this was going to happen. She'd spent the day thinking about last night's kiss, becoming more and more indignant. She'd finally decided that the next time she saw Mr. Duncan Campbell, she would greet him with such frigidity that he'd think the cold stone walls he complained of were hot coals by comparison. She'd let him know in no uncertain terms that while the castle may be his, the mistress of the castle definitely was not. And never would be.

Then she'd watched him stride into the room, and her heart had sped up, and her palms had grown moist and she'd felt that undetermined *ache* again somewhere in her middle.

Now he was going to kiss her again. "You haven't been doing it right," he'd said. There'd been no smugness in the tone, just certainty.

He slipped to his knees next to the sofa and put his arms around her, then lowered her to the pillows. It was all done with no hurry. There was plenty of time for her to call a halt. But as if she was in some sort of trance, she let him position her in the downy softness and said not a word as he took her mouth with his. *Took* it, this time. This was not the respectful pressing of lips of the previous evening. He took her with lips and tongue and teeth until her mouth was burning and the rest of her body vibrated like a tightly pulled bow.

She had no idea how long it lasted, but suddenly he pulled away, breathing heavily, his eyes narrowed.

"I'm still not apologizing," he said, his voice thick. Then he stood and walked swiftly out of the room.

She lay against the pillows, unable to move. She'd planned a stern reprimand, a showdown, an *end* to what had begun between them yesterday on the road and last night in her bedroom. Instead, she'd capitulated. There could be no denying it—she'd participated. Now what?

She closed her eyes, suddenly tired, though she'd been lying on the sofa all day. She'd call for Malcolm to help her up to her room and eat supper there, she decided. Perhaps tomorrow things would be clearer. Tomorrow she could face Duncan on her own two feet, literally, and tell him that this nonsense had to stop.

It wouldn't be an easy task. The kisses—there had been more than one—had shown her that Mr. Duncan Campbell had been correct about one thing. She'd kissed Alasdair many, many times. But she hadn't been doing it right.

*D*uncan's head was reeling. *What the devil had happened to him?* Ever since he'd had his first schoolboy crush at age thirteen, he'd been meticulously careful not to get too invested in any woman. His longest affair had been the four years he'd spent with Isabelle, a former French courtesan who had made enough money to move to New

York for an attempt at respectability. He and Isabelle had suited perfectly. They'd been stimulated by each other's company and had enjoyed each other's prowess in bed. Though he'd be loath to admit it, she'd taught him things about a woman's body that he'd never even have thought to investigate.

Eventually they had parted by mutual agreement when she'd had the opportunity for marriage to a scion of society. It was her lifelong dream, and Duncan didn't begrudge her choice. He'd been rather relieved, since it once again freed him from being accountable to anyone but himself.

Isabelle had been tall, dark, ravishing, worldly wise . . . and worldly weary. She and Fiona could not be more opposite.

It was nearly time for supper. He should have waited to ask Fiona if she needed help reaching the dining room, but he'd had to get away. He wandered into the portrait hall. A few minutes of looking at the faces of the stern MacLennan ancestors should cool his ardor enough for him to return to the solar to assist her.

Down the row of portraits the one Fiona had called Black Guin seemed to be turning his head in Duncan's direction and looking at him with fierce reproach. "I just kissed her," Duncan said aloud to the lacquered face. "There's no crime in it."

"Who are you talking to?" Robby was entering at the opposite end of the hall.

Duncan smiled sheepishly. "To your ancestor here. He's a fearsome one, isn't he?"

Robby came to stand beside him and they both looked up at the painting. "He must've been as brave as they come. And this one's his son—Geordie the Meek," Robby added, pointing to the adjacent painting. "Isn't that odd? Do you suppose the son was cowardly because he was afraid of his father? I'd be afraid of a father like that," he added.

Duncan thought for a moment. "Well, now, we don't know why they called him Geordie the Meek. Perhaps he was a good man, looking for peace. That wouldn't make him a coward."

Robby looked as if he'd never considered it from that angle. "My father hated everything that meant change, but I like new things. I always worried that it would make him angry with me."

"I'm sure it did nothing of the sort. Fathers and sons can have very different ideas. It doesn't mean that one way is better than the other."

Robby had apparently had enough of the topic. He pulled on Duncan's arm and led him down the row to stop in front of another large painting. This one was of a young lad, not much older than Robby himself. He was dressed in a kilt and tartan and carried a claymore, but his expression had none of the ferocity of Black Guin. He wore a jaunty hat with a white cockade.

"That's Jaime," the boy said.

Duncan raised his eyebrows. "Our ghost?"

"Yes."

"He's young."

"He was only eighteen when he went off to fight at Culloden."

"And he never came home."

Robby grinned. "Well, he *did* come home, just not alive."

Duncan put his hand on the boy's shoulder. "So you really believe that Jaime's here in the castle somewhere?"

"I know he is, only—" He stopped, his smile fading.

"Only what?"

"I slept up in the Tower Room last night. I was hoping

if I stayed there all night, he might make an actual appearance."

"But he didn't show."

Robby looked dejected. "Nay. I'm going to try again, though."

He was a brave boy. Duncan wasn't sure that he himself would be willing to spend a night alone up in that tower if he truly believed in ghosts as Robby did. "That must have made for a long night," he said. "Were you scared?"

Robby's shrug served as a noncommittal answer.

"What did you sleep on?"

This received a more enthusiastic response. "Oh, I've fixed things up just fine. I brought some bedding and candles and a chamber pot. When the lights are out, it's kind of like sleeping out in the open. You can hear the wind sighing through all those windows."

"You're sure it wasn't Jaime sighing?" Duncan teased.

"No. I'd have known if it was him," Robby said with utter conviction.

At a sudden impulse Duncan said, "How about if I join you up there tonight? Do you suppose we'd have more chance of catching sight of him with two of us?"

Robby's face brightened. "Maybe we would. That would be *swell*."

"Fine. Now let's go find your stepmother and help her into supper."

Fiona's plan for a peaceful supper in her room had not withstood Robby's pleading. In a way, it was for the better, she realized as she sat at the table, laughing at a remark made by one of the maids. It was better for her to be with people than to be shut away with her own thoughts. She'd had enough of those for one day.

In fact, the gathering was allowing her to forget her meeting in the solar with Duncan. She watched as he led the conversation. He obviously was feeling more comfortable with the Castle Glen family each day.

When Jane made a teasing comment to Elspeth about the increasingly ardent attentions of her swain from town, Duncan told all three of the maids who were still single that he couldn't see why there wasn't a line stretching all the way down the hill waiting to call on such pretty girls.

He paid close attention to Hamish's report on the gardens, a topic that usually drew glazed eyes from the rest of the group. Duncan appeared to have genuine interest.

The Bandys obviously were captivated by their new master. When Duncan himself told the story of trying to ride away from the mill with his horse still tied to the hitching post, the stable men roared with laughter. Baird promised to put a little sign on Duncan's saddle that said "Untie first."

This drew a smile even from stiff-necked Malcolm.

All in all, it seemed that the people of the castle were beginning to accept their new master, even to like him. Fiona wasn't sure if that was entirely a good thing since she would soon be taking steps to send him away. But as she looked around the table of happy faces, she realized that the big dining hall at Castle Glen hadn't seen that much merriment since before Alasdair had become ill. For the moment, it felt good.

Duncan *was not about to admit to a fourteen-year-old* boy that he was beginning to feel that the idea of spending the night in the Stuart Tower was slightly creepy. He'd made the offer, and Robby had obviously been enthusiastic about having a companion in his ghost hunt. Now there was no help for it.

The previous evening Robby had apparently slept on the floor of the Tower Room with only a couple of blankets, but Duncan decided that if he was going to sleep with a ghost, at least he'd be comfortable. He and Robby together dragged a heavy feather mattress all the way up the winding stairs.

"It might be that Jaime prefers to come out and play only when he's by himself," Duncan told the boy. "No one has ever actually seen him, right?"

Robby gave a stubborn shake of his head. "Some of the old-timers in town claim to have seen lights from the tower in the middle of the night."

"Lights? But that could have been anything."

Robby looked at him warily. Apparently he was beginning to realize that his partner for the adventure was less than enthusiastic. "You don't have to stay," he said.

Duncan looked around the room. They'd set two candles at opposite sides of the mattress. The lights illuminated a warm circle around their makeshift bed. The rest of the room was lit only by dim moonbeams from the slanting windows that made eerie dark patterns on the floor and walls.

By the time they had arranged their bedding, Robby's eyelids were drooping with fatigue. Duncan suspected that the boy had gotten little sleep the previous evening when he had stayed here alone.

"Do you want to go to bed?" Duncan asked.

Robby blinked hard. "No, I'll stay awake."

They sat on the mattress, leaning up against the stone wall, and neither spoke for several moments.

"I was just thinking about something," Robby said. He sounded concerned.

"What's that?"

"They say Jaime comes to play for his bride, Bethia."

"Well, that makes sense. They only had a short time together—it must have been tragic for her to lose her husband so young."

He could see the boy glancing at him sideways, obviously reluctant to continue. "Bethia MacLennan fell in love with a Campbell," he blurted out finally.

"With a Campbell?"

"Aye. Didn't you know the story? Shortly after Jaime died, the king gave Castle Glen to a Black Watch loyalist named Fergus Campbell. When he came to claim his prize, he and Jaime's widow fell in love."

When the Scottish solicitors had contacted Duncan in New York about his inheritance, he'd paid little attention to the old stories that had led to his windfall. All he had cared about was that he'd somehow acquired a sizable estate in Scotland, the country his father had spent his life yearning for.

Suddenly, sitting with the MacLennan descendant in the old Stuart Tower, waiting for the ghost of his ancestor to appear, the griefs and loves of those olden days seemed more real to him.

"That was when the agreement was signed about Castle Glen," he confirmed.

"Yes. Fergus Campbell loved Bethia MacLennan so much that he agreed that the baby she was carrying—Jaime's baby—would retain the rights to Castle Glen, as would his son and grandsons through five generations."

"Up to you."

"Yes, up to me." It still seemed remarkable to Duncan that the boy held no resentment about having his fate decided generations ago by the whim of a lovesick soldier. Of course, if Duncan had been in Fergus Campbell's position, Castle Glen would have been in Campbell hands one hundred and fifty years ago.

"Well, it's a romantic tale," he said, leaving his latter thought unexpressed.

"Aye."

Robby still seemed to be disturbed about something. "So what's troubling you?" Duncan asked.

"I'm thinking that Jaime might not be so happy about the man who came to take his place with his new bride."

"The Campbell," he confirmed, suddenly understanding Robby's worry.

"Aye, the Campbell."

"And perhaps you think that Jaime might not want to come show himself to you if you're with a Campbell."

Robby gave him another sideways glance, obviously embarrassed. "Well, I—"

Duncan smiled. "Don't feel bad, Robby. It's no insult to me. I'd never even heard of Fergus Campbell until I saw his name in the legal papers a few weeks ago."

"But 'tis your family. You're a Campbell."

"In America we don't think that way," he explained. "Most of us scarcely know who our grandparents are, much less our great-great-great grandparents. If ghost Jaime hates Fergus Campbell, I take no offense. And I can't say as I blame him, either. If a man took my woman while I was scarcely cold in my grave, I'd not be likely to sit down to tea with him."

Robby laughed, sounding a little relieved. He looked around the shadowy room. "Maybe Jaime will hear you say that and decide to visit us after all."

They were quiet a moment, then Robby asked, "Were you happy when you found out about inheriting Castle Glen?"

Duncan glanced over at the boy, wondering if he'd been wrong about the lack of resentment, but the question appeared to be straightforward. "I wasn't sure at first."

"Because you had to leave your home to come here?"

"Yes, and because I wasn't sure I wanted to go back to Scotland."

Robby looked puzzled. "Had you been here before?"

"No, I meant back to my father's homeland. He came from here, and never stopped longing for it his whole life. Never stopped talking about it, either."

"That must have been tiresome," Robby observed with youthful perceptiveness.

Duncan chuckled. "It was. At least I always thought so. But the odd thing is that once I found out about Castle Glen, it seemed as if I was meant to come back here. To do it for him, somehow."

"It's because we love our fathers, even if we're different from them."

Duncan wondered how the young boy had become so wise. "My father's name was Robert," he told him.

"Like mine."

"Yes."

They were silent for a long time when suddenly Robby sat up straight. "Has it gotten colder in here?"

Duncan noticed it, too. It was probably just the wind picking up the cooler evening air and bringing it through the window slots, but the room had definitely dropped in temperature. "It is cold," he said. "Are you sure you want to stay up here?"

Robby started to say something, then jumped to one side as the candle on his side of the mattress fell over, igniting the starchy linen coverlet.

"Watch out!" Duncan shouted, pulling the boy out of the way of the flame. He jumped up and began to stomp on the fire with his boots.

Robby scrambled out of the covers to help him, then he grabbed his arm and said, "Look!"

In front of their eyes the candle on the opposite end of the mattress tumbled over, lighting the covers from the other side.

chapter 10

Fiona was just leaning over to put out her lamp when there was a cursory knock on her door, followed instantly by Robby barreling into the room. Duncan came behind him at a more decorous pace.

The boy jumped onto the end of her bed and perched on his knees as he shouted, "Jaime tried to set Duncan and me on fire!"

Fiona listened in surprise as Duncan gave a more measured account of the incident, but Robby couldn't keep quiet. "If I hadn't brought up a pitcher and washbasin last night, we'd never have been able to put it out, Fee!"

Duncan took a seat in the chair next to the bed. "The fires were small, but Robby's right, it could have been a problem. The old feather mattress was dry as kindling."

Fiona looked from one to the other, her eyes wide. "How did you manage to knock the candles over?"

"We *didn't*!" Robby said, emphasizing the words. "I tell you, it was Jaime. I was just telling Duncan that I feared

Jaime might not be happy having a Campbell stay in his tower, and then *pffftt!* We were on fire!"

"Careful of my foot," Fiona cautioned with a wince.

"I'm sorry," Robby said, pushing himself away from her bad ankle.

"It was drafty up there," Duncan added. "You yourself said those tower windows do odd things with the wind currents."

Fiona couldn't tell if he gave any credit to Robby's theory about the cause of the fire. At least he wasn't mocking it.

"I've never seen wind currents that could push over a heavy candlestick," she replied.

"I'll admit, it was exceedingly odd," he said.

Robby gave another bounce. "It was Jaime. I'm afraid he didn't want you there after all, Duncan." His expression dimmed. "Maybe he didn't want either of us there."

Duncan smiled at the boy. "If there was malevolence, I'm sure it was directed at me, lad. After all, I'm the interloper here at Jaime's castle."

His answer seemed to reassure the boy, who was visibly exhilarated by what he considered the first tangible proof of the ghost's presence. It took awhile to calm him down, but eventually he began to yawn.

"Do you think he'd come back if I go up again?" he asked, without much enthusiasm.

"I think you've had enough excitement for one evening," Fiona said. "You'd best sleep in your own bed tonight."

"And no doubt the room is still smoky," Duncan added.

Robby nodded agreement. His shoulders suddenly drooping with exhaustion, he got off the bed, leaned to give Fiona a kiss on the cheek, and left the room.

"It was nice of you to humor his notions," Fiona said when the door had closed behind him.

"His faith is almost enough to make one into a believer."

"What *do* you think happened up there tonight?"

"Damned if I know. Robby and I might have jostled the second candle when we were stomping out the fire on the other side of the mattress, but I have no idea why the first one tipped over."

"So maybe it *was* Jaime trying to drive you away."

"Maybe it was." He gave her one of those grins that she found so difficult to resist.

Now that the initial shock over the fire was fading, she was having trouble keeping her mind off the kisses he'd given her that afternoon in the solar. Once again they were alone. In her bedroom.

"I suppose you're tired, too," she said. She knew the words had come out sounding rushed and nervous.

He smiled, leaned back in the chair, and folded his arms. "Not at all. I'm not the one who spent all last night waiting up for a ghost."

"Poor Robby. I almost wish that Jaime would make an appearance. He's hoped for so long." This, at least, was a safe topic.

But Duncan was evidently not inclined to stay on safe ground. "How are *you* feeling?" he asked in a deep tone that told her he was not only talking about her foot.

At supper they'd been surrounded by people, and she'd managed to act as if nothing unusual had passed between them, but she couldn't avoid the subject forever.

Although she could try. "My ankle? It's better."

He tapped his fingers together and waited.

After a moment of awkward silence, she added, "I'm just fine."

He nodded and then stood up, pacing to the other side of the room to take a closer look at an oil painting on her wall. "I wondered if you'd done any more thinking on that subject we were discussing this afternoon," he said casually.

"I don't suppose you're referring to the subject of my taking a rest from household duties."

He turned and gave a slow, deliberate shake of his head.

"Then you must be referring to the topic of . . . of—"

"Kissing," he supplied.

She took a deep breath. "Yes, I, er, remember."

"I should hope so," he said with a smile.

It was easier talking about it when he was standing across the room, but he turned away from the painting and walked toward the bed. "Why did you tell me that you didn't like it?"

She was still covered by blankets and had begun to feel hot. Her face was growing flushed and her neck was sticky. "I—I don't know. I suppose I was trying to keep you from being forward."

He pursed his lips and nodded. "It might have been a good plan. The lady's not interested because she doesn't fancy the activity. Problem is, I decided to discover for myself, and I found out that you were not telling the truth."

A bead of moisture ran down her neck. It *was* hot. She was longing to throw back the covers, but she wasn't about to do so with him standing over her.

"You do like kissing," he continued calmly. "At least, you liked kissing *me*."

"Mr. Campbell, I don't think it's proper for you to be here in my bedroom talking about these matters." She tried to keep her tone cool and dignified, but she heard her voice crack as she finished the sentence.

He heard it, too. He sat down on the bed beside her and reached for her hand. "What is it, Fiona? Exactly what are you afraid of?"

All trace of predatory male had disappeared. There was nothing but concern in his eyes. Tears welled in her eyes. "I—I'm not sure. I *was* telling the truth this afternoon. I don't like kissing. Or, at least, I didn't think I liked it."

His smile was gentle. "But you may have started to change your mind?"

She managed a teary smile in return. "It was . . . nice."

He tipped his head and raised one eyebrow. "Nice. I guess I've had more enthusiastic endorsements in my day, but it will do for a start."

She gave a nervous giggle.

"Because we *are* just starting, Fiona MacLennan," he continued in that low tone that thrummed inside her stomach. "You know that, don't you?"

She shook her head. He still held her hand. Slowly he raised it to his lips and kissed the back of each finger, just below the knuckles. Then he turned it over and gently bit the fleshy part of her palm. She felt as if her insides were dissolving like hot gelatin.

Her mouth fell open as she leaned back against the headboard. "You mustn't—" she began.

"Why not?" he interrupted. Then he continued making love to her hand with his mouth. Just her hand.

"This isn't . . . proper," she said finally, pulling her hand away from him.

"Proper." He appeared to be considering the word as he moved slightly back from her. "Fiona," he asked briskly. "How many men have you kissed in your life? Before me, that is."

The question was impertinent, but she figured that he already knew the answer. "One," she said, her lips tight.

"And that would be your husband, correct?" At her nod he continued. "How old were you when he first kissed you? I mean really kissed you, the way lovers kiss. The way I kissed you this afternoon."

This forced a rueful smile. "I reckon Alasdair never kissed me the way you did this afternoon. Remember, he was a gentleman."

"A gentleman? What the hell's that got to do with it? I know the hackles will stand up on that pretty neck of yours if I say one word against your revered late husband. But gentleman or not, if he was married to you for ten years and he *never* kissed you the way I did this afternoon, then the man was either a fool or just too damned old to be married to you."

Strangely, she didn't feel the rush of anger she had when Duncan had first made comments about Alasdair. Alasdair had been her savior, her mentor, her protector, but she was beginning to see that marriage to him could never have included some of the elements that were most important to the union of a man and a woman.

Still, she felt she had to defend him. "He took care of me," she said simply.

"He gave you a house, you mean, and food and a name. But he didn't take care of you the way a woman needs to be taken care of."

She was silent.

"You've been missing out, lassie," he said.

"I was happy in my marriage."

His tone softened. "I'm sure you were. Maybe it was lucky that you weren't much more than a babe yourself when he married you. But now you're a woman."

"I'm a widow, Mr. Campbell. I'll ask you to remember that."

"Yes, but you're a widow with some time to make up, I'd say. You gave ten years of your life to your aging husband. I don't think you owe him more than that."

She thought about that for a minute and then said softly, "Oddly enough, I think he would say exactly the same thing."

Duncan smiled. "From what I've heard about Alasdair MacLennan, I think he would, too."

They looked at each other, lost in their own thoughts. What now? Fiona wondered. If she was free to explore this new world of the senses that Duncan had opened for her, what did that mean? Did it mean she should allow this man whom she had sworn to defeat continue his onslaught until she succumbed to an illicit union with no promise of a future? Perhaps it meant that she should accept Graham Maitland's proposal of marriage.

To her surprise, Duncan abruptly stood up. He had an odd look on his face. "You're tired," he said, "and no doubt your leg aches from moving around today. I'll let you sleep now."

"All right," she said, uncertain.

He bowed his head briefly, then spun around and left the room.

She sat staring after him, both relieved and disappointed by his sudden departure. She clenched her hand around the last bit of moisture from his gentle biting. He *had* bitten her. She hadn't imagined it. Alasdair would never even have thought of such a thing.

The sweat on her body had dried and she felt a chill. Sliding down, she pulled the covers tightly around herself and tried to keep from shaking.

*H*ampton Sinclair is a dunderhead," Graham Maitland told his father as they sat together following a late-night supper. "He's had almost four months to do something about the MacLennans' inheritance mess, and he still claims he needs more time."

Logan swirled the brandy in his glass. "Perhaps he does. He's dealing with records that are over a century old."

"In the meantime, this Yankee troublemaker has all the time in the world to come in here and make changes, turn everything topsy-turvy."

His father smiled. "You mean he has all the time in the world to charm the lovely Fiona."

Graham drained his own snifter. "That, too. You wouldn't be happy if the woman you loved was living with another man."

"If the woman I loved was living with another man, I'd take her out of there by force and, along the way, make the other man sorry he ever dared look at her."

"Ever the warrior, Father. Would you have me challenge the bloke to a duel? We live in more civilized times now."

Logan shrugged. "You're the one in love with the chit."

"I don't intend to fight anyone or to kidnap my own bride, but I'm beginning to think you may be right about a more direct approach."

"The loans?"

Graham nodded. "If we called them all in, would it be enough to break the estate?"

"I should think so, but I don't know the full extent of their resources. They couldn't get a tuppence of credit based on that dilapidated old mill, that's for sure."

Graham poured himself another full glass of brandy. "I heard an odd thing in town today. They're saying that Campbell is planning on updating the old factory."

Logan's solid ridge of eyebrow rose an inch. "Then the bastard must have money somewhere. That's interesting." He continued to swirl the liquor without drinking. "Well, son, you may need to see what cards your American is holding before you play your hand."

"Which means more time for him to ingratiate himself with Fiona."

"I wouldn't worry about it," Logan said with a yawn.

"From what I've heard, Americans are more interested in their businesses than their women."

*I*t had been nearly a week since the night of the fire, the night Duncan had come to her room and engaged her in the most intimate conversation she'd ever had with a man. Nearly a week, and he'd barely spoken to her.

She saw him everywhere—in the kitchens talking with Emmaline, in the dining hall leading the conversation at supper, out in the gardens conferring with Hamish. He'd been taking riding lessons from the Bandys, much to the amusement of everyone on the estate. He had helped Robby clean up the fire debris in the Tower Room and cheered the boy up when Robby had dejectedly decided not to resume his nightly vigil. He'd ridden down to the mill almost daily to confer with Jock.

Duncan Campbell seemed more than willing to talk to everyone in Glencolly *except* her.

At least her ankle was almost back to normal, she thought as she hobbled down the stairs without assistance for breakfast. Today she should actually be able to get some work done. After a week of inactivity, the notion sounded incredibly appealing. Perhaps she'd ask Emmaline if she'd like help cleaning out the winter pantry. Before long there would be summer produce coming in from the Castle Glen gardens.

She walked to the front door and opened it, drawing in a deep breath of cool spring air. It smelled of rich earth and early flowers. She hadn't been outdoors in a week. The winter pantry could wait another day, she decided suddenly. After breakfast she was going riding.

"How about going for a ride today instead of studies?" she asked Robby, who was seated at the dining table eating an enormous plate of coddled eggs and ham. "The day is too beautiful to sit closed up in the schoolroom."

Robby looked up with a smile. "I'm glad you think so, Fee, because I was going to ask you for permission to miss my lessons."

"So you'd like to go for a ride?"

Robby shook his head. "Diamond is in labor. Baird and Blair said I might help birthing the new colt if you said it was all right. You could come, too."

Fiona thought for a moment. She wouldn't mind seeing the new colt, but sitting in the hay all day waiting for the birth did not seem as appealing as a brisk ride across the spring meadows.

"Rufus is coming up from town to help," Robby added.

That decided her. Fiona knew that the ill-tempered blacksmith provided valuable service to the estate, but she didn't particularly enjoy his company.

"I really want to ride, Robby," she told him apologetically. "I'm so sick of being stuck on the sofa with this bad foot, it will feel good to be moving again. And Sorcha needs the outing." Alasdair had given Fiona the beautiful silver mare on her sixteenth birthday, and no one else rode her.

Robby nodded agreeably. "It might take all day. You should go for your ride and then check with us at the stables when you get back. You might still be in time to see the birth."

It was a sensible plan. She finished breakfast quickly while Robby was still in the middle of his mountain of food. Then she limped back upstairs and donned her riding clothes. It would have been fun to ride out with Robby, but there was also something appealing about riding alone, just she and Sorcha racing up into the gentle hills of Glencolly Valley.

Duncan hadn't been at the breakfast table, and she didn't

bother to ask where he was. If he wasn't interested in speaking to her, she didn't want to speak to him, either. But as she opened the front door to leave, there he was. She gave a jump of surprise.

"I was looking for you," he said.

"What for?" she asked bluntly.

He gave a little smile. "It sounds as if you're angry with me."

"Why would I be angry?" she asked.

"I've made it a practice not to try to guess the reasons a woman might find to be angry."

"I'm sure that's been a convenient system for you."

He grinned. "Aye."

The man was impossible.

He tipped his head and regarded her. "How's your ankle?"

"Fine, thank you."

He nodded. "Well enough for a ride?"

She was wearing riding clothes, so she supposed the question was logical. "Yes. In fact, I was just on my way out to the stables."

"I was hoping you would join me."

"Another phaeton ride?" she asked dryly. "No, thank you."

His smile twisted. "No. I meant on horseback. I'm ready to show off my new abilities."

For just a moment he reminded her of Robby when he felt particularly proud of his lesson. It softened her reply. "I had planned to ride out this morning. You may join me if you wish."

"Good," he said. "Just wait here a moment."

He went quickly down the hall and returned shortly with a package wrapped in oil paper and a flask of wine. "Sustenance," he said, holding it up with a grin.

He slowed his stride to match her still-halting steps as they made their way up the hill to the stable.

"Are you sure your foot is well enough?" he asked.

"I can put full weight on it," she told him. "I'm just being careful so I don't twist it again."

She could see that he was studying her gait, and she made an attempt to walk normally. By the time they reached the stable, he seemed satisfied.

"Wait here and I'll ask the Bandys to saddle our horses. I ride one called Daisy," he added with a rueful smile.

"She's a good mount," Fiona assured him. She'd spent the week getting madder and madder at him, but found it difficult to hang on to her anger when he was suddenly acting like a young pupil eager to please the teacher. "But let's go saddle the horses ourselves. The Bandys are busy with a pregnant mare."

They walked into the shadowy stable. Fiona quickly saddled Sorcha, a task she'd accomplished many times in the past. Duncan was taking more time, but seemed to be in control. While he finished, Fiona wandered down to the opposite end of the stables, where the Bandys were sitting on a stall divider watching a restless black mare.

"How's she doing?" she asked the stable men.

"She's taking 'er time about it," Baird said, "but she'll be fine. She's a trooper."

Fiona nodded and told them that Robby would be out shortly once he had finished devouring every egg in the kitchen.

"He do have an appetite of a sudden, don't he?" Baird noted with a grin. "He puts my brother and me to shame."

"He's excited about spending the day with you two. I may join you later, but first I'm going on a ride with Mr. Campbell."

The Bandys exchanged a glance.

"He says he wants to show me his riding prowess. You two have been teaching him, I understand."

Both men were silent for a moment, then Baird said, "Miss Fee, there's things that can be taught and there's things that can't be taught."

"But he's getting better, isn't he?"

Both men shifted uncomfortably on their perch. Finally Baird said, "Let's put it this way, ma'am. Every man had his particular talents. And I do believe Mr. Campbell must be one mighty fine businessman."

Fiona left the two with a grin and a wave, then walked back to where Duncan was standing proudly next to his fully saddled mount. "She's all ready," he said cheerfully, that note of little-boy pride still in his voice.

They led the horses out of the stable, then Fiona swung easily up on Sorcha's back. Duncan's approach to his mount was more deliberate, but he was confident. "I know about not mounting from the off side," he told her, pulling himself into the saddle.

"Good," she told him with a smile, and once again had the sensation that she was a teacher praising a star pupil.

"Where do you want to ride?" he asked.

"I'll take you up to Sullivan's Meadow," she said. "It should be covered with spring wildflowers by now. Just let Daisy follow Sorcha's lead."

She reined Sorcha to the right and headed around the corner of the barn, then turned back as she heard a strangled exclamation and half-curse from behind her.

Duncan was clinging to Daisy's mane as he tried to stay seated in his saddle, which had slipped down to the horse's side. Before she could say anything, Daisy began to move forward and stepped into the left stirrup that was dragging on the ground. The horse kicked in confusion as the saddle slipped farther around her middle, and Duncan slid off into the dirt.

Stifling a laugh, Fiona dismounted, remembering only at the last second to be careful of her bad foot. Then she hobbled quickly back to the agitated horse, freed the animal's tangled hoof, and soothed her with reassuring words and strokes. Finally she turned to look at Duncan, sprawled on the ground.

"I swear that saddle was tight as can be," he said, utterly indignant that his show of skill had been spoiled before he'd even started.

"Did you wait for the bloat?" she asked.

He looked mystified.

"Horses usually bloat their stomachs when you tighten the girth. You have to wait a minute or walk them around a little, then tighten again."

"No one told me that," Duncan muttered.

He looked so crestfallen lying on the ground that Fiona tried to keep her reaction hidden, but it was impossible. The laughter finally bubbled up from her.

After a minute he started laughing, too, and continued to laugh as he picked himself up and dusted off his hands. "I may have a few minor things still left to learn," he admitted.

chapter 11

Once Daisy was saddled properly, the ride went smoothly. Duncan was slightly chagrined that his show of equestrian skill had been spoiled, but it wasn't enough to dampen his spirits. Fiona was once again walking and healthy, and he was alone with her. He'd been thinking about this moment for a week.

"This must be just about the prettiest valley outside of Eden," he told her as their horses fell into step side by side crossing a meadow. It smelled of spring.

"I won't argue with you on that one, Mr. Campbell."

He leaned toward her, making sure he was still balanced well on Daisy's back. He wanted no further mishaps. "Most women I know are willing to call a man by his first name once they've been thoroughly kissed by him."

He grinned as she straightened indignantly in her saddle. "I suspect those women you are so familiar with may number in the hundreds, *Mr.* Campbell, but I'm not one of them."

"Hundreds? No, you give me too much credit. Remember, I'm a businessman. I've allowed myself little enough time for the softer pleasures of life."

"Dozens, then," she snapped.

He grinned again. "That's at least a more reasonable sum."

He knew that teasing was one way to lead to intimacy, but he wanted to be careful not to push her so far that she would be too angry to be appeased. Though her face was set and her lips tight, he didn't think he'd crossed the line yet.

"However, I can't remember a single one who kept me tossing in my bed every night for a week like a certain Scottish lassie."

Her head whipped around and she looked at him, dumbfounded. "I beg your pardon?" she said.

"It serves me right for trying to act the gentleman and not take advantage of a lady who is laid up with an injury and can't rightly defend herself."

She didn't say anything. He could see her swallow, and from her expression, it was as if she'd swallowed a toad. Duncan frowned. He'd always prided himself on unerring instincts about women, but as he told himself daily, he wasn't in New York anymore. Could he have been mistaken about the attraction between the two of them? He thought back to that last night in her bedroom when he'd watched her eyes as he'd caressed her hand with his mouth. He hadn't been mistaken. The attraction had definitely been there. And she'd felt it.

He'd made himself stay away from her all week long, knowing that if he got near her again, he'd have a hard time restraining the impulse to act on that attraction. Of course, he had every intention of acting on it, just not when she was confined to a bed or a sofa and at the castle where anyone could come along at any time to interrupt.

He figured that she'd be willing enough. From her ready response, he suspected that it had been a long time since her elderly husband had been able to please her. She would be ripe for a romp with an eager partner—a partner who was strong and healthy and *young*. She'd been a married woman, so he didn't have to worry about considerations of virginity and reputation. As long as he was careful not to start a babe growing inside her, they should be able to act as two adults desirous of mutual pleasure. Of course, she would take a little coaxing. That was one of the best parts of the game.

"Come now, sweetheart," he said in a low voice, reaching out from his horse to take her hand. "I think you'll agree we left matters unfinished the other night in your bedchamber."

He could see that she was biting her lip. Finally she said, "I'm not sure I know what matters you're referring to, Mr. Campbell, since it was a *week* ago, and you've not seen fit to speak to me since."

He relaxed back in his saddle, his doubts gone. She'd mistaken his discretion for inattention and it had piqued her feminine sensibilities. This he could remedy. "Then I shall just have to remind you about those matters I'm referring to. Where can we find a good place to stop around here for lunch?"

She looked at him warily.

"You may be used to all day in the saddle," he said, shifting in his seat, "but this tenderfoot could use a rest."

They rode for another few minutes to reach a stream, a smaller branch of the river that went from the hills down through the village of Glencolly. "I like to sit by the water," she told him as she pulled her horse to a stop and lightly jumped off. Before he could dismount, she had walked over to him as if to offer assistance.

"I honestly do know how to get down off a horse," he

said. "That is, if the saddle is on top of the animal where it's supposed to be."

She laughed. If she retained any anger over his teasing on the road, it was hidden. Mostly, he decided, the banter had served its purpose, which was to get them back to the same intimate plane they had been on that night in her bedroom. He sensed the success of his tactics in the way she tensed when his hands touched her as he handed her the packet of food. He could see it in the way she had to lick her dry lips several times, in the heightened color of her cheeks, in the way her fingers fluttered at her throat.

She may not be as eager as he, he calculated, since that would hardly be possible. He'd told her the truth about tossing in his bed all week long. But she was eager enough.

The notion made him ravenous. Emmaline had packaged cold chicken and cheese. He devoured it, while Fiona sat without taking a bite. "Aren't you hungry?" he asked when he stopped eating long enough to notice that she was not following his example.

She shook her head. "I believe lying around all week long made me lose my appetite."

"So you need some vigorous activity to restore it. Hmm, I wonder what we could find for you to do." One eyebrow went up as he said the words, leaving no doubt about the innuendo intended.

To his surprise, her lower lip began to tremble as if she were about to burst into tears. "Sweetheart!" he cried. Then he swept away the remains of their picnic and reached to pull her into his arms. "What's the matter?"

Fiona was not entirely sure that she could explain. Especially not to Duncan Campbell. She knew that his teasing was not meant to be malicious. If she were one of the sophisticated women in New York City he was used to, she would be able to laugh at his sallies and tease back without feeling this knot tightening in the middle of her stomach. She'd be able to let the teasing lead to more kisses, as he obviously intended, and to more ardent attentions after that.

But though she was a widow, she felt as timid and bewildered as a young girl with her first menses. She realized now that though they had made love, Alasdair had never been her lover. He'd been a father figure, kind, gentle. In all their years together, he'd never produced in her the feelings that Duncan had in a few casual encounters.

And they *had* been casual, she reminded herself. This had nothing to do with love. The worst of it was, though she felt she should be scandalized by his suggestions, they made her stomach jump with illicit pleasure.

He was holding her in his arms without pressing further. "Will you tell me what's bothering you?" he asked gently.

She'd managed to blink down the tears. "I'm not used to this," she said. "I don't know how to act."

He held her away from him so that he could see her face. "You don't mean to say that you and your husband . . . ?"

She shook her head. "Our marriage was consummated, if that's what you mean. But I'm beginning to see that there are feelings . . ." She couldn't finish.

He was silent a long moment, then he lifted her from his lap and set her beside him on the blanket. "Sweetheart, I'm beginning to see that I may have made a bit of a miscalculation."

Miscalculation? The word irritated her. Did he think this was one of his business deals?"

"No harm done that can't be repaired," he added. "We'll just start back toward the beginning and take things a bit slower."

Though it sounded like exactly what she needed, it rankled that he seemed to be approaching the whole notion of making love to her as if it were some kind of game.

"I think it would be better if we simply didn't start at all," she said. "If you're finished with your lunch, perhaps we'd best head back."

He looked at her for a long moment. Then he nodded. "We'll leave in a few minutes. Just give my poor posterior a bit more time for a reprieve."

He had that little-boy tone again, and it forced a smile. At least, he appeared to be backing away from the dangerous suggestions of earlier. "We may stay longer, if you need the rest," she agreed.

He lay back on the sloping bank and reached for the flask of wine. "It makes one thirsty to ride all day in the sun," he said. "Would you like some?"

She was leery of drinking too much, especially since she'd eaten practically nothing, but she was thirsty. Taking the flask from him, she took a deep, fruity swallow, then handed it back.

Duncan had closed his eyes. "I need to do this more often," he said with a contented sigh. "A man can only do so much business without losing an important part of himself."

"That day on the road you said that business is what makes you happy."

He opened his eyes and looked up at her. "It does. But I find that it also makes me forget that the earth smells different in the spring, and that wind rustling through trees is prettier than chamber music. It makes me forget that when one is hungry, cold chicken can taste better than the fanciest dish from a fine French chef."

She smiled. There were apparently sides to Duncan Campbell she had yet to learn.

He lifted the flask again. "Or that wine drunk from a

flask by a country stream is more heady than any served in a crystal goblet in a stuffy drawing room."

He passed her the flask again, and she obliged by taking another drink. She already could feel the liquor stretching out along her limbs. It felt good after the tenseness of the past few minutes.

"It *is* heady," she agreed. "Alasdair always kept good wines."

"You're spoiling my poetry, lass," Duncan teased. " 'Tis the surroundings that make it heady, not the vintage. The surroundings and the company," he added.

He was still lying back on the grass. He looked relaxed and content, not at all the predatory male she had sensed earlier. Perhaps she'd been silly to be afraid, she told herself. It could be that he'd meant to go no farther than teasing. Then she pictured the night in her bedroom when he'd bitten her hand. The memory brought instant heat to her cheeks.

"Have you rested enough now?" she asked, trying to sound normal. "Are you ready to ride again?"

He sat up and took another drink of wine. When he pushed the flask toward her, she shook her head.

"I'm fine," he said with a smile. "The question is—how are you?"

"I apologize for the . . . for, you know, earlier." She stumbled over the words. "As I told you, I'm not very good at this kind of thing."

He was sitting with his face inches from hers, his dark eyes studying hers as if trying to see inside her head. "I'm beginning to understand that, Fiona, and I don't want to make you uncomfortable."

She nodded, relieved. He *did* understand, and she was grateful.

"On the other hand," he continued, setting aside the wine and taking both her hands in her, "sometimes when we're afraid of something, the best thing to do is face it. I think we should face it together."

Once again she could feel herself stiffening. "I didn't say I was afraid."

"You didn't say it, but it's there in your eyes. I won't question you any more about your marriage, but I can assure you that when I make love to you, you will feel nothing but pleasure."

When, he'd said, not *if.*

He took her head between his two hands and kissed her on the mouth with such exquisite tenderness, it made the back of her throat ache. She stayed perfectly still, letting his kisses stoke that longing in her middle that she was just beginning to know. He kissed her lips, her eyes, her cheeks, her temples, the tip of her chin, then her mouth again, until her entire face felt . . . cherished. It was utterly seductive.

Finally he took his hands from the sides of her head and sat back. She opened her eyes and looked at him. She could see his desire in the flare of his nostrils, in his lowered eyelids. But he said, "That's as far as we'll take it today, my skittish little mare. You liked that much, I take it?"

She couldn't remember Alasdair ever asking her if she had liked anything he had done to her. "Aye," she admitted through shallow breaths.

He nodded, then grinned. "It wasn't the wine, was it?"

She shook her head slowly.

He stood and reached his hand to help her up. "We'll try another lesson tomorrow. If I can get over my fear of riding, you can get over your fear of lovemaking."

She let him pull her up, stuttering a reply to his totally outrageous implication that he intended to continue his efforts at seduction. "But I can't——"

He just shook his head and put a hand on her lips to

stop her words. "Don't think about it. Take it from a hard-nosed businessman who knows what he's talking about. Lovemaking is for doing, not for strategizing."

If that was so, Fiona thought as they mounted their horses for the ride home, why did she have the feeling that Duncan Campbell was a master strategist whose current business objective was her?

W hen Fiona and Duncan had returned to the stable the previous day, the new colt was finally making an appearance. They'd immediately joined a circle of people who were watching the proceedings, which, to Fiona's relief, had eliminated any need for further exchange with Duncan.

But she'd had difficulty getting to sleep that night. She tried to tell herself that it was because of her ankle. The ride had proved to be hard on it after a week of no activity, and it had been aching. But deep down she knew it wasn't her ankle that was keeping her awake. It was the memory of what had transpired that day by the stream with Duncan and his promise of "another lesson tomorrow."

How dare the man? she'd think one minute. Then the next she'd be wishing that tomorrow would come faster so that she could find out if he'd really meant it.

She'd finally fallen asleep in the wee morning hours, and when she awakened her body was sluggish from not enough sleep. Nevertheless, she forced herself to get up and dress. She wasn't going to have Duncan think that she was hiding. Though she still hadn't decided what she would do if he made good his promise. Would she slap his face? Or would she begin that mindless melting that she'd already experienced with him more than once? The indecision was making her head ache.

The best solution, she decided finally, was simply to ensure that the two of them weren't alone together. With that resolve made, she went downstairs and directly to the kitchens. That way she wouldn't risk encountering Duncan alone at the breakfast table.

Emmaline was, as usual, up to her elbows in flour. "Why, there she be, walking pretty as a sparrow with barely a limp," the cook greeted her.

Fiona smiled. "I'm recovered finally, Emma, and intend to make up for my week of slacking by helping you clean out the winter pantry."

"God luv ye, Lady Fee, but 'tis no work fer yer first day back on yer feet. Ye'll have that ankle all swole up agin."

Fiona lifted her skirts and waggled her foot in the air. "It's fine, look. And I want to do it."

"Ye canna, even if 'tis what ye want. Malcolm's waitin' to give ye a message from the Maitlands. An invitation to dine at their place today."

Fiona had been surprised that she had not yet heard from Graham after she had asked him to check with her solicitor. Perhaps the invitation was to discuss what he had discovered.

"Was Mr. Campbell invited as well?"

"Aye." The little cook's fleshy, flour-covered forearms shook as she laughed. "I reckon 'twill come to a showdown between those two." At Fiona's confused look, she continued. "Between Mr. Maitland the Young'un and yer new American swain."

Fiona gasped. "Mr. Campbell is not my beau, Emma."

Emmaline tipped her head and continued rolling out her dough. "Not yet, but I can tell ye that when Mr. Maitland sees how Mr. Campbell watches ye with them mooncalf eyes, there'll be a showdown. Mark my words."

Fiona walked slowly out of the kitchens to search for

Malcolm. Servants were always trying to make drama of a household, she told herself. She had never seen Duncan look at her with anything resembling mooncalf eyes. The very idea was preposterous. He'd looked at her with desire a time or two, but so had many men, even while she'd been married to Alasdair.

Malcolm was not in the front part of the castle, and as she turned to go up the stairs in search of him, Duncan emerged from the dining hall.

"We've an invitation to have dinner with your neighbors," he told her.

"I heard from Emmaline." He looked his normal self. Brisk, efficient. Looking forward to the day's business. Certainly not mooncalf.

"I assume you'll want to go," he said.

She nodded. "I haven't visited in a long time. And it would be good for you to meet Mr. Maitland. Logan Maitland," she clarified. "That is, if you intend to accept the invitation as well."

He nodded. "Of course. I suppose the road to Maitland Manor is as bad as the road to town?"

She smiled. "Yes, it's best to go on horseback." Robby would be with them, she told herself firmly. This would not be a repetition of yesterday's scene. "Are you . . . up to it? You're not too stiff?"

"No. Even though she pulled that saddle trick yesterday, Baird and Blair were right to pick Daisy for me. She and I are starting to come to an understanding." He grinned and for a moment he resembled her companion from yesterday's picnic.

As the vein along her throat began to pulse, she turned away quickly. "I'm going up to the schoolroom to tell Robby."

"I suppose he'll go with us," Duncan said.

She shot him a wary glance, but there didn't appear to

be any deeper motive to his question. "Of course. It will do him good to pay a visit. We've stayed in the castle too much since his father's death."

"Very well then. I'll be about my work so that I can enjoy the afternoon with both of you."

Then he turned down the hall to his office, whistling. If he was disappointed that he wouldn't be traveling alone with her, it didn't show. If he had had any plans of continuing where they had left off by the river bank the previous afternoon, it was certainly not apparent to her.

D*uncan sat at his office desk, tapping his pencil idly on* the account books in front of him. After an hour he'd scarcely looked at them. He tried to remember if any of his pursuits of women back in New York had turned into such an obsession. There had been one time when he was not much more than twenty that he'd been entranced by an older opera singer and had sent flowers to her dressing room every night for weeks in exchange for the few amorous nights she agreed to spend with him. For a time he'd found himself daydreaming about her at inopportune times. He was already a successful businessman and found the infatuation to be most disruptive.

But even that hadn't been like this. He told himself it was because he was under the same roof with her. When he lay down to sleep at night, he knew that she was doing the same at the other end of the drafty castle corridor. And she was imminently available—an independent widow who was neither a virgin nor, apparently, looking for another husband. There was really little to prevent him from walking down that corridor and joining her for a night of reciprocal satisfaction.

Nothing but the reluctance of the woman herself. This was new to him, and he wasn't sure exactly what to do about it. Hellfire, he knew with utter certainty that she had liked his kisses. He suspected that if he'd pressed the issue, she would have let him make love to her. But he didn't want her to *let* him. He wanted her to *want* him.

In the end, he decided, it was a matter of strategizing, just like with any business he'd undertaken. He needed to plan in advance to arrange all the elements to ensure a favorable outcome.

It would not happen today. He would have no opportunity to convince Fiona to act on what he was sure was their *mutual* desire when they would be traveling with Robby and visiting her overly protective neighbors. So why couldn't he concentrate on his books? he asked himself, slamming the big ledger with disgust.

He stood up and went over to add some wood to the fire, which was already burning bright and hot. It was a mystery to him how the library could stay so damned cold when they kept the fire burning all day.

Straightening up from the fire, he went over to gaze out the bay window. A cold drizzle misted the glass.

It was too bad that he'd already invited Robby to accompany him to Glasgow to buy the mill equipment, he thought. That could have been the perfect opportunity. . . . But the boy was looking forward to going. He couldn't disappoint him.

Perhaps she would come along with them. Would she want to stay in the same room with Robby? Dammit, Campbell, he told himself. Stop acting like a lovesick boy. It was all just a matter of time. She'd kissed back. Happily. There was no doubt about it. She just needed more time.

chapter 12

It wasn't often that Duncan Campbell left important factors out of his business strategies. But he'd left out Graham Maitland, he realized, as their neighbor greeted them in the curving front driveway of Maitland Manor. The manor was a handsome brick building with white gables. Dark green shutters lined the neatly symmetrical windows.

Duncan had not been looking forward to the visit. When it had begun to rain in the morning, he'd hoped it would have to be put off for another day, but by midmorning the sun had come out, warming the countryside. By the time they reached Maitland Manor, it had turned into a warm day.

There was a proprietary look in Graham Maitland's eyes when he took Fiona's hand in greeting. After a cursory greeting to Duncan, he tucked her hand into his arm and walked with her up the steps to the front door as if he were welcoming the future mistress of the place.

Duncan lingered behind with Robby while a groom

took the three horses off to the Maitland stable. "Do you visit here often?" he asked the boy.

Robby shook his head and said in an undertone, "To tell you the truth, I don't think my father was that fond of the Maitlands. And I don't think he liked the way Mr. Maitland looks at Fee."

So it was not all his own imagination, Duncan thought, climbing the steps behind the couple, who had now disappeared through the front door. He felt a nip of conscience. Perhaps he'd been wrong about Fiona's independence. If Graham Maitland intended to make her an honorable offer of marriage, wouldn't it be wrong for Duncan to continue his own pursuit, which had no other object than physical satisfaction?

Perhaps that was the true reason why she had resisted him. His mood had been high on the ride as he enjoyed the company of Fiona and her son and took satisfaction in the fact that he and Daisy were managing the rough road with ease. But by the time he entered the cavernous front receiving hall of Maitland Manor, his good humor had disappeared.

"I'd like you to meet my father," Graham said with a polite smile. He was playing the careful host, but Duncan had heard warmer voices across the table at cutthroat negotiations.

He shook hands with Logan Maitland, who was an older version of the son.

"Welcome to Scotland," Logan Maitland said. Unlike his son, he made no attempt to disguise his curiosity in pleasantries. He looked the American up and down, taking his measure. "I reckon the Highland stock shines through even in America," he said finally.

Duncan could find no complaint in his treatment by the Maitlands. They were courteous and pleasant. Without dominating the conversation, they managed to entertain with stories of their days in India. They asked numerous questions about his life in New York. To all appearances it seemed to be a perfectly friendly gathering of close neighbors. Yet there was something underlying the veneer of good hospitality that had Duncan puzzled.

By the time they had adjourned to the parlor after the meal, he decided that his judgment was clouded from the continued attentions their young host paid to Fiona.

"I have a gift for you, Robby," Graham said. He had taken a seat on the sofa next to the boy.

Duncan had the impression that Robby thought little more of Graham than Duncan himself, but he showed the typical boy's interest in the idea of a surprise present.

"It's not my birthday for months yet."

Graham clasped a hand on his shoulder. "It's not for your birthday. It's just something I want to give you. With your stepmother's approval, of course."

Robby cast a slightly wary glance at Fiona, who looked mystified. "My approval?" she asked.

"We could go out to the stable now to see him," Graham added. He looked pleased with himself.

"To see him?" Robby parroted, his hesitation replaced with excitement.

Graham stood up. "Well, you've lost all the MacLennan horses in this inheritance switch," he said with a glance at Duncan. "I figured I'd give you one of ours. He's a stallion, just a two-year-old, but already one of the smoothest mounts I've seen in a long time."

Robby jumped from the sofa. "Criminy! A stallion! May I, Fee?"

"Are you sure he's gentled, Graham?" she asked.

"You can see for yourself," he answered. "We'll go have a look right now."

Duncan sat against his straight-backed chair feeling as

if he'd been smacked. Robby and Fiona had the run of the Castle Glen stables, but he hadn't thought about transferring ownership of any of the animals back to them. He could have done so easily—he cared little how many animals he possessed. Now Graham had come in and trumped him. With great success, if the looks on Robby's and Fiona's faces were any indication.

"What a lovely gesture, Graham," Fiona said, standing. "Of course we'll go see the horse. But I'm sure it's far too valuable for Robby to accept."

"Nonsense," Graham disagreed. "It will give pleasure to both me and my father to see that Robby has his own horse again. It's the least we can do—in memory of Alasdair."

Under those terms, it would be impossible to refuse, Duncan saw immediately. He also saw that Fiona was secretly relieved that she wouldn't have to refuse the gift that had put such a huge smile on Robby's face.

"Let's go, then," Graham said, reaching for Fiona's hand. She gave it to him willingly, but turned to address Duncan. "Are you coming?"

Logan Maitland lifted a decanter of brandy from the cart next to his seat. "You'll keep an old man company, won't you, Campbell? I'd like to hear more about your plans for the old Glencolly mill."

Duncan looked from his host to Fiona, still grasping Graham's hand, to Robby who was practically jumping up and down with eagerness to see his new acquisition.

"Of course, I'd be pleased to stay with you, Mr. Maitland," he said pleasantly. Then he reached to take the snifter of brandy his host had already poured for him.

"This is far too generous of you, Graham," Fiona said as they watched Robby ride around the Maitland corral with his new stallion, a small but perfectly formed sorrel with a white blaze.

"His name is Phantom," Graham had told Robby, pointing to the distinctive white spot. "Some say that looks like a ghost. But you may change it if you like. He's yours now."

Robby had been delighted with the name and with everything else about the trim animal.

"Some day I hope to be able to give you far more than a horse, Fiona," Graham said, his voice low. "I'd have given you one today, but I thought I'd have better luck convincing you to accept one for Robby."

She smiled at him. "You were right. Though I'm still hoping the day will come when all of the Castle Glen horses will belong to him again, along with the rest of the estate."

"I know. That's another reason I invited you here today."

"Did you have a chance to send word to Mr. Sinclair?"

"I went to see him, as I promised you. But I'm afraid I wasn't that impressed with the solicitor your late husband chose."

Fiona was surprised. "Alasdair worked with him for years. He always said he would trust Hampton over all other men."

"Well, that may be the problem. The man is getting on in years. I just don't think he's got enough fight left in him to help you through this battle."

This was not good news. Fiona herself had been getting impatient with her attorney's slow progress on the case, but she had at least trusted that Alasdair had left her in the hands of someone who was capable enough to help her. "I should go into Glasgow and meet with him myself," she said.

Robby came riding up to the fence. "He's smooth all

right, Mr. Maitland," he said excitedly. "Smooth as cream. You're swell to give him to me."

Graham smiled. "You're welcome, lad. perhaps we can ride together soon."

"Sure thing," Robby called as he turned Phantom away for another gallop around the corral.

"You can talk with Sinclair, but it would be better for you to see the Maitland lawyers. It's a large firm, and they'll be able to be of more help. I'd be happy to take you to Glasgow," Graham added casually. "Now that we can go by train, it's an easy trip."

The idea made Fiona uncomfortable, and she wasn't sure if it was the prospect of the train ride or a trip with Graham. It was generous of him to offer to involve his family attorneys, but she wasn't yet ready to give up on Alasdair's old friend, Hampton Sinclair.

"It would be wise not to delay much longer," Graham cautioned. "Every day your Mr. Campbell's hold on Castle Glen becomes stronger."

"I know." Fiona's head had begun to ache. She knew that she wanted Castle Glen back for Robby. She knew that she needed to consult with Mr. Sinclair. She knew that Graham would help her in any way possible. So why was she hesitating to accept his offer? "I'll let you know," she said finally.

D uncan's ill humor remained as they made their way home. Robby rode on his new horse, leading the one from the Castle Glen stables behind him. Fiona had told them that she had a headache, and apparently it was true since she hardly said a word through the entire trip. Once they reached the castle, she dismounted immediately and disappeared inside. Duncan stayed at the stables for a few minutes listening to the Bandys exclaim over Robby's new horse, then he, too, went in the castle.

All in all, his first social call in the neighborhood had not been a great success. When the others had left, Logan Maitland had grilled him about his plans for the mill. The man had seemed satisfied with the knowledge Duncan had gained about the industry, but he had given a low whistle when Duncan had told him how much labor the new equipment would save.

"Which means you'll discharge people?" the older man had asked.

At Duncan's nod, Maitland had leaned back with a skeptical twist of his head. "That will be interesting" was all he said.

What did they expect him to do? Duncan thought angrily as he reached his bedroom and began to take off his riding clothes. The mill was losing money, and he couldn't change that without getting rid of the antiquated methods that were causing the loss.

He sat on the edge of the bed and pulled off his boots. It shouldn't be this hard to run a modest castle and to modernize an old village factory. But if Logan Maitland's reaction to the necessary worker dismissals had been reserved, he knew Fiona's would not be. Perhaps it was time he told her about what was going to happen.

But he'd not do it on the same day Graham Maitland had put that warm smile on her face by giving her stepson a damn horse.

Her headache had gone away, but Fiona still couldn't sleep. She seldom remembered being this confused. The visit to Maitland Manor that afternoon had erased any doubt. She had only to ask and she would have the immediate support of her wealthy neighbor in fighting this inheritance battle. Why was she so reluctant?

Alasdair had always said that she was stubborn. Was it merely stubbornness that kept her from asking for help? Or was it something else? A horrible thought had begun to take form somewhere deep inside her. Did she in some perverse way not *want* to go to battle with Duncan Campbell? Had his kisses so altered her that she no longer was willing to stand up for the cause of justice for her stepson?

"I wish you were here, Alasdair," she said aloud. "Just for a short visit. Just to give me strength and help me put this muddled head of mine back into order."

Her words were followed so immediately by a knock on the door that she felt a superstitious rush. It had been a real knock, she assured herself, tying on a robe and walking across the room, nothing otherworldly.

Indeed, it was not her late husband on the other side of the door, but his heir, Duncan Campbell.

"I know it's late," he said, "but I thought I heard you talking to someone."

"From the other end of the castle you heard me talking to someone?" she asked dryly.

"No, that is, I came here to talk to you, then I was worried that it might be too late, but then I heard your voice . . ."

He was so uncharacteristically nonplussed that she took pity on him. "Obviously I'm awake," she said. "What did you want?"

He peered into the room, evidently looking for her conversation partner.

"I was talking to myself," she said bluntly. "I couldn't sleep."

He grinned. "I've been in my room talking to myself, too. We would probably both be less bored if we talked to each other. How's your headache?" he asked, sauntering into her bedroom without an invitation.

She watched him indignantly. "I'm not dressed, Mr. Campbell."

"Duncan," he corrected automatically. "I'm not, either." He held out his arms to show off his dressing gown. Then he wandered over and stood by the chair next to her bed looking as if he expected her to join him for a chat. "So we'll be casual."

She couldn't believe the man's audacity, but then, was coming to her room in the middle of the night any more audacious than kissing her in the shocking manner he'd already demonstrated?

"What did you want?" she asked again, still standing by the door as if ready to see the conversation finished quickly.

"I would have given Robby a horse," he said. "Hell, he can have as many horses as he wants. So can you."

This was the last thing she had expected him to say. The man continued to confuse her. When he'd first arrived, she'd believed him to be a greedy American. Now she no longer knew what she believed. "The horses are part of the estate," she said. "Why would you give them to us?"

"Why did Graham Maitland give a horse to Robby today?" he asked in return.

She hesitated. "I think he did it to please me," she answered honestly.

"He wants to impress you," he agreed. "Perhaps I do, too."

Their gazes held for a minute across the room.

"I'm not the kind of woman who is impressed with gifts."

"Nonsense. Everyone is impressed with gifts. Not just

women. It's human nature. I saw the look on your face today when Maitland made the gesture."

"That was pleasure over seeing Robby so happy."

"Exactly. Maitland's clever enough to know that a gift to Robby would make you happier than one to yourself." He looked down at the chair. "Are we going to sit down?"

"No," she said bluntly.

He shrugged. "Do you prefer talking to yourself?"

"I wasn't really talking to myself," she said, surprising herself with the admission. "I was talking to . . . to my husband."

Duncan's gaze flicked briefly to her empty bed, then back to her. There was a glint of sympathy in his eyes. "Does it help?" he asked gently.

She looked down at her hand, which still tightly grasped the doorknob. "I don't know," she said. "At times I wish he were still here to give me advice."

He walked toward her. "Advice about what?"

Advice about you. "I don't know—life, Robby, castle business, other things . . ."

"Maitland?" he asked, cocking his head.

She lifted her chin. "Perhaps."

"He's not for you, Fiona," he said, pulling her hand away from the doorknob.

She drew in an indignant breath. "You know nothing about him."

"It's just an instinct. One man to another. In business you have to be able to size a man up quickly. Graham Maitland isn't man enough for you. Now the father, that's another story. But the father is too old for you, and besides, he bases his every move on self-interest."

She'd had her own reservations about the Maitlands, wondering why she'd never been able to warm up to them when they'd always been perfect gentlemen and immensely helpful. But to hear Duncan disparaging her neighbors when he himself was the one who had come to take over their home was too much. "That's outrageous—all of it! And if this is your idea of pleasant conversation, then I'd thank you to—"

She broke off as an eerie sound drifted toward them from down the hall.

They both listened for a minute, then Duncan said, "I believe your ghost has decided to pay a visit."

Fiona frowned. "It sounds like piping," she agreed, "but it's not coming from the Stuart Tower."

"It almost sounds as if it's in the front parlor."

"But that's impossible. Everyone retired for the night hours ago."

Duncan seized her hand. "I don't believe ghosts sleep," he said with a grin. "Shall we go see if we can catch him this time?"

She let him lead her down the hall, both of them still in their robes. The piping had grown louder. At the top of the stairs he let go his hand and said, "Perhaps I should go down first."

He started down, quickly, but Fiona stayed close behind. As they both reached the bottom, the music stopped. Duncan put his finger to his lips as they slowed their pace and crept toward the archway that led to the big front parlor. Peering around the corner, Fiona could see at once that the room was unoccupied.

"No one's here," she said, her voice slightly shaky.

Duncan walked into the room and looked behind the two overstuffed sofas. "Apparently not," he agreed, "but look." He pointed at the hearth, where a freshly stoked fire was burning brightly. The fireplace screen had been moved to the side. "You said everyone had been asleep for hours."

"Someone has been down here."

He nodded, then walked over to the fire and used a

poker to stir the logs. "You don't think it was your ghost?"

"I can't imagine why a ghost would build up a fire," she told him. "Besides, the tales of Jaime MacLennan have always placed him in the Stuart Tower."

Duncan continued to stir the fire, spreading out the logs so that it would begin to die down. "Well, maybe he *is* getting restless, like Robby said. Someone's put this wood on recently."

She had a sudden suspicion. "You didn't come down here and make this fire before you came to my room, did you?"

He laughed. "To what purpose, my suspicious Lady MacLennan?"

"I don't know—to play a joke or something."

"And just how did I manage to be talking with you in your bedchamber and playing the pipes in the parlor at the same time? Granted, I'm a remarkable fellow, but playing ghost is not among my talents." He straightened up and set the poker aside. "Nor is piping, I'm afraid. Though my father always wanted me to learn."

"Your father played the pipes?" It was odd. She knew everything about the story of Bethia MacLennan and Duncan's many-times-great grandfather Fergus Campbell, but she'd never thought about his more recent family.

"Yes."

"Was he born in America?"

"No, he was born here. And never stopped cursing the day that he left the Highlands."

That was surprising news. She considered Duncan utterly American, yet his father had been a true Scot. She was curious to know more about him, but it didn't seem the time for further questions. It was the middle of the night, and they were standing in the parlor searching for a nonexistent ghost.

Struck suddenly with the absurdity, she began to laugh. "I'm afraid my father didn't think it all that funny," Duncan said, sounding miffed.

Fiona's laughter continued as she put a hand up to her mouth to stifle it. "No, I'm sorry—forgive me. I wasn't laughing about your father. I was just laughing—" Tears formed at the corner of her eyes as she dissolved in helpless giggles. "At us," she gasped, gesturing to herself, then to Duncan and the fireplace, "chasing downstairs in our nightclothes to look for a ghost."

After a moment Duncan started to laugh with her. "I'd have a hard time explaining this at a New York soiree," he agreed.

Slowly getting her giggles under control, Fiona wiped at her eyes and said, "I imagine your life was very different back there."

Duncan moved to place the screen carefully in front of the fire. Then he dusted off his hands and turned back to her. "You have no idea," he said wryly.

Her stomach ached from the sudden bout of hysterical laughter. She wiped away the last of the tears and tried to adopt a serious tone. "Do you wish you were back there?" she asked.

"Not right at the moment," he said.

She watched as he began to walk toward her. The look in his eyes told her what he was going to do long before he actually took her in his arms.

chapter 13

*O*nce again she felt small and silky and potent in his arms. Once again he couldn't explain the peculiar combination of desire and protectiveness. Something that went beyond passion. It was new and uncomfortable to him. He tried to dismiss it from his mind and concentrate on the physical sensations.

That wasn't difficult. It was as if their lips had been made to mate. The first couple of times he'd kissed her, she'd been surprised and hesitant, but this time she seemed to be ready for him. The touch of their mouths brought instant heat. He caught her up against him. Her bare feet rested on his leather slippers as they clung together. He could feel the tantalizing tips of her breasts against his soft dressing gown. Surely she could feel his erection against that silky thing she was wearing.

She pulled back for a moment of air and looked up at him with teasing eyes. "So you don't wish you were back in New York, Mr. Campbell?" she asked.

He couldn't muster a smile. His need was that strong.

But he swallowed and managed to answer, "No, ma'am, I don't."

Then he kissed her again and didn't stop for several long minutes. They were standing only a couple of feet away from an utterly convenient sofa. He let her slide off his feet to the ground and nodded in that direction. By God, he wanted her naked.

She looked at the sofa, and for the first time since he'd begun kissing her, he saw signs of doubt. "We could just sit for a spell," he told her, feeling the acquiescence slip away. His hoarse voice betrayed a desire to do more than *just sit*.

She looked over at the fire, then back at the sofa. Finally she said with a tone of regret, "I don't think so."

Duncan wanted to groan in frustration, but he managed to stay in control. Lightly, he kissed the tip of her nose. "I wouldn't do anything you didn't want me to," he told her.

She nodded. "I believe you. The problem is that I might want you to. And I don't want you to. If that makes any sense," she ended with a little helpless shrug that he found totally endearing.

"Sorry, sweetheart, but no, it doesn't make sense," he argued. "If you want and I sure as hell want, then what's stopping us?"

She looked around the room again. "Well, for one thing, we may not even be alone," she said with a mischievous grin.

His body had begun to cool enough for him to share her humor. "If your damn ghost decides to start wandering all over the castle, we can't be responsible for what he's going to see."

"It is odd," she said slowly. "The piping sounded like Jaime, yet it definitely came from here. And there was the other night with the candles in the Tower Room. And now this fire. Perhaps he is getting restless."

Duncan shook his head. Fiona seemed to have moved on from the subject of their lovemaking with frustrating ease. But at least she'd been receptive. She certainly hadn't kissed him like a woman who was falling in love with another man, namely Graham Maitland. Perhaps she just needed further wooing.

On a sudden impulse he asked her, "Would you like to go to Glasgow with me? That is, with me and Robby, of course. We're going to purchase the new equipment for the mill. We're planning to go day after tomorrow and stay overnight in a hotel. You would have your own room, of course," he explained carefully, "or you and Robby could stay together, however you prefer."

She hesitated, and there was an odd expression on her face that he couldn't read. Finally, somewhat to his surprise, she accepted.

"Yes, I'd like that," she said. "I have some business in the city myself."

He started to ask her what business, but she yawned and raised her arms in the air. "I do believe that's been enough excitement for one night. I'm going up to my bed." She turned toward the door and added, "Pleasant dreams, Mr. Campbell." Then she disappeared around the side of the archway.

E mmaline *looked sternly at the giggling row of girls.* "'Tis nae a fittin' subject fer the likes o' servants."

May giggled and gave a nudge to Elspeth, the maid with whom she shared downstairs duties. "I reckon 'tis as fittin' that we talk o' it as that they do it."

"Do ye reckon they'll truly be *doin' it*, if ye take my meanin'?" asked Lizzie, her upstairs counterpart.

"Hush your mouth, Lizzie Travers," said her upstairs partner, Jane. "Emmaline's right. 'Taint fittin'."

The four house girls had spent the morning helping Emmaline clean out the winter pantry. When Fiona had shown up to help, Emmaline had lifted her apron and literally shooed her out the door. "Ye need to be gettin' ready fer yer trip on the morrow, lass. I dinna want to see yer pretty face downstairs all day."

Without the mistress of the house present, the young girls had been free to speculate about the significance of the new master taking Lady MacLennan with him to the city. *Overnight.*

"Fer meself, I dinna think there's naught to it," May said finally with a sigh. "He's handsome as sin, the man is, but I dinna think he's got much o' the romantic to him."

"I think he's romantic," Lizzie disagreed with a roll of her eyes.

Departing from her role as the voice of decorum, Emmaline leaned close to the circle of young faces and said in a low voice, "If he has none o' the romantic in him, 'tis mighty odd that he come home from the Maitlands yesterday looking like a bull whose cow's been lured away by a steer from the next yard."

"Lady Fee's nae a cow," Jane chided.

"I dinna say she was, luv," Emmaline clarified. "I'm just sayin' that she's caught the master's eye. There's no doubt o' it."

May gave a little jump and clutched the cook's arm. "So ye do think that he asked her to travel wi' him fer—"

"Don't be puttin' words in my mouth, girl. I think nae such thing. They be goin' wi' the boy, ben't they?"

The girls' excited expressions dimmed. "Ah, so they be," May said. "I'd forgotten. Well, that puts a cap to it, I reckon."

"Puts a cap to what?" Malcolm appeared at the door to

the kitchen, standing erect, as always, his wool coat buttoned in spite of the warm spring day.

The four maids burst into laughter.

"To nothin'. They're just talkin' nonsense," Emmaline told him, though she was smiling herself.

Malcolm's expression didn't change. "I've come to offer my services," he said. "I calculated that you might need the help of a man."

Emmaline looked from the tall manservant to the still-giggling girls.

"Thank ye kindly, Malcolm," she said. "But I warrant we've got this covered."

He gave a stiff nod, then withdrew from the doorway.

"Now, *there's* a romantic," May said. Her words set off a fresh round of laughter among the four younger girls. None of them noticed that Emmaline had blushed to the roots of her gray hair.

*R*obby wanted to walk to the front of the row of handsome blue and red train cars to see the big engine that would pull them. Duncan fell into step beside the boy, and Fiona followed behind. She stood back and listened as the two males admired the powerful machine.

"Look in that door, Robby," Duncan told him. "They shovel the coal into that little door. It heats the water tank to produce the steam that moves the pistons."

He pointed to the big front wheels. "The pistons move these driver wheels."

Robby looked down the train. "What moves the wheels on the other cars?"

"The wheels on the other cars have no power at all. They are simply pulled along the tracks by these two big driving wheels."

Robby gave a low whistle of amazement. "Think of how strong they are!"

"Yes, it's a wonderful machine," Duncan agreed.

He smiled over his shoulder at Fiona as if to share adult amusement over the boy's enthusiasm, but the truth was, Fiona was as dazzled as her stepson.

Though it still seemed to her that she was somehow being disloyal to Alasdair, she had to admit that she was excited about the train ride. She'd been to Glasgow before, but she'd traveled by horseback over the poor Scottish highways that were worse than ever now that the railroad was becoming the transport of choice.

If Alasdair had lived, she decided as they walked back down the platform to their first-class car, he would eventually have changed his mind. It simply made no sense not to take advantage of a system that could get them from Glencolly to Glasgow in less than half a day.

She was dressed in her accustomed gray, but at the last minute the previous evening, she had packed a blue evening gown. It was still dark, not disrespectful to her mourning status, but the color made her eyes bluer and her suntanned skin paler.

Robby had decided that the pace of his two adult companions was too sedate, and he began to skip along the edge of the cars, reaching his hand out to slap each one as he passed. He'd grown up a lot since his father's illness, but occasionally she still saw glimpses of the carefree, chubby little boy who had brightened her first dark days at Castle Glen after the death of her mother. She'd been little more than a child herself, and the four-year-old had been a welcome diversion from the weight of suddenly facing a grown-up life.

Duncan nodded at the boy. "It makes you want to recapture childhood, doesn't it?" he asked her, as if reading her thoughts.

"Aye. He's tremendously excited about this trip. Alasdair took him to Glasgow a couple of times, but, of course, never on a *train*."

"It's easy to forget the enthusiasm of youth," Duncan said thoughtfully. "I get on a train and it seems that I'm spending the entire time looking at my watch to see if they're keeping schedule so that I won't miss whatever is awaiting me at the end of the trip."

Fiona smiled. "When you first came to Castle Glen, it seemed as if you were pulling that watch out of your pocket every ten minutes. Now I rarely see you do it."

Reflexively Duncan patted his watch pocket. "Damned if I haven't forgotten the thing entirely!" he exclaimed.

He was carrying both her valise and his, but he set them on the platform to assist her in mounting the high steps up to the train car. Fiona felt a rush of excitement, which she told herself had nothing to do with the sudden touch of his hand between her arm and the side of her breast.

The train car was larger inside than she had imagined. The comfortable seats looked not too much different from those of a plush carriage. But the big windows were magnificent. It should be a spectacular trip through the hills, seeing the panorama from all sides without worrying about wind or rain or runaway horses down the steep inclines.

"Would you like to sit by the window?" Duncan asked her, his expression amused. She apparently had not been able to totally hide her excitement.

She nodded, and took the seat he indicated, running her hands over the smooth leather seat. The train churned to life, and she sat up eagerly in her seat.

"How fast are we going?" Robby asked.

Duncan smiled at him. "Ten or twelve miles an hour, I should say. We'll be going faster when we finish climbing out of the valley."

After several minutes Fiona took her spectacles from her reticule. The vista was too beautiful to worry about vanity. She and Robby sat transfixed as the train passed the Glencolly Loch, then chugged upward alongside the turbulent black waters of a mountain stream. As they came out of the valley and headed across the flat moorlands, the wildflowers sprinkled alongside the tracks blurred with the speed of the cars.

Robby looked at her, beaming like a toddler with a sweetmeat, and she calculated that her own grin was probably just as big. Alasdair had been wrong about the railroad, she thought suddenly. It was a wonderful invention.

B*y the time the train pulled into the station at Glasgow,* Duncan suspected that his two companions were ready to end their first experience with train travel. Unlike the relatively easy trip when he had arrived at Castle Glen, this one had been plagued with problems. They'd made the first unscheduled stop about a half hour out of Glencolly. A piece of track had been out of alignment, and by the time a crew came to repair the rail, they'd sat for most of the morning.

Then they had encountered the obligatory herd of sheep for further delay. At noon the porter had come around with sandwiches and bags of dried fruit to distract them, but Robby had grown restless and had climbed off the train. He was still outside when the big engine moved forward again.

Fiona had stood up in a panic. "He's not going to make it back on board!" she'd exclaimed, lowering the window and sticking out her head and half her upper body to yell at her stepson.

Duncan had rather unceremoniously hauled her back

inside just as the train started to move. "He'll be fine," he said. "He's young—he can jump."

"But he might fall off—"

"No, he won't," Duncan said firmly. "Just concentrate on the scenery. Look at that pretty little glen through those trees over there."

And, sure enough, seconds later Robby had come bouncing back to his seat, face flushed. "I almost got left behind!" he said.

Duncan had blocked Fiona's more melodramatic reaction by saying simply, "Stay close next time."

The scare had not prevented the curious lad from climbing down when the train stopped yet again for mechanical difficulties. This time even Fiona let herself be persuaded to get off for a few minutes to stretch her legs as the repairs dragged on for over three hours.

"I guess it's lucky I didn't bring my watch," Duncan said ruefully. "I can pretend this isn't happening."

Finally, weary from the rocking motion of the train and grimy from the smoke and engine soot that seemed to reach even to the first-class cars, they heard the hollow blast of the steam whistle that signaled their arrival at Glasgow Central Station.

Taking one look at his drooping companions, Duncan flashed enough bills to ensure an immediate cab to the hotel, but by the time they had registered for their two adjoining rooms, it was late.

"We won't be able to get any business done today," Duncan told them as they walked toward the new electric elevator that would take them up to their rooms.

Fiona eyed the wrought-iron cage with wariness. "Are those tiny wires strong enough to hold this big thing?" she asked.

Duncan assured her that the device was safe as he ushered her inside.

She held on to the railing as the odd apparatus began to hum, lifting them upward to the third floor.

"Swell!" Robby said as they stepped out. "Could we go again?"

"Tomorrow you can go up and down as many times as you like," Duncan said with an indulgent smile. "But tonight we're all too tired."

When they reached their suite, Duncan said to Robby, "You can bunk in here with me. We'll give your stepmother a room to herself."

"Do you mind, Fee?" Robby asked, obviously pleased with the arrangement.

She smiled and nodded. "I'm so tired, I doubt I'll know where I'm sleeping."

Fiona had been certain that she would fall immediately to sleep, but after an hour of tossing on the unfamiliar hotel bed, she was still wide awake. Perhaps it was the strange surroundings, she told herself. She'd stayed in a hotel once before, but she'd been with Alasdair. She smiled at the memory. He'd been excited about showing her the city of Glasgow. The trip had renewed his strength, which had been flagging as he seemed to grow older with each passing month.

In fact, she remembered with a flush, he'd made love to her in the hotel that night—something he hadn't tried for a couple of years. She'd been so pleased to see him feeling well enough for that kind of vigor that she had actually almost enjoyed the activity for once.

Dear Alasdair. She *had* loved him, and she believed that he knew that, even though their physical encounters had always left her curiously unsatisfied.

She stretched out her arms. The bed was much larger than her own in Castle Glen. And warmer. The sheets felt pleasantly cool to the touch rather than icy like she was used to at home.

What was wrong with her? Her head was full of such an odd mixture of images—of Alasdair that night at the hotel, of Alasdair on his deathbed.

"Now ye must find the man who can truly make ye happy, my dearest Fee," he'd said.

"No man could ever make me happier than you have, my love," she'd told him. And she'd believed it. But he had just smiled and shaken his head.

She sat up and struck a match to light the table lamp next to the bed. It was time to banish these specters, she told herself firmly. Alasdair was gone.

But why was she feeling this peculiar ache in the lower portions of her body? Why was the memory of Alasdair getting mixed up in her mind with the image of Duncan Campbell's face coming closer as he prepared to kiss her?

The ache intensified. She didn't even particularly *like* the man, she told herself. *Aye, but you liked his kisses,* argued a warring voice in her head.

She lay back against the pillows with a smile. Her breasts had grown hard, she realized with bemusement. Experimentally she touched one peaking nipple and felt a twinge of response in her abdomen. What was wrong with her? She let her hand stroke along the silk of her night rail toward the center of her body. When it reached below her stomach, she stopped, feeling the warmth of her palm through the thin cloth.

The flush in her cheeks grew hotter as she brought her other hand to cover her left breast. The ache in the lower portions of her body had intensified. She closed her eyes and pictured how it had felt when Alasdair had entered her body. Oddly, when she had actually been with Alasdair, she had never felt anything approaching this full-body fever.

Her breast was a tight globe under her hand, the nipple utterly sensitive. She started to make idle circles with her fingers, then opened her eyes in horror at a sudden knock and the sound of the adjoining door opening.

Cheeks burning, she jerked her hands away from her body and whipped them out from underneath the covers.

Duncan's head appeared around the edge of the door. "I saw a light," he said. "I wondered if there was something wrong."

She shook her head, too embarrassed to try words.

He seemed to be studying her. After a minute he walked in the room. He was wearing trousers, but was barefoot and without a shirt. She gathered the blankets into a bunch over her chest to disguise the fact that her breasts were stiff and full.

"Are you sure?" he asked with a slight frown.

"Aye, nothing's wrong," she finally managed to answer. "I just couldn't sleep."

"It's sometimes difficult to sleep in a strange bed."

"Yes, I suppose that's the problem."

He stood watching her for another long moment, then he reached back and softly shut the door behind him.

chapter 14

Y ou aren't afraid here by yourself, are you?" he asked, walking toward the bed.

Not until I saw you, she told herself silently. Alasdair's chest had been sunken, his shoulders bony. Duncan Campbell's bare chest was huge, his arms strong and muscular. A sprinkling of hair down the center veed and disappeared under the waistband of his trousers.

"You—you shouldn't be in here," she stumbled, mouth dry. "Robby—"

"Robby fell like a rock," he told her with a smile. "One of the sweet advantages of youth. He's out until morning."

He now stood right next to her bed. "But you were still awake?" she asked.

He gave a humorless laugh. "*Aye*," he said, using her Highland inflection.

She wanted to sit up instead of lying there with him towering over her, half naked, but she had the feeling that if she removed her protective coverings, he would know exactly what she'd been doing and thinking before he came in. The very idea mortified her.

"What—why couldn't you sleep?"

He reached down and pried one of the hands from the bunched covers, then clasped it between his own. "I discovered it was even more difficult to sleep with you in the adjoining room than it was back at the castle with you a long corridor away."

She shouldn't have asked.

"What was keeping *you* awake?" he asked. She thought the question was accompanied by a slight quirk of his lips, but she couldn't be sure.

"I . . . well, I . . . I've only been to a hotel once before. As you say, it's a strange bed."

Now there was a definite upturn to the lips. "I'm disappointed in you, Lady MacLennan. I thought Highlanders never lied."

She pulled her hand out of his grasp, and heedless of what might be revealed about the state of her body, she sat up. "I'm sure I don't know what you mean," she told him with a huff. "But now that you've ascertained that nothing is amiss here, I'll thank you to return to your own room and let me try to salvage some rest out of what is left of the night."

He put one knee on the bed, took hold of her left shoulder with one hand and slipped the other behind her neck. "You may not want to admit it, but I believe you're suffering from the same malady as I. And until we remedy it, neither one of us is going to get a good night's rest."

Her head bumped gently against the backboard of the bed as he started to kiss her. The minute he began, she realized that he had been absolutely right. She wanted this, no, *needed* it. Her body was ripe and aching. For eight years of lovemaking with Alasdair, her own desires had lain undiscovered, and in just a few short weeks Duncan

Campbell had managed to make them erupt with a fierceness she would never have thought possible.

She made no further protest as he eased himself beside her on the bed and continued his caresses. Now it was his hands that were on her hardened breasts, his fingers plucking at her nipples.

She let her own hands explore his taut male nipples, the soft hair of his chest, the bulge of his arms, the prickly stubble along his jaw.

"You've captured me, my Highland lassie," he whispered to her. "I want to make love to you." He pulled back the covers and threw them off the end of the bed, then ran his big hand down the length of her. "I want to make you moan with pleasure."

His words made her do just that as his fingers reached a sensitive spot at the juncture of her legs. She closed her eyes while he teased her with his hand.

Within seconds the feeling had become so intense that she arched as incredible waves burst inside her body. Her eyes flew open in surprise. "My God," she breathed.

Duncan chuckled. "I had the sense that you were, um, needy, sweetheart, but I didn't realize how much. We still have our clothes on."

Fiona felt as if she were lying in a warm bath of sensation. Her limbs were limp and tingly as though she'd drunk whiskey. Duncan's words reached her through a haze.

"Is that supposed to happen?" she asked finally, her throat dry.

For a moment he looked confused by the question, then he asked carefully, "Have you not felt that before?"

She'd felt nothing that could remotely compare, she thought to herself, but she answered his question with a simple shake of her head.

It appeared that Duncan wanted to ask further details,

perhaps to ask why she was so inexperienced when she'd been married for ten years, but in the end he simply pulled her into his arms and whispered in her ear, "The next one will be without clothes and with me inside you."

Her stomach rolled. The feeling had returned to her arms and legs, and her breasts were already hard again. She helped him as he removed her nightdress, then rid himself of his trousers. He had no small clothes underneath them, only a flagrant erection that made her eyes widen.

The next hour was like nothing she had ever dreamed. It began with a twining of their bodies and their legs and their tongues. It seemed that his mouth was everywhere, nibbling at her now sensitive lips, sucking her nipples, one after the other, then kissing her neck and the soft underside of her chin as his hand readied her swollen folds to receive him. When he finally entered her, she gave a long sigh of contentment that made him give another of those deep chuckles.

"I think I've just found the most beautiful place in Scotland," he teased, moving slowly within her.

Then there was suddenly no time for teasing. The feeling began to spiral. He thrust faster and she dug her nails into his arms as they crashed with climax.

It seemed once the barrier had been broken, they couldn't get enough of each other. They had hardly finished when Fiona looked down to see that his penis was again hard. She touched him there, and he flipped her over with a growl.

"Would you keep me at it all night, wench?" he asked.

She grinned. "So this is my fault, is it?"

"Aye, lassie, that it is. I never knew when I set sail for Scotland that I'd be caught in such a snare. Are you one of the silkies they tell of?"

She laughed. "The silkies are seals that turn into men. Plus, they come from the sea," she pointed out.

"Ah. Then 'tis a Highland faerie who has snagged me. For surely there's some otherworldly influence at work here." He looked down at his erection ruefully. "Something has bewitched me."

They laughed together, until their play led to another coupling and yet another climax.

Fiona lay against the bed next to him, exhausted and sated and amazed. "I had no idea," she said weakly. "I hardly believe it."

Once again, Duncan seemed to be holding back his questions. "I'll be happy to try to make you a believer one more time, princess, though I have to tell you that—"

She pushed him back as he tried to roll above her.

"Nay, I'm convinced. And fully satisfied, thank you very much."

He lay back. "That's just as well, because if we start in again, I fear your stepson next door will be waking up to a shock."

Fiona sat up with a rush of guilt. "Lord, what time is it?"

Duncan remained prone. "I don't know," he answered with a grin. "I don't have a watch, remember?"

She clasped the sheet to her bare breasts and gave him a budge. "You have to go back to your own room. Gracious, it must be almost dawn."

With a groan, Duncan sat up on the edge of the bed and reached for his discarded trousers.

"Hurry!" she urged.

He turned around and gave her a kiss on the tip of the nose. "Don't worry about it, sweetheart."

"But if he wakes up—"

"He won't."

He finished buttoning his pants, then leaned over to pull her against him for a final long kiss. "Try to get some sleep," he told her. "We have a busy day ahead of us."

"We do?" she asked.

He grinned. "I plan to make it busy enough to ensure that Robby will sleep soundly again tonight."

H *ssst. Aren't you going to wake up?"*
Duncan heard the voice as if from far away. He struggled to open his eyes. It seemed as if he'd put his head down on the pillow only seconds before, but he could see through the hotel window that the sun was already high in the sky.

Robby sat on the edge of the bed, fully dressed. "I thought you said we'd be off early today," he said with a slight sulk.

Duncan blinked the sleep from his eyes and stretched. The stretch brought immediate memories of the previous night with Fiona. His lethargy disappeared instantly, and he sat up, smiling.

"Aye, but I said that before we knew we'd be on a train for fourteen hours. I thought you'd be tired."

Robby laughed.

"What's the matter?"

"You said aye instead of yes. You're starting to sound like a Highlander."

Duncan grinned at him. "I feel like a Highlander today, Robby, me boy. And I intend to eat a breakfast worthy of a Highlander. I may start with an entire roast pig."

He washed up and dressed quickly, whistling. He couldn't remember when he'd been so hungry, he decided. Or so full of energy, in spite of having slept little more than three hours.

"I don't hear anything from Fee's room. Shall I knock?" Robby asked.

Duncan glanced at the closed door between the rooms. "We'll let her sleep a while longer."

"She'll want breakfast, too," Robby protested.

Duncan nodded. "We'll bring her up some when we've finished." He knew exactly how he'd like to wake her up, he thought with a sudden erotic rush, but he may have to restrain his impulses until they could be alone again tonight after Robby had gone to sleep.

F*iona sat up in bed with a start. For a minute she didn't* know where she was. Then she remembered that she was in the hotel, and all the other memories of the previous evening came flooding back. She lay back with a smile of contentment and stretched. Certain parts of her body ached from unaccustomed activity, but it was a good ache, she decided.

She wondered why she hadn't heard anything from Duncan and Robby. She felt as if she'd slept for a few hours, which meant it must be the middle of the morning. She wouldn't question it. The extra sleep had been delicious.

Everything felt delicious. As she'd admitted to Duncan last night, she'd never even imagined the feelings he'd been able to produce in her. She didn't blame Alasdair. She'd been perhaps too young and innocent to understand the true nature of intercourse between a man and a woman. And he'd been frail for much of their marriage. But now that Duncan Campbell had come into her life . . .

She sat up again, more slowly. Now that Duncan had come into her life . . . what? He'd said nothing about wanting anything more than to satisfy their mutual desires. There had been no talk of love. He wasn't in love with her, and she certainly was not in love with him. Was she?

The elation of her first awakening minutes faded. For a few hours she'd forgotten her mission in coming to Glasgow. She'd come to see Hampton Sinclair. She'd come to ensure that Duncan would lose Castle Glen. To ensure that he would soon be on his way back to New York City where he belonged.

She flopped back against the pillow. Last night when he'd taken her in his arms, she'd forgotten that, but as sun streamed brightly into her room, it all came back—the Campbell inheritance papers, the appointment with Mr. Sinclair, her campaign to regain Robby's inheritance.

She had just spent the most incredible night of her life with Duncan Campbell, and today she was on a mission that would turn him into an enemy.

She turned and pressed her face hard into the pillow, hoping the pressure would somehow clear the muddle in her head.

I believe we finally have the documentation we need, Lady MacLennan." Hampton Sinclair's spectacles had slid down his nose as the elderly lawyer leaned forward in obvious excitement.

"The codicil was not filed with the original Campbell will, which is why we've had such difficulty in tracking it down. But it was filed in Edinburgh, two years before Fergus Campbell's death. We also found the record of his marriage to Bethia MacLennan."

"Jaime's widow."

"Yes. The marriage took place in 1752, five years after the Battle of Culloden. It appears she gave her husband an honorable term of mourning."

Fiona gave a guilty flush. Had she given Alasdair honorable mourning by sleeping with Duncan last night?

"Are you all right, Lady MacLennan?" the lawyer asked. "You look a bit unwell. Would you care for some tea?"

She shook her head. Tea would not solve her problem. "Let me go over this one more time, Mr. Sinclair. When Fergus Campbell married Bethia, he withdrew the future Campbell claim to Castle Glen."

Hampton Sinclair began to rise from his leather chair. His thin arms wobbled as he pushed on the desk in front of him to assist himself. Hampton Sinclair was an old man, she realized suddenly. He and Alasdair had been close friends and the same age.

She gave him an affectionate smile as he moved carefully around to her side of the desk and spread the papers out in front of her.

"The codicil says that if Fergus Campbell has no children *or* if his only children are also children of Bethia Campbell, then the document that passed Castle Glen to the Campbell descendant in five generations is null and void."

"And since he married Bethia, his children were also hers."

The lawyer nodded. "They had one child, a son. He would have been half-brother to the son of Bethia and Jaime. I suppose Fergus didn't want to begin a feud between brothers."

A thought occurred to Fiona as she looked at the yellowed papers in front of her. "If Duncan Campbell is the descendant of Fergus and Bethia, then he and Robby are cousins in a way."

"Distant ones," Hampton Sinclair agreed. "Bethia MacLennan was a many-times-great-grandmother to both."

"It's too bad they can't share the inheritance," she said, without intending to voice the thought out loud.

"Share it!" the old lawyer exclaimed. "My dear Lady MacLennan, what are you saying? Hasn't the purpose of all this investigation been to secure the inheritance for Robby?"

"Of course," she agreed hastily. "It's only—" She hesitated. "It is true that the estate has numerous problems, and Robby's only a boy."

Hampton gathered the papers into a pile and placed them carefully back into their folder. "You know I'm happy to be of service in any way I can to both you and Alasdair's son. It's the least I can do for a dear old friend."

He hobbled around the desk and took a seat again in his chair. Fiona feared she had disappointed him with her comment about sharing the inheritance, but as soon as she'd said it, she realized that there was a lot of truth to her words. The estate *was* in trouble. And it had been comforting to have Duncan around beginning to tackle some of the problems.

However well intentioned, Mr. Sinclair was miles away in Glasgow. He couldn't be of much help.

"Mr. Campbell has taken measures to straighten out some matters that Alasdair left in some disarray. Alasdair himself before he died apologized to me for the condition of the estate. He told me he was leaving me nothing but problems."

"And you think Duncan Campbell will be able to solve them," the lawyer stated, his cloudy blue eyes suddenly sharp.

Fiona sighed. She wanted to believe that the softening of her attitude about Duncan had nothing to do with what had passed between them in her bedroom at the hotel, but the argument wasn't very convincing, even to herself.

"He's here in Glasgow buying spinning machines and steam looms for the woolen mill, which I understand has been in dire straits. The hand looms don't produce enough to stay competitive," she said.

Now she was beginning to *sound* like Duncan, she realized with a start.

"Power looms?"

"Aye. He and Robby are at the factory now making the order."

"Has he told you what that will entail for the workers?"

"What do you mean—for the workers? I would imagine it will make things easier."

Mr. Sinclair reached in his pocket for a handkerchief and plucked the spectacles off his nose to clean them. "For those who are left."

Fiona got a sudden hollow feeling in her stomach. "For those who are left?"

The lawyer waited while he finished his cleaning, replaced the spectacles on his nose, and adjusted them to his liking. Then he stared through them, his gaze once again sharp. "Surely you must know, Lady MacLennan. If your Mr. Campbell is replacing the hand looms at the mill with steam, he'll be putting most of the town of Glencolly out of work."

I *s it true?" Fiona sat facing Duncan in the carriage he had* rented to take them around Glasgow. He and Robby had returned in high spirits from their trip to the loom factory, but their smiles quickly faded when they saw her stormy countenance.

"Yes," he said, meeting her gaze. "That's part of the reason we're buying the power equipment. It costs less to run machines than to pay people."

"And what are the people supposed to do while the machines take over their jobs?" she asked him, feeling even sicker than she had in Hampton Sinclair's office. "It's not as if there are a number of other places they can work in Glencolly."

"Perhaps in the neighboring towns—"

"Some of these people have worked for the MacLennans for generations. Now you propose to simply turn them away?"

Robby was listening to the two adults with a worried expression. "Maybe we should keep the hand looms after all," he said.

Duncan shook his head. "I've investigated this thoroughly. Glencolly is one of the last mills in Scotland to use hand weaving. That's why it's not been able to keep up with the competition. When we install the new looms, Glencolly will be able to regain its reputation in the wool marketplace."

Fiona clutched her hands tightly around the folder of papers Hampton Sinclair had given her, copies of all the evidence he'd found about the Campbell inheritance. "Who cares about the wool marketplace if it means that people won't have jobs?"

Duncan gave an exasperated sigh. He looked nothing at all like the man who had been beside her in her bed all night. Even his voice sounded different as he said, "Without improvements, there will *be* no jobs, Fiona. For *anyone*. And without income from a prosperous mill, there may be no Castle Glen."

She understood what he was telling her, but she didn't want to believe it. "You say you've investigated thoroughly. Do you know who the head weaver is at Glencolly Mill?"

He looked startled. "Well, no. My dealings have been with Jock MacLennan, the mill manager."

"The head weaver is John Strahorn. Brother of Malcolm Strahorn."

Duncan winced. "That would be *our* Malcolm?"

"Aye, that would be our Malcolm."

"But, of course, nothing will happen to him. Good God,

the head weaver—we'll need his skills more than ever to make the transition—"

"And who do you suppose the other weavers are?" she interrupted. "Let's see, there's Magnus Gemmel. That's our maid May's brother. And Seamus, Emmaline's son. And Tavis MacLennan, Jock's son, another MacLennan cousin, and all three sons of Hamish, the gardener, and the Bandys' mother, Margaret, works in the spinning room—"

Duncan held up a hand to stop her. "I get the idea, Fiona. Glencolly is a family. But sometimes you have to make hard choices about individual members to ensure that the family as a whole survives."

Robby was hunched down in his seat, looking as miserable as Fiona felt.

Duncan looked from one unhappy face to the other. "Perhaps the new looms will help the mill make enough profit to provide some kind of payment for the people who lose jobs," he said finally.

"Nay, these are proud Highlanders," she reminded him. "They'll not accept charity."

At that Duncan lapsed into silence and lifted the carriage reins to steer the horse out into the busy Glasgow traffic.

chapter 15

❦

Fiona could see that Duncan was trying hard to rally their spirits as he drove them around the impressive civic buildings of Glasgow's Merchant City district and past the big cathedral with its majestic spire of ancient stone.

Robby finally did perk up when they headed down the Broomielaw to view the big ships docked along the River Clyde piers.

Normally Fiona would have been fascinated with the tour of the bustling city, but her thoughts kept returning to everything she had learned that day at her solicitor's office . . . and everything she had learned the previous evening in her bed at the hotel.

By the time Duncan asked her if she wanted to try shopping at the Argyll, she had no need to invent an excuse for her refusal. Her head was pounding.

It continued to throb all through the uncomfortable dinner at the hotel restaurant. She felt a bit guilty when she glanced at Robby's worried face. He'd so looked forward to this trip, and she hated to dampen his enthusiasm. But she had to make some decisions that would affect not only his life, but the lives of everyone in Glencolly Valley. Robby would have other chances to enjoy a visit to the thriving city.

When they reached their rooms, she once again pleaded her headache. She had the feeling that Duncan would have liked to speak with her alone—or perhaps he expected to resume their lovemaking of the previous evening, but before he had a chance to speak, she said a hasty good night and escaped into her room.

A s little rest as he'd had the previous evening, Duncan once again found it impossible to fall asleep. Last night Fiona had been a welcoming, sensual lover. He couldn't remember lovemaking that had been so intense. It was as if they couldn't get enough of each other in the few hours they had before dawn.

When she had emerged from the solicitor's office today she'd been a different person. Once again she'd been the stiff-necked widow of Alasdair MacLennan who was fighting him at every turn. He could scarcely believe the change. He'd tried hard all day to pull her out of her thorny mood, but nothing had worked. Robby's presence had only made things worse, since he had the feeling that the old question of him stealing Castle Glen from the boy was again causing contention.

Hellfire and brimstone, he said to himself as he gave a punch to the pillow beneath him. It wasn't *his* fault that he'd inherited the bloody old castle. He'd been perfectly content with his life in New York City before all this had come along. He could be content with it again if he decided that saving Castle Glen was not worth the trouble. He could just up and walk away from the whole blasted mess and leave Lady Fiona MacLennan to sort out the

problems that her husband had been too old or too old-
fashioned to deal with.

He sat up in bed and rubbed his burning eyes. Robby's
breathing was deep and even beside him.

He was tired from lack of sleep and frustrated from a
day of trying to placate his traveling companions. Perhaps
that was exactly what he should do, he thought. Just leave
the wench to her problems. He'd head back to New York
City to his own friends and his own world. Perhaps he'd
look up Isabelle again, see if her marriage had worked out
as she had expected. At least with Isabelle, he didn't have
to put up with a prickly temper the next day.

But much as he tried to conjure up a memory of Isabelle's long dark hair and tall, lithe body, all he could
think of was Fiona. Fiona bustling around the castle with
a sense of responsibility that belied her years, making sure
that everyone—her *family*—was happy and cared for.
Fiona glancing back at him with a brilliant smile as she
raced across the moors on Sorcha. Fiona looking up at
him with wonder in her blue eyes as she reached a sexual
pinnacle that she'd evidently never known before.

She'd learned quickly, he remembered with a chuckle.
Once she'd gotten the idea, she'd been both giving and
demanding. It had been an erotic match between equals
that had been quite unlike any encounter he'd had before.
Exhausted as he was, the memory made him swell with
desire.

Confound the woman! She was as sharp as any businessman he'd ever dealt with. There had to be a way to
make her understand that there were times when money
had to take precedence over sentimentality.

With a glance at Robby, still sleeping, he slipped from
the bed, donned his robe, and walked to the adjoining
doors. Perhaps the best way for the two of them to com-
municate was in bed, the way they had begun the previous

evening. With that resolve made, he quietly turned the knob.

The door to Fiona's room had been firmly bolted shut.

W e can begin to clear out the old looms next week," Duncan told his mill manager as they walked through the factory making plans for the placement of the new equipment.

"Aye, sir. I've made a list of the people who won't be needed any longer." Jock MacLennan's expression was gloomy. "But I have a proposition to make ye."

Duncan turned his head, trying to stretch the tiredness out of his neck. The train ride home from Glasgow had been long and silent. Even Robby had shown little of his earlier enthusiasm for the new transport. Fiona had disappeared as soon as they had arrived back at the castle, and Duncan decided to ride down to the mill to talk with Jock about his purchases. He knew the mill manager wasn't happy about the changes, but at least he understood the need for them. And he didn't look at Duncan as if he were a masked executioner carrying a sharp ax.

"What kind of proposition?" Duncan asked.

"The goodwife and me find ourselves with fewer needs these days. The bairns are grown-up and gone, and me goodwife is takin' in plenty o' money wi' her candymaking. If I stop takin' me salary here at the mill, we should be able to keep on payin' two o' three more o' the boys."

Duncan fought back an angry retort. "That's no way to run a business, Jock. You pay for the workers you need, not the ones you don't need. The one we need here is you."

"Aye, but I dinna think it a bad idea to keep a few more on, even with these fancy new machines yer bringin' in.

We can always use the extra hands. And, as I say, the wife and me—"

"We'll talk about it later, Jock," Duncan interrupted. "No one is being let go until we get all the new equipment up and working, and by then I may have a few ideas for the ones who are no longer needed."

Jock's thick brow rose in surprise. "What kind o' ideas might those be, Mr. Campbell?"

Duncan smiled. "All in good time, Jock. First we get the new looms installed and decide what is needed to make this place into a profitable enterprise again."

Jock nodded slowly. "Aye, I'd like to see that, sure enough."

Duncan extended his hand. "Then we're in agreement, my friend."

There was little point in delaying, Fiona decided as she headed from the far side of the castle toward Duncan's office. She knew what she had to do. She'd always known, really. It was just that Duncan Campbell had confused her for a time with his seductive charm.

She'd send word to the Maitlands tonight and tell Robby after supper. He'd not be happy about moving to Maitland Manor, but when she explained the whole thing, he'd understand that it was all part of the process of securing Castle Glen for him legally and for good.

The Maitlands would help her work with the lawyers and file the necessary papers. She supposed it would take a few weeks for a legal judgment to be rendered. Until then, she wasn't about to stay under the same roof with Duncan Campbell. It would be awkward and difficult for everyone concerned.

She could demand that *he* leave until the judgment was issued, she supposed, slowing her steps while she considered this new angle. Duncan had nowhere else to go, but that wasn't her problem. However, he had been legally awarded the castle by one court, so she supposed he would be within his rights to refuse to leave. All in all, moving in with the Maitlands was her best choice.

Of course, she had to tell Duncan that she was leaving. In her present mood, she was looking forward to that task. She hadn't spoken to him much since she'd learned about the upcoming firings at the mill, but she'd had the time to become more incensed about his role in it. He'd known all along that the upgrading meant putting people out of their jobs, but he'd never said a word to her. He'd even invited her along on the trip to Glasgow where he would buy the cursed power looms. Perhaps he'd even seduced her in order to soften her up for the news that was to come.

That was probably unfair, she decided after the momentary flare of temper faded. He was the owner of the estate, at least as far as he knew, and he could do anything he wanted with the mill. He didn't have to sleep with her in order to carry out his plan.

"Still, he was a cad," she said aloud to the row of MacLennan ancestors as she marched through the portrait room. "Nothing like Graham Maitland."

Unlike Duncan, Graham had made it clear that he wanted to make her an honorable offer of marriage. He'd never once stepped out of line in his attentions to her, even though she'd seen the look a time or two on his face. Graham Maitland was a gentleman, whereas Duncan Campbell was . . . an *American.*

W*hat do you mean, leaving?"* Duncan looked up from his desk in astonishment.

"Robby and I will be moving to Maitland Manor tomorrow," Fiona said quietly.

"Why in blazes would you do that?" He tried to keep his tone down. In business, he'd learned, it was the one with the calmer voice who won the negotiation. And Fiona sounded calm as a windless topsail.

"I have my reasons."

"Would you care to share them with me?"

"Nay."

Calm as a sleeping tortoise. Duncan gripped the edge of the desk and leaned toward her. "Sit down," he said brusquely.

"No, thank you."

"Fiona, we need to talk. I know you're angry that I didn't tell you about the firings at the mill, but—"

"This has nothing to do with that."

He sat back, confused, then opened his eyes wide with sudden realization. "You're not going to marry that sycophantic bastard, are you?"

"If you're referring to Graham, the truth is, I haven't decided. Not that it's any of your business."

She remained standing in front of his desk. He got up and walked around to her. "This has something to do with the other night at the hotel." He grasped her shoulders. "Fiona, what we did together was—"

"That's over and done with, Mr. Campbell," she interrupted once again. "I won't say that I regret that night, because that would be a lie. But I will say that it's over."

Once again she was the staunch little Scotswoman—stubborn, sure of herself, her spectacles firmly in place. He wondered suddenly if he had dreamed that she had once melted in his arms.

Perhaps he should tell her about the plans he had for further changes in Glencolly. Would that soften those tight lips?

"Now, if you'll excuse me, I have a lot to accomplish before tomorrow," she said.

"I think we have more to discuss."

"Perhaps," she said, turning to free herself from his grasp. "But it will have to wait. I have packing to do."

"What does Robby have to say about this?"

For the first time she looked uncertain. "I'm going up to tell him now."

"He won't want to go."

"Maybe he won't, but Robby is still a minor, and I am his guardian. He goes where I go."

With that, she spun around and marched out of the room.

Duncan walked back to his chair and sat down heavily. What in blazes had gotten into the woman? He picked up a pencil from the desk and broke it in half.

It had been the devil's own luck that she had learned about the mill firings so soon after they had first made love. He knew women were sensitive about things like lovemaking, and he should have been able to spend the day paying her lavish attentions instead of defending himself against charges of callousness.

He rested his head on his hands. This was exactly why he had always been meticulously careful never to mix his business dealings with his women. The creatures didn't think the same as men, and they had trouble separating one area of life from another.

He raised his head at the sound of a knock on the door. His first thought was that Fiona had returned, but then he'd realized that it had been a *timid* knock.

"Enter," he said.

He recognized the slight girl as one of the maids, but he still sometimes had trouble with the names.

"Beggin' yer pardon, sir."

He could hardly hear her soft voice. "Of course, come in, er, Elspeth, isn't it?"

She looked directly up at him for the first time. "Aye, sir. I be the one who brings yer coffee in the morning."

"Of course. What can I do for you?" He looked at the young girl more closely and gave an inner groan as he recognized the telltale signs of tears. Her eyes were puffy and the tip of her nose was red. "What's the matter?"

"Is it true, sir?"

He had a feeling he already knew what she was talking about, but he asked, "Is what true, lass?"

"About the dismissals at the mill."

"Your brother works there, right?" he asked, more sharply than he had intended. "Or is it your father or uncle or—"

"Me fiancé," she answered softly. "Hugh Cullen. We were to be married at the Midsummer Fair, but now Hugh says he may no' be able to hae me since he may no' hae a job by then."

Duncan looked down at the broken pencil on his desk. It was not turning out to be a good evening. "You go ahead with your wedding plans, Elspeth, and tell your young man not to worry. I'm sure something can be worked out for him to stay on at the mill."

Her pale eyes brimmed. "Truly, sir?"

"Aye, er, *yes*. Truly."

"Oh, I thank ye kindly, sir. Hughie and I will be ever so grateful to ye. I canna wait to tell 'im."

It took a few more minutes before he could usher the appreciative girl out of the office. Then he sat back in his chair, lost in thought. He'd helped Elspeth, but he knew he couldn't continue to make exceptions to the dismissals. From what Fiona had said, if he made an exception for everyone who had connections at Castle Glen, he wouldn't be able to let any of the mill workers go.

So far he hadn't told anyone about the additional meetings he'd had his last morning in Glasgow or the follow-up letters that had come in today's post. He had a feeling that many in Glencolly would think him crazy, perhaps Fiona among them. But his plan would mean jobs. It would be a way for Glencolly to have a thriving, cost-efficient woolen mill and full employment for the people as well. He'd been called crazy a time or two back in New York, and it had never bothered him as long as the final results were successful.

The room had grown chilly, which was odd, since the fire appeared to be burning brightly. He started to get up, intending to add another log or two, but suddenly it seemed that something pushed him backward into his chair. A chill started up the sides of his neck. He'd seen strange things happen in the castle before, but he'd never before had quite this sense of a tangible . . . *something* all around him.

The late spring sun had set and the sky outside the window was dark. He wasn't afraid, he told himself. But he had this strange feeling of something not being right.

As he stared out the window, he could swear that in front of the blackness the air was turning grayish. Was it smoke from the fire? he wondered, jerking his head to look. The fireplace appeared totally normal.

He rubbed his eyes and swallowed, telling himself that his throat was not unusually tight. This was nonsense. He was simply too tired and crabby and letting his bad humor from Fiona's visit give him some kind of rare vapors.

That decided, he gave a firm nod and stretched his arms up over his head. There, he felt better already. He looked at the fire. It looked the same as it had a minute ago. He looked at the window. It was still dark outside. He smiled and began to shift his gaze to his papers, then suddenly whipped his head back in the direction of the window.

The sill had disappeared. That is to say, something was covering it. His jaw slack, he stood and walked over to it.

It looked like the top of the window seat. It had been opened to reveal a storage compartment hidden inside the seat. He ran his fingers along the edges to see if there was some kind of spring mechanism that had made it pop open just now, but as far as he could tell, the top was opened only by lifting it manually.

He gave another little shiver. This was *not* a ghost, he told himself. There was some other explanation. There was no such thing as ghosts. Still, he knew his breathing was slightly faster than normal.

There was a folder of papers inside the compartment, he saw. He bent over and picked them up. Shuffling through them, he could see that some appeared to be copies of older documents. The phrase "Campbell Will" caught his eye. What the hell?

Closing the top of the bench, he went back to his desk, spread the papers out, and began to read.

chapter 16

"S o Castle Glen is truly mine?" Robby asked, looking around his bedchamber with wonder. "But . . . what about Duncan?"

Fiona winced. She realized that Robby was too young to understand the full import of the news she had just told him, but she hadn't expected his first question to be about the interloper who had almost taken everything away from him.

"What about him? He can go back to America, where he belongs. I reckon he'll be just fine."

Robby bounced back on his bed and looked up at the ceiling. "I was kinda liking things the way they were," he admitted after a moment. "I'm not sure I *want* to be master of Castle Glen."

Fiona smiled. It was a big responsibility for Robby's still-slender shoulders. "I know 'tis daunting sometimes. But I'll be here to help you. And Graham Maitland has offered help, too."

Robby wrinkled his nose.

"And you have Malcolm and Emmaline and Hamish and everyone else at Castle Glen," she added quickly. "You know that any one of them would do anything for you."

"I know." His tone was gloomy. "Duncan said I was to help him make the changes at the mill. And we talked about doing a lot of things here at the castle. I was going to be his right-hand man, he told me."

"Well, now you'll be the one in charge, and you'll have all kinds of other people who will be *your* right hands." She gave him a playful slap on his knee. "You'll have more right hands than you know what to do with. Including me."

"Have you told him yet?"

"Duncan?"

"Aye."

"Nay, I haven't told him. I want to wait until we are established at Maitland Manor."

"But if Castle Glen belongs to us, why do we have to leave?"

"Because a judge said that it belonged to Duncan. Now we have to wait until we can get another judge to say that the first judge was wrong and that it actually belongs to you."

Robby suddenly had that grown-up look in his eyes that still startled her. "In other words," he said, "we have to have a fight with Duncan in court."

"It may not be a fight. Once Duncan sees the papers, I believe he'll realize that this whole thing has been a bad mistake. We'll just file the new papers and that will be the end of it."

"What about all the mill equipment I helped him pick out in Glasgow?"

She hadn't thought about this, but it was one more reason why things had to be done quickly. "I suppose there's still time to cancel the purchase."

Robby gave a sigh of exasperation, and Fiona realized that for just a moment he sounded exactly like Duncan. "We can't cancel it, Fee. The Glencolly mill will fail unless it gets modernized."

"We'll have to look into it, of course. Perhaps Jock has some other ideas, but in the meantime, we don't want to put half the village out of work."

"But Duncan says—"

Fiona stopped him with a raise of her hand. "We don't have to decide this tonight, Robby. We'll discuss it with the Maitlands tomorrow when we get there."

"I don't want to go live at Maitland Manor." Now he was back to sounding like a little boy.

Fiona shook her head. Her stepson's moods were much like his voice these days. You never knew exactly what you would get. "It's for the best, Robby. Until all this is settled." His expression was reproachful as she stood up and kissed him good night. "You'll see," she told him, "it will turn out fine. Duncan Campbell will go back to his own country, and the rest of us will be here at Castle Glen, just like when your father was alive."

"My father is not alive," Robby said. Like quicksilver, his eyes suddenly looked old again.

Duncan bunched together the pile of papers and put them carefully back in their folder. He'd read through them twice. Carefully.

Did Fiona know about this? he wondered. Who had left these in the window seat? He remembered that she had had a sheaf of papers when she had come out of her solicitor's office in Glasgow, and she had not offered to show them to him. In fact, looking back on it, he now had the feeling that she'd been careful to be sure that he hadn't caught a glimpse of them.

He drew in a long breath. If these papers were authentic, it meant that Castle Glen was not his after all. His troublesome ancestor, Fergus Campbell, who had started this whole inheritance tangle in the first place, had evidently changed his mind. He'd fallen in love with his MacLennan widow and decided to let her bloodline continue on as masters of Castle Glen. Lord Almighty, what a fiasco.

But if Fiona had known all this, why hadn't she told him? He supposed these papers had been unearthed after the initial judgment in his favor, but how long had they been sitting right under his nose in the window seat? He glanced over at the dark window, and another chill went up the back of his neck as he remembered how the top of the seat had opened apparently by itself.

"I'll be well out of this bloody country!" he said aloud. He didn't need to try to stay here and make sense of a place where everyone was kin to someone and ghosts wandered at will—a place where a woman would let you in her bed one night and plot to vanquish you the next.

Why hadn't she told him?

After several scowling minutes of thinking, the only answer appeared to be that she was playing the good adversary—keeping her enemy unaware of her weapons until the appropriate moment. What a fool he'd been thinking that she was nothing more than an innocent Highland lass. Yesterday she'd had a determined look in her eyes when she'd come out from seeing her lawyer. Her move to the Maitlands probably meant that she was now ready to begin the fight.

Well, fighting was one thing he knew well. He hadn't acquired over a dozen businesses in the cutthroat climate of New York City without learning how to fight for them.

He tapped his fingers on the folder in front of him. Then he reflexively pulled his watch from his pocket to see the time. Nine o'clock. Too late for action tonight. First thing in the morning he intended to pay a visit to *his* lawyers. If Fiona MacLennan was looking for a fight, he was ready to oblige her.

Logan Maitland opened his desk drawer to put away the Indian hookah he'd been showing Graham for the hundredth time. "We slogged through those mountains with the sun burning the skin off our necks. It burned right through our clothes," he told his son, who appeared to be only half listening to the often-told tale.

"And the only thing to keep me going was the idea that if I came through, I was going to get myself a knighthood and a castle."

"You got the knighthood," Graham pointed out, leaning back in his chair.

"And I intend to have Castle Glen!" Logan roared. "Mind you don't let these foolish romantic notions spoil the plans I've worked so hard on."

Graham did not appear affected by his father's temper. "I know, Father. Castle Glen will belong to the Maitlands eventually. But by then Fiona and I will be married. I want her to have no hint of our intentions until she's my wife. I doubt she'll be any happier to have us taking the place away from her stepson than she was to see the New Yorker come."

"Fiona's no milksop. You may be sorry to be tied to her if she decides to make you miserable once the deed is done."

"She's not like that. Once she's pledged herself in marriage, I'm sure she'll honor that and try to make me happy. She may protest when we actually take the place away from Robby, but she'll get over it."

Logan shook his head. "In some ways it might have been easier to take it away from the American."

"No. Duncan Campbell would have been a more formidable opponent than a boy and a widow. I intend to do everything possible to help Fiona overturn the court judgment and secure Robby's place as owner of the estate. Then, when her gratitude has finally convinced her to marry me, we can regretfully bring out the IOUs and take the place over."

Logan looked amused. "You're the one building a wasp's nest for yourself, son. And you're the one who'll have to bed the queen wasp. As long as we end up with Castle Glen, I don't care how you go about it."

Duncan noticed many more somber faces than he'd seen on previous visits to the mill. Of course, some of these people would be without jobs once the new machines were in place. He'd hoped to be able to make an announcement about his plans to offer alternative employment, but he was still waiting for word from New York. He was the owner of Campbell Enterprises, but he wanted his board of directors to give final approval to his investment in the Scottish railway company.

Even the usually genial Jock was having a difficult time putting on a good face.

"I've promised a few o' the spinners that they could buy their jennies," he told Duncan. "I reckon I shouldna made the promise without askin' first, but I reckon we hae nae use fer them here once the spinning machines are workin'."

Duncan nodded agreement. "Give them a good price, Jock," he said. "But I want you to keep three or four of the old spinning wheels. And I intend to keep a couple of the old style looms."

"Why would ye do that, sir, if ye dinna mind my askin'?"

Duncan looked around the factory. Everywhere workers were busy dismantling the old equipment. The boxes with the new steam-powered looms were stacked in front of the building, ready to be assembled. "You once told me that weaving is an art, Jock. I don't want to lose that. People will want to come here to Glencolly Wool to see how things used to be done."

The idea had come to him in the middle of the night. The mill was not only a business in Glencolly, it was a way of life. Most likely people for generations to come would be interested in seeing a glimpse of the way things were done in the olden days. Preserving some of the old methods at the mill would help ensure that the Glencolly pride in their wool and their art would not be forgotten.

"Beggin' yer pardon, sir, but everyone in Glencolly has seen this hundreds of times."

Duncan smiled. "I know. I'm talking about people from outside Glencolly."

Jock gave a resigned nod, as if to say that it wasn't his place to question the crazy ideas of the owner. "Does that mean I'm to keep on a couple more spinners and weavers?" he asked.

"Yes. Who's your best weaver?"

"That'll be Hugh Cullen. He's young yet, but I never seen a man with such a natural touch."

"Hugh Cullen? That's the one who's to marry the little maid up at the castle?"

"Aye, sir. Elspeth and Hugh are planning to be wed on Midsummer's Eve."

"Perfect. I want you to tell Hugh that he's in charge of a new section of the mill that will operate strictly using the old methods. He can set it up any way he likes and choose the people he wants to work with him."

"I reckon he'll be verra, verra happy," Jock said with a satisfied grin. "And 'twill soften the blow for all o' us to see a few o' the old wheels still spinnin' away."

For a fleeting moment, Duncan wished that Fiona were here to see Jock's nod of approval. He wasn't doing this for her, he told himself. He was doing it for Glencolly. But as his plans progressed, he found himself wishing that things had turned out differently between them. He suspected she would be pleased at his plans, and he knew that Robby would be excited. Until the two MacLennans had left to go to Maitland Manor, he hadn't realized how much he'd come to enjoy sharing things with both of them.

They'd been gone almost a week, and he hadn't heard a word from them.

"I'm glad you approve," Duncan told Jock. "Now let's go over those books of yours one more time and see exactly how many people will be out of a job beginning next week."

There's no more reason for delay, Fee." Graham's tone was uncharacteristically harsh. "The papers are all in order. We have the lawyers ready to go to a court fight, if necessary. Why won't you let me ride over to Castle Glen today and tell Campbell to start packing?"

Fiona looked at her host, who sat at the opposite end of a gilded settee. The Maitlands were fond of gilt, she'd decided. Every other piece of furniture at Maitland Manor was golden, as were all the frames that housed the precious artwork Logan Maitland had brought from all over the world.

It was much more luxurious than Castle Glen, but after

living amid all the splendor for a week, it had started to feel slightly suffocating.

"I just want to be sure we're not missing anything," she told him. "I want our case to be so perfect that Duncan will have no choice but to withdraw."

Graham moved closer to her and took her hand. "Are you sure there isn't some other reason for your reluctance?"

"I'm not sure I know what you mean," she said. Though she did know.

Graham was simply asking the same question she'd asked herself everyday since she'd left Castle Glen. Did she want Duncan Campbell to "start packing," as Graham had said? She wanted the castle for Robby, of course, but did she want Duncan to go back to New York? To never see him again?

"Ah, Fee, don't play with me. It breaks my heart. You know what I'm asking. Is there some reason why you don't want to finish this thing with Campbell?"

Graham Maitland had been a good friend for several years. By accepting his help, she supposed she'd given him the right to ask questions. But she simply did not want to discuss her complicated feelings for Duncan Campbell with him.

"I'll talk to Duncan when I'm ready," she said finally.

He scowled. For a moment he looked nothing at all like the gentlemanly neighbor she had come to know. "If I thought you had feelings for this man . . ." he began, his voice shaking. Then he stopped and took a deep breath.

"Let me take all of this off your shoulders, Fee. You know how I feel about you."

He put an arm around her back and leaned so close that she could see his moist breath on her spectacles. She found herself grateful for the slight barrier the glasses represented. She pushed backward, only to discover that she was trapped at the end of the sofa.

Slipping around him, she stood up. There was no help for it. She simply did not share the feelings that he so obviously had for her, and she finally realized that it was not fair to him or his father for her to continue to accept their hospitality.

"I do intend to get Castle Glen back for Robby," she said calmly. "But I've decided that I have to do it my way. I'm appreciative of all the help you've given us, but I think it would be best if Robby and I went home."

Graham stood up, his face growing red with anger. "You *are* smitten with the Yankee bastard, aren't you, Fee?" He took her shoulders in a hurtful grip. "Tell me the truth."

Fiona pulled away from him. "I'm sorry, Graham. I consider you my friend, but I can't talk with you when you're like this. I'm going to find Robby, and we'll make arrangements to be gone by this afternoon."

Graham became immediately contrite. "Fee, no! I didn't mean to hurt you. It's only because I can't bear the thought of you—"

She held up her hand. "I know, Graham. I'm not angry with you. But this is for the best. Robby and I are going back to Castle Glen where we belong."

I'm glad you changed your mind, Fee. I didn't like it at Maitland Manor."

Fiona and Robby were riding across the moor that was halfway between the Maitlands' and Castle Glen. The nearer they got, the more nervous Fiona became about seeing Duncan again. She hadn't sent word about her change in plans. Perhaps they wouldn't even be welcome there after the way she had left so abruptly. But she didn't think that he would turn them away.

She tried to keep her mind on what Robby was saying. "I thought the Maitlands were very nice to you," she told him.

"They were all right, but it's just not comfortable. The older Mr. Maitland is always sitting back and watching everything like some kind of spider ready to pounce on a fly."

The assessment surprised Fiona. She'd always found Logan Maitland to be a courteous, if somewhat reserved, gentleman. "You like Graham, don't you?" she asked. "He gave you your horse."

Robby wrinkled his nose. "I know, but that's just the problem. I get the feeling that he thinks of me as some kind of little boy he has to win over with sweeties, when it's obvious what he really wants is you."

Fiona didn't know how to reply. Poor Robby. He was having to grow up entirely too fast. Now she'd mixed him up in her confused relations with two different men. She'd fled Castle Glen because of one man. Then she'd fled Maitland Manor because of another.

As if reading her mind, he said, "That's why you decided to leave, wasn't it? Because of Graham?"

How much did a boy know of such things at Robby's age? Probably a great deal, she decided. "Partly. I'll admit it had become slightly . . . uncomfortable."

"I don't blame you. It's downright creepy the way he looks at you."

She laughed. "I don't think there's anything creepy about him, but he may have affections for me that I don't return, and that makes it difficult."

Robby nodded. "Aye, I could see that. And it's especially difficult when you're falling in love with Duncan."

Sorcha gave a toss of her head in protest. Fiona loosened the reins she'd been unconsciously gathering tighter and tighter in her hands. "What makes you say that?" she asked sharply.

Robby rolled his eyes and didn't answer.

They rode in silence for several minutes. Was it as obvious as that? she wondered. Or was it that Robby knew her so well that he could see what she herself had been refusing to admit?

Was it possible that she could have fallen in love so soon after losing Alasdair? She'd made love to Duncan, but that was not the same as falling in love. Or was it? She glanced over at Robby. How did he feel about another man taking his father's place in her heart?

"Does it make you angry?" she asked.

He looked surprised. "Angry? With you?"

"With me or with Duncan or with . . . life. Your father's only been gone a few months."

Robby gave her one of his warm smiles. "If I could talk with Father about it, what do you think he'd tell me? You know how important it was to him to see you happy."

"Aye, but he wanted to see you happy, too."

Castle Glen came into view up the path.

"I am happy, Fee. If it had been Graham, I don't know . . . But Duncan is different. He talks to me. I get the feeling that he . . . he thinks I can do things." Robby chuckled. "And, anyway, watching you two I figure I'm learning things that can't be taught in the schoolroom."

Once again she was impressed with his sudden maturity. It was comforting to think that her stepson was showing early signs of the wisdom she'd loved in his father.

"I'm not sure how I feel about Duncan," she admitted. "But I don't think it's going to matter. I need to tell him about the changed will, and once I do that, I imagine he'll go back to New York and we'll never see him again."

"You don't think he'll fight it? After all, you said the courts did give him Castle Glen. It was all legal."

"Aye, but now they'll have to change their opinion. Duncan is a reasonable man. When he sees the evidence, I believe he'll realize that the castle does not truly belong to him."

At least that was what she had been telling herself all day. She had finally realized that she didn't *want* to have the fight with Duncan that Graham had sought with such relish. She planned to talk with him, calmly and rationally. She would present him with the codicil to the old Campbell will and the copies her lawyer had given her of its registration. He would understand that disputing it would be futile.

And he would go home.

chapter 17

Duncan looked down at the several-page letter he'd received that afternoon from his Glasgow attorneys. It appeared likely, the letter said, that a court would eventually uphold the validity of the codicil to the old Campbell will. Which meant that Castle Glen could be returned to Robby MacLennan.

Duncan could sue for compensation for his time and the personal money he had already invested in the estate. He could force the Glencolly mill to return the equipment that had been purchased with his funds. It would all take time to sort out, the lawyers had said.

Or he could fight the case. The "other party in question" might have difficulty coming up with the means for an extensive court battle and therefore agree to some kind of settlement. They would be happy to represent Duncan in such a fight. Of course they would, he thought grimly.

He set the letter aside and once again picked up the old papers that he had found in that mysteriously opened window seat. He didn't need to read them—he knew the words from memory by now. Instead he ran his fingers along the edge of the frail, yellowed page. It had been well over a hundred years since his ancestor, Fergus Campbell, had written these words giving away his own progeny's right to Castle Glen in order to please Jaime MacLennan's widow, Bethia. He must have loved her very much.

He looked up as a knock sounded on the door. This time he recognized the little maid.

"Good morning, Elspeth," he greeted her.

She responded with the same blushing smile she'd used every time she'd seen him since the day he had promised that her young swain's job at the mill was secure. "Good morning, sir," she said with a bob of her knees. "I come to tell ye . . . that is . . . they'd not be visitors, a course . . ."

Duncan tapped on the desk with his pencil. "Yes, what is it, lass? Out with it."

"It be the mistress, sir. The, er, the *old* mistress. Lady MacLennan and Master Robby. They be back."

The pencil dropped from his hand. "Do you mean they are paying me a social call?" Had she finally come to throw down the gauntlet? he wondered. To tell him that she was going to sue to win back Castle Glen? If so, what was he going to do in response? He'd never in his life been one to give up on a fight, but his taste for the battle had diminished over the past week.

"I dinna think 'tis a social call, sir. They came wi' all their things. I believe they've coom back to stay."

Now, that was an interesting development, he thought, standing. Fiona must be more certain of victory than he had expected.

He started to walk around the desk intending to go out to meet them, then changed his mind. A good fighter chose his ground. "You may bring them to me here," he told the girl, resuming his seat in the master's chair behind his desk.

Another rule of business—have more information than your opponent. He had one advantage. Fiona had no way of knowing that he had found the old papers. He wondered when she intended to tell him.

Had she known about all this when she had slept with him at the hotel in Glasgow? Of course she had. He frowned. Somehow he could not bring himself to believe that she would have let him into her bed simply to keep him off guard while she went about plotting his defeat.

His lawyers were right. He could fight this, if he chose. But as the memories of that night in Glasgow came flooding back to him, he wondered if he wanted to fight it. Then again, did he want to go back to New York with his tail between his legs, admitting that he'd failed in his efforts to recapture a piece of his father's homeland?

For perhaps the first time in his life, Duncan realized, he didn't know *what* he wanted.

F*iona was anxious to talk with Duncan alone, but she* knew that Robby wanted to see him. The boy had missed the companionship he'd established with the American. Somehow Duncan had managed to fill part of the void left by the death of Alasdair in a way that Graham Maitland had never been able to do.

When Elspeth told them that Duncan was waiting for them in his office, the misgivings that had plagued her on the way back to the castle returned in full force. She didn't know what she had expected. It made no sense to think he would come rushing out to greet them with open arms when they had left so abruptly. But as she and Robby walked the familiar route through the halls back to the office, it felt as if she were once again the supplicant, needing the new master's goodwill to stay on here.

Well, that was about to change, she told herself, lifting her chin. Soon everyone would know who had the right to this place.

They passed Malcolm in the hall. His face brightened with an uncharacteristic smile of surprise. "Welcome back, milady, Master Robby," he said.

"Thank you, Malcolm." Fiona returned his smile.

"We didn't like it at Maitland Manor," Robby added.

The old butler's face resumed its reserved expression. "I should think not, Master Robby." He hesitated, looking at Fiona. "Have you come back for good, then?"

She gave a firm nod. "Aye, we're here for good."

"I'm sure Mr. Campbell will be pleased. He hasn't been the same since you two left. I'd not be one to spread the kitchen gossip, but word is that he's asked every day if any word had arrived from Maitland Manor. I warrant he's missed you."

"I missed him, too," Robby put in.

Fiona was silent. *Had* he missed them? she wondered. Of course, she knew he'd grown fond of Robby. Had he missed her, too?

By the time they reached the door of the office, she realized that she was more than a little anxious to see him again. She lifted her hand to knock, but Robby had already reached for the knob and opened the door.

Duncan sat behind Alasdair's big desk looking very much like the lord of the castle. The sight of him set a pulse beating at the side of her neck.

He waited for them to speak first, and Robby obliged.

"We've come back, Duncan! Nothing was any fun at Maitland Manor."

Duncan had a smile for the boy at least. "It's good to

see you, Robby," he said. "I missed having you with me at the mill this week. The new equipment came."

"I know! Darn, I wanted to be there to see it come."

"There's still a lot of assembly work to be done. Two men from the factory will be here helping for a few days. We'll go down tomorrow, if you like."

"That would be swell!"

Fiona waited patiently while Robby and Duncan caught up on the happenings they had missed, then she said quietly, "Robby, our things should have arrived by now. Would you mind seeing that they are brought up to our rooms?"

Robby agreed with a smile and dashed out of the room, giving Duncan a happy wave and saying, "I'll see you at supper!"

When he had left, the smile faded from Duncan's face. He motioned to the chair in front of the desk. "Won't you have a seat, Lady MacLennan?"

She couldn't tell if his cool tone was masking anger. "Are you willing to take us back?" she asked, keeping her own tone neutral.

One dark eyebrow rose. "Are you asking for permission to stay in your own home?"

She hesitated. "It's not ours. The courts gave it to you."

"Ah, yes. I'd forgotten."

A sardonic smile flitted around his mouth. It confused her. "Robby didn't like staying at Maitland Manor," she explained.

"*Robby* didn't like it?"

"Nay. And I—I found it uncomfortable."

For the first time his composure broke. He leaned forward in his chair with a frown. "Uncomfortable? Was there a problem? Did Maitland try—?"

She stopped him. "Graham was a gentleman, as always.

But I'll admit that he'd like a deeper relationship between the two of us than I am willing to accept at this time."

He didn't respond for a long moment. Then he stood, came around the desk, and sat on the edge of it, his knees practically touching her. "He would be a good match for you," he said softly.

Her chin went up. "Thank you for that opinion, Mr. Campbell, but I prefer to make my own romantic choices."

He took the tip of her chin between his thumb and forefinger. "You chose me in Glasgow."

She could feel the heat rushing to her cheeks. Turning her head away from his grasp, she said, "That was probably a mistake."

He seemed to flinch, then he moved away from his perch on the desk and walked over to look out the window. "This view is more spectacular than ever now that it's spring," he said. "I've never seen anything so green."

She had little interest in the spring countryside. Did he agree with her that Glasgow had been a mistake? There was no indication from his calm tone. She twisted her hands together in her lap. There must be something she could say to get a response from him.

"I suppose, after all, it was nothing to you. You've had many women."

He turned around to look at her, and his gaze was not quite as steady as it had been earlier. "Yes," he said slowly. "I've been fortunate enough to have many women friends over the years."

She nodded. What else had she expected? She stood up and shook out her riding skirt. "I should go change for supper," she said. "Thank you for offering us the hospitality of . . . of your castle again."

"It's my pleasure, Lady MacLennan," he said with a courtly nod.

She waited for him to say something else, but when he

remained silent, watching her with that raw gaze, she hurriedly left the room.

He *should have confronted her that afternoon in his office*, Duncan reproached himself. There was no point in delaying the matter. The sooner he found out what she was planning to do about the will codicil, the sooner he could decide his own strategy.

But now was certainly not the time to bring up that subject. He sat at dinner with Robby and many of the typical castle crew. They seemed to be aware of the fact that something was wrong between the new master and the former mistress. Conversation was limited, and people seemed to be hurrying to finish their plates of stew.

Even Robby was subdued, casting worried glances first at Fiona, then at Duncan. He'd sent the boy a smile of reassurance, but it hadn't seemed to help.

Fiona herself looked every inch the lady of the castle. Her hair was piled high on top of her head, leaving only a few tendrils to fall along her slender neck. She was wearing one of her low-cut gowns. The light from the table candles flickered across her white bosom, bringing him flashes of memory from the night when his own head had rested there.

No, this was definitely not the time or place to do battle. It might, however, be a perfect time to broach his latest ideas. He cleared his throat. "I know Castle Glen means a lot to all of you," he began. Every head turned to look at him. "I want to tell you about a plan I'm working on.

"As most of you know, we're going to have to make some big changes at the mill. It will mean some people will lose their jobs."

He looked around the table at the gloomy faces.

"Which is why I'm happy to announce that the railroad has decided to put one of their station inns at Glencolly."

"An inn? Here?" Robby asked, his face brightening.

"Yes. More and more people are wanting to travel now that the railways are in. Glencolly will be one of the spots they will come to stay. We'll have tourists, shooting clubs, hiking enthusiasts. And I'm thinking that many of them will want to come up and see the famous Castle Glen if we open it up for tours."

No one spoke.

"It would only be for a few months each year. The extra income would help us keep things going and pay for some badly needed repairs here. A two-hundred-year-old castle doesn't get by without some changes."

Robby was the first to speak. "I wouldn't mind," he said. "We don't get many visitors here. It might be kind of fun."

Duncan looked around the table. "Some of you may not like the idea," he acknowledged. "But city folks are willing to pay good money to get a taste of the Highlands. Especially to see a real castle with a *ghost*."

"I thought you didn't believe in ghosts," Fiona said. Her expression gave no hint of her reaction to his plan.

"I don't. Most of the visitors probably won't, either, but they'll enjoy taking the stories back to their city friends."

"You mean they'll enjoy laughing at the quaint country folk with their superstitious fancies," she said.

Duncan shook his head. "What difference does it make what they think of us if their ready money will help keep Castle Glen alive?"

Fiona noticed that Duncan had included himself when he'd said "what they think of *us*." It was obvious that he felt part of this place. His plan to open the castle to the public came from a genuine desire to save the place from financial ruin. It was the interests of everyone around this table that he was trying to protect.

Hamish, the gardener, put his hands together and tapped his two forefingers on his lips, pondering. "I believe it could work," he said. "We'd have to make some rules. Like not tramplin' in the garden and no shootin' near the castle. But I reckon 'twould be rich folk who'd come, and I reckon we could make good use o' their money."

Malcolm had sat up even straighter than normal in his seat. "Lord MacLennan would *never* approve."

Fiona spoke up. "No, he wouldn't, but then he's not around to see it happen, is he?"

Duncan gave her a surprised smile. "I know this is something new," he said, looking around the table. "I'd like you all to think about it, and then I'd like to hear from each of you what it would mean for your position." He nodded to the little buttermaid. "May, I'd like to meet with you and Emmaline to see what changes would have to be made to accommodate visitors."

"With *me,* sir?" the girl asked with one of her nervous giggles.

"Yes, I want to hear from all of you." He turned to the Bandys. "We might have to think about acquiring a few more horses for the inn guests to ride. I assume they'll come by train and need to rent mounts while they're here."

The twins exchanged a glance. Then Baird said, "Lord MacLennan had to sell off some of our best horses over these past few years. It would be wonderful to be able to bring them back."

Malcolm's expression was cloudy, and there were still some faces full of doubt, but the initial resistance had disappeared.

Duncan looked across the table at Fiona with a satisfied expression.

She bit her lip. Once again Duncan was making plans to ensure the future of Castle Glen. What would he say when she told him that she intended to take it back from him?

She had to tell him, and delaying was not going to help matters. Would he be furious? Hurt? Would he fight her? Not her, she corrected, Robby. He'd left his home and his country to inherit Castle Glen. Would he now fight to keep it?

He looked big and powerful sitting in the carved master's chair. In the reflection of the table candles, his face was strong and craggy, much like the faces of the old Scottish warriors that lined the walls of the portrait room.

One by one, the castle staff, their expressions happier than they had been at the beginning of the meal, finished eating and made their excuses to leave.

When she, Robby, and Duncan were the only ones left, Robby looked anxiously at each of them. "Are you two going to stay mad at each other?" he asked with the bluntness of youth.

"I'm not angry," Duncan said after a moment.

"I'm not, either," Fiona agreed.

Robby put his hands on his hips and gave an exasperated sigh. "Then why did you come into supper scowling at each other?"

"I'm not scowling," Fiona said. "I think Duncan may be right. The inn at Glencolly and the castle tours will solve a lot of problems."

Robby turned to Duncan. "Are you mad at Fiona?" he asked.

Duncan let out a long stream of air and took a long time to answer. "I appreciate her support for the new plans," he said finally.

Robby frowned. "But you look like something is still wrong. What is it?"

Duncan was sitting more stiffly in his chair. "You might want to ask your stepmother that question."

Fiona suddenly felt cold. "What do you mean?"

Duncan turned to her. "When did you intend to tell me that ever since I arrived you've been planning to take Castle Glen away from me?"

Fiona gasped. "How did you—?" She stopped. "You make it sound as if I was involved in some kind of treachery when I've only been trying to see to Robby's interests."

"Label it what you will," Duncan retorted. "Label it anything but honesty."

Both their tones had escalated, and Robby put his hands over his ears. "Stop it, both of you!" He looked from one adult to another, his eyes full of misery. "If all it means is fighting, maybe I don't even *want* Castle Glen!" Then he jumped up from his seat and ran from the room.

Duncan and Fiona looked at each other.

"I should go talk with him," she said.

"Give him a while to cool down," Duncan advised. "He didn't mean what he said. The boy loves this place."

"He always thought it would be his."

"I know. So when *were* you going to tell me about the changed will?" he asked.

"I—I was just waiting for the right opportunity."

"But you've known about this since I arrived?"

If his tone had held even the slightest bit of the warmth he had once used with her, she would have tried to make him understand the confusion she'd had, to tell him about the indecision she was feeling. But instead, she said simply, "Aye, the papers were found shortly after the court awarded the inheritance to you."

He nodded, as if confirming something to himself.

"My lawyer says the codicil was registered in accordance with the law of the times. It will be held to be legal and binding."

Duncan remained silent.

"But I . . . we'll owe you something for all your work. The mill and now the plans for the inn and the tours. I . . . Alasdair would never have thought of all that. I've begun to realize that Castle Glen would have been in dire straits if you had not come here."

He gave a brief, humorless smile.

"What are you going to do?" she asked.

He stood up. "I haven't decided," he said. Then without another word he stalked out of the room.

chapter 18

Logan and Graham Maitland walked down the stairs from their Glasgow bank and stepped into the waiting carriage.

"I assume you've finally realized that my way is best," Logan told his son with a smile of satisfaction.

"They've done a good job of gathering up the MacLennan debts," Graham replied.

"Yes, the estate should be ours for the taking. So if you've finally realized that these romantic approaches are not going to work with the stubborn chit—"

"Father, I'd appreciate more respect for the woman who is going to be my wife."

Logan signaled to the driver to move. "There's only one thing I respect, boy, and that's money. A commodity in which Fiona MacLennan is sadly lacking."

"There is more to life than money, Father. Fiona has other qualities that I *do* appreciate."

"That may be, but the fact remains that the chit continues to resist your best efforts. It's time you listened to me. Get her to marry you first. The romance can come later."

Graham ran his hand over the folder of papers they'd brought out of the bank. "You may be right," he admitted grudgingly. "We hold enough paper on Castle Glen to take over the entire estate."

"So you tell your Lady Fiona that the only way to save the estate for her precious stepson is to marry you. Once you're married, we take it over anyway. I doubt that will set well with your new wife, but—"

"But by then she'll *be* my wife," Graham interrupted. "And, as you say, I'll have all the time in the world to placate her."

"If you continue to be so inclined." Logan took off his hat and settled himself back in the carriage seat. "Frankly, I can't see how it would be worth the trouble." Then he folded his arms, closed his eyes, and went to sleep.

"*The machines are purrin' away like so many kittens.*" Jock looked considerably happier than the last time Duncan had visited the mill. The manager grinned as he came out the front door to escort Duncan into the refurbished factory. "I' truth, 'twould have ta be lions, not kittens, fer they do make a racket. But except fer the noise, they're a wonder. The wool practically spins and weaves itself."

"I'm glad it's going well." Duncan shouted to be heard over the pounding of the new steam looms. "And you've kept some of the old equipment like I asked?"

"Aye, that we have, sir. Hugh Cullen be in charge, just like ye said, and we've left our best people there spinnin' and weavin' just like they used to. It's made everyone feel better knowin' that the old ways aren't totally gone."

He led the way into a room that had been set up to

house several examples of the old style carding, spinning, and weaving.

Duncan smiled at the workers who looked up from their work. There were none of the strained faces he had seen on his previous visit. He gave a wave to Hugh Cullen, who sat at a hand loom on one side of the room. "How are your wedding plans?" he asked the young man.

"Fine, sir. 'Tis to be tomorrow at the Midsummer Fair."

Duncan wished him luck, then followed Jock into his office. They shut the door to keep out the noise, then took seats on either side of Jock's desk.

"The next step," Duncan continued, "is to figure out how we're going to deal with the tours."

"The tours?" Jock asked, mystified.

"Remember I told you I was working on some ideas to find work for the people who would lose their jobs when the new machines came?"

"Aye." Jock looked wary.

"It just turns out that the railroad has decided to put one of its station inns right here in Glencolly."

"In Glencolly? Whyever would they do that?"

Duncan smiled. "They might have been persuaded somewhat."

"An inn in Glencolly. Think o' that!" Jock exclaimed.

"The inn will need people to run it, of course. It should provide employment for most of the people who lost jobs."

"But who will coom here, sir? Do ye really think people will coom to see the mill?"

"To see the mill, yes, and to hunt and fish. There are hunting and hiking clubs springing up all over England. It's the latest rage. What better place to come than Glencolly Valley? Then, of course, we have the added attraction."

"What's that?"

Duncan grinned. "The chance to catch a glimpse of the famous Castle Glen ghost."

Jock threw back his head and laughed. "Ye hope ta convince folks aboot that cock-and-bull story?"

"Don't you believe in the ghost?"

"Nay, I'm a practical man. But ye're right. Most o' the folk in these parts swear he walks up there. They claim ta hear the Stuart pipes. But the visitors would have ta go up to the castle to see him."

"Yes, they would. And many of the people who come will be willing to pay for a tour of the castle just to get the chance."

Jock gave a low whistle. "We'd have the old Lord MacLennan turnin' in his grave to hear that. Have ye told Lady Fee aboot yer plan, sir?"

"Yes." Duncan frowned remembering how his conversation with Fiona had ended the previous evening. She'd seemed almost excited about his plans, but then had come the issue of ownership of Castle Glen. In that, their business interests were diametrically opposed.

Jock's kindly eyes narrowed as he looked at the younger man. "She didna approve, eh? Too bad. I was fancying I saw a bit o' a spark between ye two. I reckon 'twould please a lot o' Glencolly folk to see Lady Fee happy again."

"I reckon it would," Duncan answered quietly. "Now let's look at those books and see how we're going to fare now that Glencolly mill has joined the industrial age."

F*iona was surprised when Elspeth told her that Graham Maitland had come to call and was waiting for her in* the front parlor. After the way she had left Maitland Manor, she had figured that it would be a while before she would see the man again.

She took a quick glimpse in the mirror. She'd been working with Emmaline all morning and was disheveled, her hair escaping in wisps from its tight bun. With a quick pat that changed nothing of her appearance, she turned away and started downstairs, grabbing her spectacles from the dresser at the last minute. Lord, what did the man see in her anyway? she thought with a rueful grin.

As usual, Graham greeted her with a smile and a kiss on the cheek. If he harbored any resentment over her abrupt departure from Maitland Manor, it was not apparent.

"You look lovely," he said.

She gestured to her gray work dress. "You are easy to please, Graham."

"I am where you're concerned, Fee. You always please me, you know that."

She sighed and invited him to sit on the damask settee. She herself took a small chair to one side. "Did you have a particular reason for calling?" she asked him when they were settled.

Shifting on his seat, he answered, "Yes. I've come to ask you to return with me to Maitland Manor."

"I already explained to you, Graham—"

"Hear me out, Fee. I'm not asking you to come as my guest. I'm asking you to come as my wife."

The proposal was not a complete surprise. In her heart she'd known that once a decent mourning period had passed, Graham would ask her to marry him.

Her mourning was her refuge and an easy escape. "It's too soon for me to even think about such a thing, Graham. Alasdair's death is—"

She stopped as she could see a subtle change in his expression. Something about the set of his face almost frightened her.

"Permit me to be blunt, Fee. Alasdair was an old man

who could not possibly have been a proper husband to you. He left you an inheritance mess that you are still trying to clear up. He also left you destitute."

She bit her lip. Before his death, her husband had admitted that he was leaving her in poor straits. In her few disloyal moments, she herself had blamed him for not doing something about the Campbell will. If he had investigated and discovered the old codicil, they might have been able to prevent Duncan Campbell from ever coming to Castle Glen. But she wasn't about to discuss any of this with Graham Maitland.

"I'll ask you not to speak with disrespect of my husband," she said quietly.

He stood up and started pacing the room. "I'm telling you, Fee, you don't know the truth about what your *husband* did to you . . . and to his son."

"What do you mean?"

He turned around to her. "Castle Glen is mortgaged beyond its worth, and the estate has outstanding loans that will ensure that your inheritance battle doesn't matter a whit. Castle Glen is already lost."

She felt the blood drain from her face. "I've seen nothing of this in Alasdair's papers. How do you know this?"

"Because my father and I hold the loans."

For a long moment she stared up at him, trying to tell herself that what he was saying could not possibly be true. But in her heart she knew that it was. Time and again she'd heard Alasdair moan about the "fiddle" he was leaving her in. She'd thought his illness had exaggerated his worries. She'd thought the only thing she had to deal with was the tightening of cash with the declining estate income.

She stood up to face him, though she reached only to his shoulder. "What exactly have you come here today to tell me, Graham?"

He looked much like Robby did when he became angry in order to disguise the fact that he knew he'd done something wrong. "I came to ask you to marry me. It's an offer that would be extremely well-received by any number of women both here and in England."

For some reason, his words helped her regain control. "I'm sure it would," she said with a quirk of her lips.

He seemed to sense her renewed confidence. His voice rose as he said, "Perhaps you won't hold my offer in such disdain when you begin to realize that marrying me is the *only* way you'll ever keep Castle Glen."

She grimaced with distaste. "In other words, I can save Castle Glen for Robby if I sell myself to you."

"I've offered marriage," he said stiffly.

"Ah, yes. I save Castle Glen by selling myself to you *in marriage,*" she clarified.

"You'll get used to the idea. Think about it, Fee. You once married an old man because you had nowhere else to go. This time you'll have a young husband."

"I'm going to ask you to leave, Graham."

He ignored her words. "I've been patient, Fiona. My father wanted to take over the estate the minute Alasdair died."

She shot him a scornful glance. "Your father professed to be my husband's friend. No doubt that's the reason Alasdair went to him when he needed money. He never suspected his good old friend would turn on him."

"Alasdair couldn't have kept Castle Glen or the mill running without the help my father gave him."

She walked over to stand directly in front of him. Looking up, she said in the firmest tone she could muster, "Graham, I do believe that you have tried to be a friend to me. That's why I'm going to refrain from telling you what I think of the *offer* you've made me today. And I'm going to ask you politely to leave my house now before I'm forced to ring for Malcolm to show you out."

The edges around his lips turned white. "Don't say anything rash, Fee. You'll have a lifetime to regret it. Because you *are* going to be my wife. I'll put it to you plain—you have no other choice."

Then he snatched his hat from the sofa and stalked out of the room.

The visit to the mill had buoyed Duncan's spirits. He'd begun putting together business deals at age sixteen as a remedy for his lonely childhood, but he'd never before spent time looking at how his dealings were affecting the people involved. Somehow the people of Castle Glen and their extended relations in Glencolly had managed to reach him in a way he'd never experienced back in New York. He was finding tremendous satisfaction in working to see that they could preserve some of their old ways, while surviving in the modern world.

As he rode up to the stable and handed Daisy to Blair Bandy, he had a sudden wish to find Fiona and tell her about his visit. He wanted her to know how well the new machines were working. He wanted to share with her the look of pride on Hugh Cullen's face when he'd shown Duncan how he'd set up the room to preserve some of the traditional methods at the mill.

Then he remembered that he and Fiona were barely speaking.

His steps slowed as he neared the front door of the castle. She *had* deceived him, he reminded himself. He'd been angry when he'd discovered she'd kept her knowledge about the codicil from him. But he didn't want to be angry with her. The truth was, he wanted to sit with her, looking into those determined blue eyes, and tell her his plans. He wanted to settle this matter of the wills.

His entire life, he'd relished the battle. It had been part of what had made him so successful. But he was finally realizing that some of the most important things in life weren't won by fighting. He had no desire to go up against Fiona and Robby in court. If Castle Glen legally belonged to Robby, so be it. For once, Duncan would take his satisfaction from the mark he was leaving behind, rather the wealth he was taking away.

He took a long, assessing look at the impressive gray stone façade of the castle before pulling open the big iron door and walking in.

The front hall was empty. Something made him glance into the front parlor. Fiona was sitting alone in near darkness. It was twilight, but she'd not lit any of the lamps. He began to move toward her, and as he approached, he could see traces of tears on her cheeks.

"What's wrong?" he asked gently.

She looked up at him and gave a long sniff, wiping her nose on the edge of her sleeve. She looked like a bedraggled child.

"Nothing," she answered.

"Oh, I can see that—*nothing*."

"Nothing important," she amended.

She was sitting on one edge of the settee, her body drooped over the curving arm. He sat next to her. "It's something important enough to have you sitting alone in the dark crying."

She shook her head and straightened up with a sigh. "Sometimes I envy Robby," she said. "He doesn't have to grow up quite yet."

He smiled and turned her shoulders so that she was facing him. "Whereas you, my poor Fiona, *did* have to grow up at exactly Robby's age. You had no mother or father or stubborn little stepmother to fight for you."

"Alasdair took care of me."

"Alasdair *married* you, which is not entirely the same thing. He could have offered to make you his ward. By marrying you, he was doing what *he* wanted to do, not what you wanted."

She looked as if she'd never considered the matter from that angle. "I was happy—mostly," she said after a moment.

"But you were missing out on a few things," he reminded her gently.

She blushed as she correctly guessed that he was thinking back to their night in the hotel when she had admitted that she had never before fully experienced sexual pleasure.

Her chin came up in that way he'd come to know. "Perhaps I was, but I wouldn't trade my years with Alasdair for anything."

"I'm sure you wouldn't. From everything I've heard about him, he was a remarkable man. But now it's time for you to have your own life."

She sighed again and remained silent. Something was definitely bothering her, but the way things had been between them, she obviously didn't feel she wanted to confide in him.

"I saw the happy prospective bridegroom of Elspeth today down at the mill," he said, changing subjects to brighten the mood.

"Hugh Cullen?"

"Yes. Now, there's a marriage that promises to be happy. He beams every time he talks of it."

She smiled. "Elspeth, too."

"He says the ceremony is to be at the Midsummer Fair. It seems an odd place for a wedding."

"In Glencolly they believe that on Midsummer's Eve the faeries come out to shower blessings on young lovers. It's a lucky time to be wed."

"Ah. Are you intending to go to the fair?"

"Everyone in Glencolly goes to the fair." Her smile was still wavery.

Duncan had dropped his hold on her shoulders. His hands itched to touch her again, but he refrained.

"Shall we talk about the will?" he asked after a long moment of silence.

"Aye, I should have told you about the codicil," she admitted, her tone resigned.

"*Aye,* you should have. But now that everything's on the table, we need to discuss what we're going to do about it."

"I know. My lawyer says our case is good."

He nodded. "Which means you intend to reclaim Robby's inheritance."

She glanced away. "I have to—I owe it to him and to—"

"To Alasdair, I know." He was tired of hearing the man's name. "I'm not going to contest it."

She looked up in surprise. "You're not?"

He shook his head. "No."

She shook her head as if trying to clear it. "You're giving Castle Glen back to Robby?" she asked again.

"Yes. As long as you'll agree to let me implement the changes—"

She put her hand to her temple. "Could we . . . could we wait and talk about all that later? I'm afraid I've developed a megrim."

She was on the verge of tears again.

He hesitated, but finally said, "Very well, we'll talk about the plans later."

She gave him a grateful look and quickly stood up. As

she turned to leave, he could see the tears begin to stream down her face.

A re you and Fee fighting again?"

Duncan looked up. Robby stood in the doorway of the parlor. He gave the boy a sad smile. "No, son. I reckon we're done fighting."

"Then why was Fee crying just now?"

Duncan sighed. "Women do that. It's sometimes hard to know why."

"Not Fee. She's not like most silly girls."

"No, she's not," Duncan agreed.

"So what was wrong?"

Robby looked older suddenly. The sleeves of his jacket rode up on his arms. Overnight, it seemed, he was growing into a man.

"I just told your stepmother that I don't intend to contest your claim to Castle Glen."

Robby's expression was troubled. "I thought that was what she wanted."

"Yes, I believe it is what she wants."

"But does that mean you are going back to New York?" The boy's voice, which a moment ago had been so deep, suddenly slid into treble.

"It might," Duncan told him.

"But what about—" He stopped, and glanced away from Duncan, blinking hard. When he looked back, his eyes were angry. "Does Fee want you to leave Castle Glen?" he asked.

If I knew the answer to that, Duncan thought wryly, I wouldn't be sitting here alone in the parlor as the room turned dark with the coming twilight.

"I don't know," he answered Robby finally. "Things sometimes get complicated between a man and a woman." That was about the best explanation he could muster.

Robby continued to watch him for another long moment, then he spun around and disappeared into the hall.

chapter 19

A walk around his favorite part of the grounds had calmed him down, but Robby was still feeling gloomy as he came up the back hill toward the castle. He diverted to head toward the kitchens. For one thing, he'd left the supper table before he'd had a chance to take one of Emmaline's sweet-cakes for dessert. For another thing, a talk with the congenial cook was always a good way to raise his spirits.

Maybe talking with Emmaline would help him understand what was happening between the two other adults he had come to care about most in his life.

There was still light burning in the kitchen, which meant that Emmaline had not yet retired to her rooms for the evening.

Robby walked up to the tiny back door of the squat stone building that still served as the main castle kitchen, even though a smaller one had been built inside more conveniently near the dining hall.

"Emmaline," he called, ducking his head under the low lintel.

Emmaline was indeed in the kitchen, but so was Malcolm. Robby's eyes widened as he saw the dignified butler and the round little cook jump away from each other. Unless he was very much mistaken, they'd just been in each other's arms.

"Master Robby!" Emmaline said, her face red and flustered. "What be ye doin' here at this hour?"

"I . . . er . . ." He'd known both Emmaline and Malcolm his entire life. They'd been old before he was born. But he'd never seen the sheepish, giddy expressions on their faces that he was seeing now.

"I didn't get any of the sweetcakes," he said, suddenly more embarrassed than the two elderly servants.

"Lord bless ye, lad, help yerself," Emmaline said, gesturing to a plate of cakes sitting on the sideboard.

Robby hastily snatched one of the cakes, then, with a mumbled good night, ducked out the door.

Emmaline and Malcolm? It was beyond belief. Absentmindedly munching his cake, he wandered toward the castle, trying to come to terms with what he had just seen. Emmaline had gone through two husbands, he knew, but he'd always thought of Malcolm as a confirmed bachelor. It had always seemed as if the old butler didn't really care about those kinds of man-woman things.

It was a subject that occupied Robby's mind more and more often these days. Particularly every time Lizzie came up to dust the schoolroom, stooping up and down between the desks with her pert young rear practically jiggling in his face as he tried to concentrate on his books.

But that had to do with . . . *sex* and those matters. Malcolm and Emmaline were *old*. Sex couldn't be what had compelled his dear old cook and proper Malcolm to seek each other's arms.

He gave a long sigh as he reached the second floor and turned toward the winding stairway to the schoolroom.

Fiona would find it amusing, but he found that he'd actually missed his studies the week they'd spent at Maitland Manor.

He grabbed a candle at the bottom of the stairs. It was almost totally dark outside. There would be no light up in the tower.

Could Malcolm and Emmaline be in love? he wondered. It was hard to picture it, but he supposed it was possible. He'd decided that the love thing was even more difficult to figure out than sex. There had been moments, especially that first night in Glasgow, when he'd thought that Duncan and Fiona might be falling in love. Apparently he'd been wrong.

Graham Maitland was in love with Fiona, and she certainly liked him, but she'd wanted to leave their house, and Robby suspected that, once again, it had something to do with that whole love-sex question. As much as Lizzie's nubile young body intrigued him, he was coming to the conclusion that the whole notion was more trouble than it was worth.

The circular stairway always looked mysterious by night. The Scholar's Tower stair was smaller than the Stuart Tower's, so the candlelight reached to the darkest parts of the winding stone. It gave the sensation of going into a tunnel that might never end. When he was younger, it had always given Robby a chill of fear to go up to the schoolroom at night.

His mind drifted back to the subject. If the story was true, Jaime MacLennan was stuck here in this world because of love. He'd been killed before he and his young bride, Bethia, could have a life together. To make matters worse, Bethia had gone and fallen in love with a Campbell. Perhaps that was what kept Jaime earthbound, Robby thought.

He rounded the final corner of the stairs into the

schoolroom. His single candle illuminated the round chamber. His gaze went to the desk where he'd left the books he'd been studying before he and Fiona had left for Maitland Manor.

Then he gasped and stumbled back, barely catching himself from tumbling backward down the stairs.

Sitting at his desk was a young man, dressed in a kilt and tartan. He wore a tam perched at a jaunty angle on his head. Pinned to the side of it was the distinctive white Stuart cockade.

"I never was much o' one fer books," the young man said casually, leafing through one of Robby's texts. "I used to make my tutors despair."

The candle trembled in Robby's hand, sending shaky shadows around the walls. "Who"—his voice cracked an entire octave—"who are you? What are you doing here?"

"Ach, now, dinna ye know me? Ye've chased me eno' these past"—he cocked his head—"how old be ye now? Fourteen?"

"Aye, f-fourteen," Robby stammered.

"Well, then, ye've been chasin' me these fourteen years past, hae ye not?"

Cautiously Robby walked over to the desk farthest from the stranger and put down the candlestick. "You aren't . . . you can't be who I think you are." Without thinking, he rubbed his eyes.

"Jaime MacLennan, at yer service, Robby, me boy. I've been thinkin' o' meetin' ye fer some time now, especially since yer father was taken. Mine was, too, did ye know? Died when I was just a bairn."

Sweat trickled down Robby's temples, but he realized that he wasn't truly *afraid*. He had no sense that this . . . apparition or whatever it was would hurt him.

"If you've been watching me, why haven't you ever shown yourself before?" he asked the figure.

Jaime grinned. "Hoot, we canna go showin' ourselves all the time, now can we? Think o' the trouble that would cause."

"But I do hear you piping."

"Oh, aye. I canna leave off me pipin'. 'Tis me tribute to me bonnie Bethia."

"Your wife."

"Aye, me bride. She never did want me to go to battle that day, but I didna want to miss the excitement."

"You wanted to fight for the Bonnie Prince," Robby added eagerly. He didn't know if this was some kind of odd dream, but whatever it was, he was finally talking to Jaime MacLennan. After all these years. He could hardly contain himself.

"I reckon I did, though 'tis hard to remember. 'Twas that long ago. We thought the Stuarts would bring back the glory o' Scotland."

"It must have been so exciting!" Robby exclaimed.

Jaime closed the book he was looking at and looked over at him. "Exciting? There were brief moments, I reckon. But Charlie Stuart, our bonnie prince, ended up hidin' in a tree and then scramblin' back to the Continent. And most o' the rest o' us ended up dead." His tone was matter-of-fact.

Robby was quiet for a moment, then said, "I'm sorry you had to die so young."

Indeed, the young man sitting at the desk didn't appear much older than Robby himself. He looked to see if he could note any other resemblance. After all, this was his many-times-great-grandfather. Jaime's hair was light brown instead of reddish like Robby's, but Robby fancied there might be some similarity in their blue eyes.

"I didna mind so much fer meself," Jaime said casually. "But 'twasn't a fair thing to do to me bride."

"Is that—" Robby searched for the words. How did one

talk to a ghost? "Some folks say that's why you stay here. Because you're looking for your lost bride."

If Jaime MacLennan hadn't already been a ghost, Robby would have said that his eyes suddenly looked haunted. "Nay, I know where she is."

"You do?"

"She's with the Campbell."

"Fergus Campbell?"

"Aye."

Suddenly the whole conversation began to feel more comfortable. Robby walked over to take a seat at the desk next to Jaime's. "Can I touch you?" he asked.

"Nay," Jaime replied sadly. "I be a spirit, dinna ye ken?"

Robby swallowed. There were a hundred things he'd like to ask this amazing apparition, but he returned to the subject that had been on his mind when he had come up to the schoolroom.

"I've wondered a bit lately about love," he confided. "You say you loved your . . . er . . . your Bethia. But then you died and Fergus Campbell came along. Didn't that make you angry?"

"Only for the first hundred years or so." Jaime's eyes danced. "I've started to coom to terms wi' the notion. As it turned out, my Bethy needed the Campbell to help her. She was bearin' me babe."

"That must have been hard for . . . for everyone. Would it have been better if you'd never fallen in love?"

"Ach, lad, then where would ye be, can ye tell me that? 'Twas me love fer Bethy that produced me son—yer great-great-grandfather."

Robby gave his head a shake. This conversation could not be happening.

"But then your Bethy fell in love with Fergus Campbell."

"Aye, 'twas a hard thing. But ye do see the harsh fact o' it, dinna ye, Robby? I was dead. My Bethy were a smart eno' lass to see that it would hae been a waste to live out her life mourning a ghost. It be hard to swallow, but I'm happy she was able to find love again. And though it galls me to say it, the Campbell were a good man."

"He was Black Watch. He could have taken Castle Glen away from your wife and her son."

"Aye, that he could."

Robby looked down at the desk where some past generation MacLennan had scratched his initials into the wood. "Maybe that would have been better," he said gloomily. "Then we wouldn't have everyone getting angry and fighting over it today."

Jaime tipped his head. The white Stuart cockade on his hat shifted. "Dinna fash yerself, Robby. Things will work out."

"I don't know. . . ." Robby began.

Jaime nodded. "They will. Do ye know the Tuiream Pool?"

Robby was surprised with the change of the subject. "At the end of the North Woods?"

"Aye. Do ye go there?"

Robby shook his head. "No one goes there much, I reckon. 'Tis said that it was where the mourning women did their keening in the olden days."

For a moment Jaime looked somber. "Aye, that they did. Well, ye should pay the Tuiream Pool a visit, and look behind it in the wee glen."

"What's there?" Robby frowned and looked down, tracing the carved letters on the desk with his fingers. This wasn't what he wanted to talk about with Jaime. He wanted to ask him about what it had been like to go to battle. He wanted to hear about Culloden and the

Bonnie Prince. "What's at the pool?" he repeated, looking up.

The desk beside him was empty.

*F*iona's *head was pounding. But it was not her headache*
that had made her flee from the front parlor. It was the
rush of feelings that had hit her. Duncan was giving back
Castle Glen. He was leaving. She would never see him
again. This, after Graham's visit, had finally made her see
the truth with total clarity.

When her neighbor had asked her bluntly to marry him,
she'd at last recognized that she could never, ever be a
wife to Graham Maitland. Because she had fallen in love
with someone else.

Fallen quite hopelessly, she added to herself as she
climbed the steep castle stairs. She'd deceived Duncan.
What was worse, she'd allowed him to invest his time, his
money, to invest *himself* in Castle Glen, all the while she
was intending to take it away from him. He probably
wished he had never heard of his ancestor Fergus Campbell or Castle Glen.

He'd be leaving soon. She'd be left to face Graham's
threats by herself. There was no way she would ask Duncan to help her. At least she had that much pride.

The gray stone walls of Castle Glen seemed unusually
oppressive as she walked down the long hall to her bedchamber. Elspeth had not lit the wall lamps. Fiona wouldn't
scold her. The girl had been giddy for the past several
days with thoughts of her upcoming wedding.

The door to Fiona's room was closed, which was odd.
She always left it open when she wasn't inside. She
walked in and looked around, but everything appeared to
be the way she had left it in the morning.

The room was freezing, she realized suddenly. It was

hard to explain why, since it had been a warm spring day outside. With a shrug, she walked over to the trunk that sat at the end of her bed to look for her wool robe. No silky night things for her tonight.

The old chest creaked as she opened it. It was carved on the sides and the top with elaborate designs of flowers and entwining grapevines. Alasdair had given it to her as a wedding present.

The robe she was searching for was buried under several lengths of plaid. As she dug for it, her fingers brushed against an envelope tucked into the paper lining of the trunk. She'd never seen it before. Mystified, she pulled it out.

Her hands began to tremble as she saw her name written on the outside in Alasdair's dear, familiar handwriting. Inside were several sheets of paper. It was a letter, and it began *My dearest Fiona . . .*

No longer cold, she sank down on her knees beside the old trunk and began to read.

> *Before I start, I will ask you to forgive me. I know you are capable, independent, and intelligent. You will be hurt by my actions and believe they show a lack of faith in you. The truth is that I am leaving behind more problems than anyone, including you, my darling wife, could be expected to deal with.*
>
> *By now you and Hampton will have found the old Campbell will in my papers. I have investigated this Campbell heir. He has considerable resources in America. More important, he appears to be a man who knows how to bring success from seemingly hopeless causes. The MacLennan estate in its present condition is such a cause. Drastic changes must be made, and I have simply not been able to*

*make them. In this, I have failed you and failed my
son.*

*My hope is that Duncan Campbell will accept the
inheritance and come to help you and Robby. He
will bring the energy and the new ways of his new
world. Glencolly needs such ideas to survive.*

*If I have been wrong about Mr. Campbell, you
have another option. There is a codicil that reverses
the old will. You will find it in the window seat in my
office. With these additional papers, you will be
able to overturn Duncan Campbell's inheritance
and regain it for yourselves.*

*I leave the decision to you, my love. My concern
is for the people of this valley, for Robby, and for
you, my dearest wife. No words can describe the
happiness you've given me. I wanted to give you the
world in return. Instead I've given you
immeasurable problems. If Duncan Campbell can
save Glencolly and ensure that you and Robby can
have happy lives, he will have my gratitude
throughout eternity.*

For several minutes Fiona sat in stunned silence. Alasdair had known all along. He had *planned* to have Duncan
Campbell come to Glencolly. He had deliberately hidden
the codicil so that she wouldn't find it with the original
will, thus causing all the trouble she and Duncan were
currently facing.

What would she have done if she'd found this letter before Duncan had ever arrived? She could have presented
the codicil from the beginning, and Duncan would never
have left New York.

Would she have been able to save Glencolly by herself?
Probably not, she admitted gloomily. She still may not be
able to save it. If Graham Maitland was telling the truth,

the estate was in such debt, even the newly refurbished mill wouldn't save it.

She looked at the letter again, feeling some of the anger and hurt Alasdair had predicted. Why hadn't he discussed all this with her? Why hadn't he told her about the mill's problems? The estate debts? The Campbell will? She would probably never know the answer.

She lifted the letter and turned it in her hand. How had it gotten into her trunk? That was as big a mystery as all the rest. Had Alasdair tucked it away there before his death? She had been in and out of that trunk a dozen times since then.

The cold in the room seemed to have eased. She threw the letter on her nightstand and slipped into bed, lowered her aching head to the pillow and closed her eyes.

Robby awoke just as dawn was breaking. He blinked a couple of times as memories of the previous evening rushed back. Had it all been a dream? Had he truly talked with Jaime MacLennan in the Scholar's Tower?

He scrambled into his clothes and ran all the way up to the schoolroom, hoping for some kind of sign. His schoolbooks were piled neatly at the desk where Jaime had been leafing through them. The rest of the room seemed normal, too. It was cold, but it was always cold up in the tower before the midday sun had a chance to warm it.

His stomach rumbled as he jogged down the stairs, but he stopped only to grab a piece of bread before heading out the door in the direction of the North Woods.

Visit the Tuiream Pool, Jaime had said, and look in the wee glen behind it. The Tuiream Pool had probably once been a regular loch, but over the generations it had been absorbed by the surrounding woods and was now not much more than a stagnant pond. Robby had been there seldom, and it was in a part of the estate where few people came. He couldn't picture the glen Jaime had mentioned, but he saw it as soon as he came upon the water—a small circle of firs surrounding a slight knoll. The trees allowed the morning sun to reach the floor of the glen, which was covered with a thick, mossy carpet of green. Robby picked his way around the rocks at the edge of the pond and walked into the circle.

At first it looked no different than the rest of the woods he had just crossed, but then his eye fell to the base of the trees at the far side. Long scraggly branches drooped to the ground. Underneath them, barely visible, were three stones. He walked over to them, pulling away a branch to see better.

They were markers of some kind, he realized. Tilted slightly from many years of settling. He knelt down on the soft ground and tried to make out the old letters.

The stone in the center was slightly larger than the other two. It said simply, "Bethia MacLennan Campbell, 1730–1782." Robby's eyes opened in wonder.

The marker on the right said, "Fergus Campbell, 1717–1779." Underneath the date was written in script, "Beloved of Bethia."

Robby reached to brush away the dirt so he could read the final stone, the one on the left of Bethia's. "Jaime MacLennan, 1729–1747," it said. Underneath were the identical scripted words as the marker on the right, "Beloved of Bethia."

Robby stood and backed up, suddenly realizing that the uneven knoll where he was kneeling could very well be the site of three graves. The center, highest part of the mound would be Bethia, lying through all eternity between the two men she had loved. Who had placed the stones? he wondered. Had it been Bethia's idea? Or had her children—the son of Jaime MacLennan and the children of Fergus Campbell—decided that Bethia would unite the fates of the two men in death the way she had in life?

He knelt again, this time in front of the knoll, and laid his hand over the slight swell in the ground that was evidently the resting place of Jaime MacLennan. "Do you lie here, Jaime?" he asked the woods. "Did they bring your dead body back from the bloody fields at Culloden to bury you here?"

There was no sound but the rustling of the pine needles around him.

Robby stretched out his arm, running his hand from Jaime's grave to Bethia's and finally to Fergus Campbell's. Duncan's ancestor.

His throat closed and tears slid from his eyes in what his father would surely have considered an unmanly display. He swiped at them angrily with his sleeve.

After a moment he grew calmer. Once again he studied each of the three markers, then looked around the empty glen. "Why did you want me to see this placc?" he softly asked the rustling trees.

chapter 20

🖤

Duncan awoke with a huge appetite. He bound down the stairs, feeling fresh after the first good night's sleep he'd gotten in a long time. When Emmaline placed a platter of oakcakes in front of him, he devoured them practically before she'd disappeared out the dining hall door.

Though it was still early, the sun was already high. Midsummer's Day—the longest day of the year. He felt curiously happy. For the first time in his life, he'd ceded victory to his opponents without even firing a shot. He'd forgiven Fiona for deceiving him, and he'd done everything possible to see that Castle Glen would survive even after he himself went back to New York.

At this last thought, his good spirits dimmed slightly. He'd lived in a number of homes, but he'd never before felt the odd attachment that he'd developed for the drafty old castle. And what about the people? Could he find a cook back in New York who would scold him if he didn't finish his dinner? How about a gardener who would linger over brandy discussing agricultural methods?

Then there was Robby. He and the boy had developed a bond that was something like the relationship he wished he had been able to have with his own father.

Well, nothing said he couldn't keep in touch, he told himself. After all, his company was now an investor in Glencolly. He could plan regular summer visits to check on things.

And to watch as Fiona became the bride of Graham Maitland or some other Highland gentry?

He looked up as she entered the dining room.

"I'm sorry I ran off so quickly last night," she said. "I didn't properly thank you for agreeing to give all this up without a fight."

He nodded. "As you said, the papers are indisputable."

"Is that why you agreed?"

He shrugged. "Are you feeling better?"

She nodded and glanced at the windows. "It's a beautiful day."

"I was just thinking the same thing myself. It looks like Hugh Cullen and little Elspeth are going to have a fair wedding day."

"Aye."

"And the Midsummer faeries will shower their blessings."

She smiled at him. "Aye."

He finished his last swallow of tea, then stood. "Will you be my escort to the fair today, Lady MacLennan?"

She looked surprised, but nodded. "Of course."

"When does it begin?"

She gave a little laugh. "It undoubtedly already has. The children will have been up before dawn bothering to be off. In fact"—she looked around—"I wonder that Robby's not downstairs already."

"Emmaline said he went out early."

"Ah, perhaps he went down by himself, then, to meet his friends."

"What time shall we go?" he asked.

"The servants have the day off. I need a few minutes to check out the household."

"I'll wait," he said.

As long as anyone could remember, the Glencolly Midsummer Fair had been set up on the moorlands that stretched to the far end of the valley north of town. Villagers from nearby communities began arriving the day before to set up their stalls for marketing various wares or offering games to win away the ready coins of the frolicking fairgoers.

The Coulter's Candy stand was the favorite of the children. From early morning you could see a stream of sticky-faced youngsters waiting their turn to hand over a coin in return for a bag of puff candy or toffee balls. The older boys bought sweetie hearts for the young village lasses.

Officially, the church bell was supposed to signal the fair cryer to declare the opening of the event, but in practice the day started early, and by the time the bells chimed at midmorning, the festive gathering was well underway.

Fiona and Duncan arrived just as the bells were sounding.

"Alasdair always loved the fair," Fiona said with a sad smile as they tied up their horses and walked toward the field of colorful flapping tents. "He liked to give out coins to all the children for an extra chance at the Wheel of Fortune or a game of Rowley-Powley."

She pointed to the stall in front of them where a crowd of village children waited for their chance to throw their sticks and knock off a penny gingerbread.

"Do you want me to win one for you?" Duncan asked.

"You'd have quite a fight getting your turn, I fear," she said.

"What's your favorite thing to do at the fair?" he asked.

She stopped to think. "Why, I don't know. I've come with Robby these past years, and we always did what he wanted. But thinking back to my childhood, I liked the Penny Geggies."

Duncan looked mystified.

"They're little shows. I remember thinking they were magical when I was a little girl."

"Well, then, the Penny Gaggles it is."

"Penny Geggies," she corrected with a giggle.

The tiny theatrical was simpler than she had remembered, but she enjoyed crowding into the tent next to Duncan. In fact, she thought as they stopped at a stall to buy a traditional black pudding, she was enjoying the entire fair. Duncan was in good spirits, and neither one of them had brought up the subject of the inheritance or the fact that his stay in Glencolly would soon be coming to an end.

"I wish we could find Robby," she said. They were sitting side by side on a log, finishing their puddings.

As if her words had conjured him he came racing across the field toward them. "Duncan, Fee!" he called.

He looked happy and more carefree than she'd seen him in a long time.

"You look as if you're having a good time," she told him with a smile.

He looked at the two of them together and gave a satisfied grin. "You do, too."

"We are," Duncan said. To Fiona's surprise, he put his arm around her.

Robby beamed.

"Terry Cullen and I are going to go ride the Dick Turpin's Horse," Robby said. "This year they'll not be able to throw me off!"

"I thought Terry would be getting ready for his brother's wedding."

"The wedding's at twilight. We've plenty of time."

He gave a quick wave and raced off again.

"It's good to see him happy," Fiona said, watching him disappear into the crowd.

"Aye," Duncan answered.

Fiona gave a little giggle. "Your New York friends will find that strange."

"What?"

"You've begun saying aye instead of yes."

He smiled. "Come let me win you a prize," he said, standing and extending his hand to help her off the log. "I'm feeling lucky today."

Duncan had never experienced anything like the Glencolly fair. He supposed there were such things back in New York, but he'd been too busy concentrating on building his fortune and his businesses to bother with them.

Fiona led him through the stalls and introduced him to any Glencolly people he hadn't already met through his work at the mill. He insisted on giving every game a try at least once. He won a wooden soldier knocking down balls at the Aunt Sally game. Several of the stalls sold "fairings," trinkets for the children or sweethearts. He bought Fiona a spinning top, and the two of them played with it like children.

Finally it was time to head toward the special tent set up at one end of the fair for Hugh and Elspeth's wedding. Fiona left him for a moment to seek out the bride to wish her luck. Duncan sat on one of the wooden benches and watched while the rest of the community assembled to bear witness as the young people embarked on their life together.

Hamish, the Castle Glen gardener, was elegantly attired in a dress kilt complete with wool knee stockings and a fine coat and tartan. May and Gavin were, as usual, lost in each other, no doubt with their own wedding still fresh in their minds. To Duncan's surprise, Malcolm entered the tent, dignified as always, but with a blushing Emmaline on his arm.

Each member of the Castle Glen family greeted him as if he were an old friend, and he was surprised to realize that he felt like one.

"Elspeth's nervous, but happy," Fiona said as she came back to sit beside him.

"No more than the groom," Duncan added, pointing to the front of the tent where Hugh Cullen stood beside his young brother. The young weaver's face looked slightly greenish.

"There's Terry," Fiona noted. "I wonder where Robby is."

Once again her stepson appeared on cue. He sat down beside them, though he muttered, "I still find all this love business bothersome. Did you see Malcolm and *Emmaline*?" he added in a loud whisper.

"Hush," Fiona told him. She looked over at Duncan, who was watching the bride enter from the far side of the tent. He had an odd expression on his face as Hugh stepped forward to take his bride's hand. The young couple looked into each other's eyes with such tenderness that Fiona felt the sting of tears.

The ceremony was simple, held over a blacksmith's anvil in the old way. Hugh and Elspeth didn't take their gaze off each other as they murmured the promises that would bind them together. They had a radiance that brightened the entire tent, Fiona decided. Fiona looked around to see many of the audience blinking back the same tears she felt prickling her eyes.

Finally she glanced up at Duncan, sitting beside her. He grinned at her and unexpectedly reached over to give her hand a squeeze.

When the ceremony was over, Hugh and Elspeth were engulfed by their kin and friends with hugs and kisses all around.

Fiona and Duncan finally managed to get close enough to offer their congratulations, then Duncan seized her hand. "There are too many people in here," he whispered in her ear.

She let him lead her out of the tent into the cooling twilight air.

"Do you think they will be disappointed that we left right away?" she asked, but made no protest as he led her across the moor toward the place where they had tied the horses.

"Hugh and Elspeth?" Duncan asked. "No. They've noticed nothing but each other since the minute Elspeth walked into the tent."

"Young love," Fiona replied with a smile.

Duncan was silent. He untied Sorcha and handed Fiona the rope, then freed his own mount. "Come on," he said. I've always fancied a moonlight ride across the moors."

For several moments they rode in silence until the noise from the wedding party and the closing down of the fair stalls was faint in the distance. The sky was growing dark and stars were appearing, one by one. In the east a yellow half moon hung over the far hills.

"Where are we going?" Fiona asked finally.

They'd almost reached the far end of the valley where one of the streams from the surrounding hills pooled to form Glencolly Loch. "This is good enough," Duncan said, dismounting.

Fiona's stomach fluttered. "Good enough for what?"

He was smiling when he came around to help her off her horse. "I told you we needed to talk about the plans for Glencolly."

Disappointment flooded through her. They were alone by a moonlit lake and he wanted to talk business?

She jumped down from her horse, ignoring his outstretched hand, and walked to the shore. The reflected moonlight stretched in a long wavy ray across the entire lake. "Fine," she said. "What do you want to tell me?"

He walked up from behind and put his arms around her. "Are you cold?"

She shrugged him away. "Nay."

"Then let's sit down," he suggested.

For several hours at the fair she'd been able to forget the problems she was facing. She'd been able to forget about the will, forget that Duncan would soon be leaving to return to his homeland. There had even been a moment sitting beside him as they listened to Hugh and Elspeth take their vows that she'd dare imagine what it would be like . . .

"Very well, Mr. Campbell," she said brusquely. "Tell me about these plans you're leaving me with."

Briskly he told her about his meetings with the railway on the inn and his ideas to use the Castle Glen tours to promote its success. When he'd finished his recital, which was as polished as if he'd been presenting it to a board of directors, she sat for a long moment in silence.

She asked the question that had been nagging her since he'd first told them the plans the other night at supper. "What exactly made the railway decide to open their inn in Glencolly? There are many larger towns in the Highlands."

"That's true."

"So why are they putting it here?"

"I believe the railway was persuaded by their business partner in the venture."

She had a feeling she knew the answer to her next question. "Who is the business partner?"

"It's an American company. Campbell Enterprises."

"As in Duncan Campbell Enterprises?"

"As a matter of fact."

She hesitated a long time before answering. Finally she said, "'Tis a kind gesture."

"Not at all. It's a good, sound investment. Tourism is going to bring a lot of money to this area."

Fiona leaned back on her hands with a sigh. "It will mean changes, just as Alasdair said." Suddenly she found herself telling him about the letter from her husband that had suddenly appeared in her wardrobe chest.

When she was finished, he observed, "So essentially Alasdair connived in bringing me here."

"Aye, he did. I'd not have thought him capable of anything quite that . . . underhanded. But he knew that he was dying, and I reckon he was feeling desperate." She turned to look directly into his eyes. "I'm sorry."

"I'm not."

There it was again. That thing between them. She could feel it all the way from her throat to the tips of her toes. And she knew that he was feeling it, too.

"I'm actually not sorry, either," she said. Her voice was husky.

It was all the invitation he needed. All at once they were lying on the bank, pressed into the cool grass, fingers clasped, his mouth searching hers. He moved on top of her and their bodies molded through their clothes.

"What was it you said about the faeries on Midsummer's Eve?" he whispered.

"They bring blessings to lovers."

"Do you think they prefer the lovers to be naked?"

She chuckled. "I think they might."

He stripped her clothes away from her and then removed his own. The moonlight shone white on their bodies as for several long moments, she lay on the grass and let him stroke her.

"Ah, my Highland lass, you're a beauty," he whispered. Then he leaned down to kiss her.

Once the kisses began, the passion built quickly. Fiona gave a little moan of longing, and he shifted their positions so that she was on top of him, their bodies joined together.

He held her hips gently, and they began the rhythmic motion that was as old as the faeries themselves.

Fiona felt flashes of heat, then cold, then heat again until the feel of his soft pulses inside her triggered her own climax. Then Duncan pulled her down and his arms were the only heat around her as her skin cooled against the grass and the night air.

"Fiona MacLennan," he said when their breathing had nearly slowed back to normal. "I love you."

A tremendous knot gathered at the base of her throat. "'Tis the faeries," she whispered, nestling against him. "'Tis Midsummer's Eve."

"Nay, my love, it's not the faeries and it's not the night. It's you. I love the bright blaze in your blue eyes when you're happy. I love the way your pretty chin lifts when you're angry. I love the way you fight for Robby and for the rest of the people at Castle Glen. I love the way you've kept going through everything that life has put you through."

He rocked her in his arms, and she rested her face against his chest feeling . . . *loved*.

She was almost afraid to believe it could be true. "But I didn't tell you about the codicil to the will—" she began.

And he merely rocked her some more and said, "You did what you thought was right for your people. But now it's time you did what was right for *you*."

"And what is that?" She honestly had never considered it.

He pulled back so that she could see his face in the moonlight. "I'm thinking it's a business partnership."

A chill ran up her spine. "A business partnership?"

"Yes. Castle Glen and Campbell Enterprises. What do you say? A sort of long-term investment."

Now she was thoroughly confused. He still held her tenderly against him. Part of him was, in fact, still within her. Why was he talking about a business partnership?

"You want to partner with Castle Glen?"

He laughed and pulled her head against his chest again. "I want to partner with Castle Glen's mistress," he clarified. "In fact, I'm planning on *partnering* every night for the rest of our lives." He punctuated his words with an unmistakable movement of his lower body, which was once again growing hard inside her.

The ache in her throat burst like a bubble. "Can we not talk about business anymore?" she asked, then moaned as he touched a particularly sensitive spot.

"I think we need to stop talking altogether," he agreed, thrusting gently. "Else we won't hear the faeries when they come to bless us."

•   •   •

*I*t was nearly dawn by the time they reached Castle Glen. Fiona could hardly remember the ride back up the valley. Duncan had kept his promise and they had done very little talking, but it had been a magical moonlit night, worthy of anything the Midsummer faeries could have conjured.

Now they lay together in her bed, willing the early sun to keep from rising.

Fiona couldn't remember ever feeling so satisfied, but even in her blissful state, troublesome thoughts hovered at the edge of her mind. She hadn't told Duncan about Graham's visit or the dire state of the estate debts.

He groaned and moved against her. "Do I have to leave?" he mumbled. "Will it be too much a scandal if the entire castle knows I slept in your bed?"

She smiled and flipped her fingers through his dark hair. "I reckon it will, Mr. Campbell."

He burrowed into a pillow. "I think when I tell them that I intend to make an honest woman of you, they'll forgive me."

"You're probably right. Especially at Midsummer's Eve. Everyone is sympathetic to lovers then."

"The season even seems to have reached old Malcolm."

Fiona laughed but then sobered as she said, "There is something I need to tell you before I can agree to marry you."

He stiffened and his smile faded. "What?"

"Graham Maitland came to see me yesterday."

The tenseness went out of his face, and he let his head drop back down to the pillow. "He told you that Castle Glen is hocked to the rafters."

"You knew?"

He shrugged. "We're going to be partners, remember? Campbell Enterprises is always careful to investigate every new venture. I've known all about the IOUs the Maitlands have been so careful to gather."

"So . . . what's going to happen?"

He pulled her down beside him. "My darling Fiona, I'll pay off the loans, and if you like, as a wedding present, I'll serve you Maitland Manor on a platter."

Her eyes grew wide. "Do you have enough money to do that?"

He laughed. "Yes, my blunt little Scotswoman, I do."

She leaned back against the pillows. "Imagine that," she said without sounding overly impressed.

Duncan shook his head with amusement. In New York, people would practically start bowing and scraping every time they learned the extent of his fortune. Here in Glencolly, it didn't seem to make that much of a difference, except for the fact that he could ease the problem of the Maitland IOUs.

"Do you mind that you're marrying a rich man?" he asked.

She looked as if she was actually considering the issue. "Nay," she said after a moment. "I suppose it's convenient to have money. It makes life easier." She lifted herself up on one elbow. "If you had so much money, why were you worried about the Castle Glen finances and the mill's problems?"

"Because problems are meant to be solved, not pasted over with injections of cash. Glencolly had to change if it was going to survive."

She nodded thoughtfully. "That's what Alasdair was saying in his letter. He just didn't have the heart to be the one to make the changes."

Duncan was reaching to pull her back down beside him when a knock sounded on the door.

"Oh, dear," Fiona said.

"Fiona! May I come in?"

It was Robby. Fiona looked at Duncan in a panic.

Duncan shrugged. "He'll know about it soon enough anyway," he said with a grin. Then he got up and quickly put on the clothes he'd discarded after their predawn arrival.

When he was dressed, he called, "Come in!"

The door opened slowly, and Robby cautiously peered inside. He glanced from Duncan, who was standing in the middle of the room in his hastily donned clothes, to Fiona, still in bed, the covers pulled up around her to hide her nakedness.

"What are you doing here?" Robby asked Duncan.

"I, er, Fiona and I were talking."

"Talking," the boy repeated. He seemed not the least bit inclined to believe their excuses.

"We were up most of the night at the wedding celebration," Fiona added, sounding slightly breathy.

"The celebration ended by midnight, and everyone commented that the two of you had ridden off long before that."

"We . . . we went for a ride," she explained.

The boy stepped inside, his good humor restored. He grinned at them both. "Don't worry, Fee," he told her. "I won't tell Malcolm or Emmaline, although if you'd seen the two of them dancing at the wedding last night . . ." He shook his head as if in despair over the foolishness of the adults in his life. He grinned at her. "In fact, I think it's an entirely fine idea."

Then a thought seemed to hit him. He turned to Duncan with a more serious expression. "That is . . . you do intend to marry her, don't you?"

Duncan did not smile at the boy's stern tone. "I certainly do. Once I ask permission of the laird of Castle Glen," he answered.

Robby gave a confused glance at Fiona, who nodded, smiling. "That's you, Robby. Castle Glen is yours again, and if we play our cards right, we just may be able to persuade a certain shrewd American businessman to become a partner and help us keep it for you."

Now Robby's grin extended from ear to ear. "That's *swell*!" he hollered. "Perfect, in fact. The MacLennans and the Campbells as partners. I think Jaime would be pleased," he said.

Duncan looked at the boy fondly. "No doubt Fergus Campbell would be, too."

"And think of how proud Bethia would be to see her heirs working together," Fiona added.

Robby gave a little bounce. "I want to show you two something I found."

Fiona pulled the blanket around her neck. "Something you can bring in here?"

"Nay, you have to come with me to see it. It'll mean a bit of a walk."

"Well then, can't it wait until—?"

"Nay, it's important, Fee. I want you and Duncan to see it."

"Very well," she agreed. "Clear on out of here, both of you, so I can get dressed. Then we'll go see this mysterious find of yours."

Fiona couldn't remember that she had ever been back to the little pond where Robby led them. It was at the far end of the North Woods, which were generally too thick and dark to be pleasant walking.

"Are you going to tell us where you're taking us?" Duncan asked as they pushed aside branches to make their way.

"It's just here," he replied, "on the other side of the pond. That glen over there."

He stopped and pointed, then he turned around to face them, his blue eyes dancing with excitement. He seemed ready to burst with his secret. "Jaime told me to come here!" he blurted out finally.

Fiona looked skeptical. "Jaime the Ghost told you to come? In a dream?"

Robby looked from one adult face to the other. "*Not* in a dream. In the schoolroom."

Duncan tipped his head and regarded the boy's eager face. "What's this all about?" he asked.

Shifting with excitement from one foot to another, he told them the story of his meeting the spirit.

"He looked just like a real person," he ended. "Kind of like me, in fact. Except he was wearing old clothes—like his picture in the Portrait Room."

Duncan and Fiona exchanged a look.

"I'm not making this up!" Robby insisted.

"I know you're not deliberately making it up, Robby," Fiona said consolingly, "but sometimes dreams can be very real. Perhaps you—"

Robby put his hands on his hips. "How would I have known about this place if Jaime hadn't told me to come here?"

Duncan looked around the pond. "What *is* this place, exactly?"

"It's called the Tuiream Pond."

Fiona had heard of it. "In the olden days there were women mourners called Tuiream. They came here after a death to wail for the departed souls."

Duncan gave a little shiver. "One of the more grim Highland tales, I must say."

Robby shook his head. "It's not grim at all. Come on, I'll show you."

He led the way around the precarious edge of the pond to the glen in back. "I almost missed the stones," he said. "They're nearly covered by the trees. I doubt anyone has seen them for a hundred years."

Duncan held back the large limb of a fir tree to allow Fiona to follow Robby into the circular glen. "There they are!" the boy exclaimed proudly, pointing across the circle to where three stone markers were barely visible beneath the trees.

"What are they?" Duncan asked.

Robby walked over to them. "Graves. Jaime, Bethia, and Fergus—lying together for the rest of eternity." He knelt beside the stones and reached out to pull away the branches to uncover them to view. Turning back to Duncan and Fiona, he said, "Do you see? Jaime wanted us to know that it's all right for all of us to be together. MacLennans and Campbells."

It was the simplistic analysis of a fourteen-year-old boy, bringing an end to a decades-old enmity. Duncan reached for Fiona's hand.

"I'll agree with Jaime," he said, his voice husky.

She looked up at him, her eyes brimming with tears. "So will I," she said.

They turned back to Robby as he gave a gasp.

"What is it?" Fiona asked in alarm.

"Look." Robby had pulled the branches back from the three stones.

Duncan put his arm around Fiona as the two walked across the circle toward the stones. When they were in front of the three markers, they stood in silence arm in arm reading the names. Jaime MacLennan. Bethia MacLennan Campbell. Fergus Campbell.

The markers were worn and muddy. The graves were slightly rounded, covered with a deep green moss. As

Robby had said, they appeared to have lain in the quiet circle undisturbed for many, many years.

Except for one thing. Robby's wide MacLennan eyes reflected his wonder as he pointed to Jaime MacLennan's grave. On the grass at the base of the tilted old stone lay a bright white Stuart cockade.

Epilogue

Glencolly, Scotland, 1888

A smart-looking young man in riding breeches and a tweed jacket pointed toward the far end of the Portrait Room. "What's that flag hanging over the doorway, Mr. Strahorn? It appears to have two different insignias."

Malcolm gave the group of visitors a stiff smile. "The flag represents both family names—the MacLennans and the Campbells. We believe it was designed shortly after the unpleasantness at Culloden, but it has only been hung here in recent years."

The members of the Mayberry Hunt Club craned their necks in unison to view the banner, then turned their attention back to Malcolm as he finished describing each of the ancestors whose lacquered faces stared impassively into the room.

He finished the recital and was leading his flock out the far doorway, when an eager young woman clutched at his arm. "Which one is the ghost?" she asked, her voice hushed.

Malcolm looked down at the hand crushing the sleeve of his Glencolly wool suit and cleared his throat. "Some people believe that Castle Glen is inhabited by the ghost of Jaime MacLennan, the young man there with the white cockade on his hat." He pointed back to the portrait, and several of the visitors moved toward it for a better look.

"Have you seen him?" asked the same young woman.

"Nay, miss, I have not," Malcolm answered, "and it has been three years since any report of ghostly activities. Now, ladies and gentleman, if you will follow me, we shall go up to the old Stuart Tower. Family legend says that Bonnie Prince Charlie himself once stayed there."

The murmur of voices faded. Fiona peered around the Portrait Room archway. "They've headed up to the tower," she whispered, then smiled as two strong arms snaked around her from behind.

"It's becoming harder and harder for a fellow to find a moment of privacy," Duncan grumbled as he turned her around in his arms and kissed her.

Fiona giggled and kissed back with an enthusiasm that left them both flushed. "We just have to learn to take advantage of the time," she said. "I thought time was your specialty. Where's that watch of yours?"

Duncan patted the pocket of his vest. "I think little Jaime ate it," he said.

"Babies can't eat watches," she protested.

He grinned at her. "I don't doubt ours could. I stopped up in the nursery to watch him playing with Elspeth's little Hughie, and I swear he's grown an inch since I went to the mill this morning."

Fiona laughed and slipped her arm around her husband's waist as they walked together up the big stone staircase. "Has Jock had any more problems with the Maitlands?"

"No, they've given up all attempts to stop the water upstream from the mill. Now that their loans have all been paid off, I think Logan is smart enough to know they are battling a losing cause, no matter what his son says. In fact, I understand they are offering Maitland Manor for sale."

"Mr. Maitland is going to go look for his castle elsewhere?"

"Apparently. Which will make me feel a sight better now that you're going to resume your regular visits to town."

She gave a nod of satisfaction and let her head drop on Duncan's shoulder. "Are you sure you want your wife supervising a woolen mill?"

He kissed the top of her head. "This is a partnership, remember? Now that the railway has made me a director, I'll be busy with the expansion plans. In the meantime, you'll be running things here, just like you did after Alasdair's death."

"I didn't do a very good job. The mill was failing, the estate was in debt—"

They'd reached the top of the stairs. Duncan stopped and pulled her around to face him. "Nonsense. You were battling the same changes and the same money problems that every big estate in the country is facing. Your husband was gone, yet single-handedly you were keeping everything together, making sure that the core of Castle Glen—its people—stayed strong. You were even ready to do battle with an interloper who had come to take away your beloved home."

Fiona gave him a grateful smile. Even though Castle Glen once again belonged legally to Robby, it would have been easy for Duncan to continue his control of the estate. It had been his money that had brought them out of their debts. He had instituted the changes that were returning prosperity to Glencolly and the mill.

"I don't think your business associates would think you've received a very good return on your investment here."

"Then they would be wrong," he told her gently. "I have you, little Jaime, Robby, and a whole family here. Castle Glen has brought me riches beyond price."

She reached out and squeezed both his hands as neither spoke for a long moment. Finally, she blinked away her threatening tears and said, "I shall enjoy working with Jock again."

Duncan leaned toward her and spoke in low tones. "Of course, you'll have to give up the mill visits again for a while when little Fee comes along to join her brother."

Fiona's eyebrow arched. "So you'd like a lassie this time, Mr. Campbell? And have you in mind a schedule for this new arrival?"

Duncan pulled her tight against him. Though it was midday his swollen anatomy told her that he was ready for the bedroom. "Robby will be off to school in London soon. I think he'd like a little sister before he leaves."

"Robby goes in the fall. I hardly think that leaves enough time—"

"How much longer will those strangers be wandering through my house?" Duncan interrupted, kissing the hollow below her ear.

She tipped her head to allow him easier access to her soft skin. "I'm not sure. Malcolm can get quite long-winded with his family stories." She gave a little moan of satisfaction as his lips brushed a particularly sensitive spot. "I do know," she continued hoarsely, "that Malcolm never brings the tours into our bedchamber."

He pulled away to look at her. Even in the darkness of the hallway, she could see his eyes shine. "Well, now, isn't Malcolm the wise fellow? What about Jaime?"

Fiona smiled back at him. "Elspeth is watching him. He'll be fine for a half hour."

Without waiting for further invitation, he swept her into his arms and headed down the hall toward their bedchamber. Fiona laughed as he fumbled at the doorknob. She pushed the door open when he had unlatched it and pulled it closed behind them. He thanked her with a hard kiss while he carried her across the room.

"A half hour, it is, Mistress Campbell," he told her with a grin, setting her in the middle of their big bed. His eyes never left her as he ripped impatiently at his cravat. "Though I should warn you—I don't have a watch."

About the Author

~

Ana Seymour has been a lover of history since childhood, an interest she says has been fostered by her genealogy-loving parents. Her father has traced the family ancestry back to the Scottish hero, Robert the Bruce! Ana is delighted to continue the family tradition by adding fascinating touches of history to her popular romances, which have been published around the world.

Ana lives in the country near one of Minnesota's fifteen thousand lakes. She appreciates hearing from readers at P.O. Box 24107, Minneapolis MN 55424, or by e-mail at anaseymour@aol.com.

Berkley Books proudly introduces

Berkley Sensation

a **brand-new** romance line
featuring today's **best-loved** authors—
and tomorrow's **hottest** up-and-comers!

Every month...
Four sensational writers

Every month...
Four sensational new romances

Every month...
**Four romances—
from historical to contemporary,
suspense to cozy.**

With Berkley Sensation launching in June 2003,

**This summer is going to
be a scorcher!**